Also by Craig Lancaster

600 Hours of Edward
The Summer Son
Edward Adrift
The Fallow Season of Hugo Hunter
This is What I Want
Edward Unspooled

the art
of departure

stories

CRAIG LANCASTER

MISSOURI BREAKS PRESS

In memory of David Brockett and Bill Petter,
a couple of guys who loved a story.

And for Elisa, who makes every day beautiful.

TABLE OF CONTENTS

foreword

Imagine we're strangers on a bus, you and I. We have boarded the Greyhound in Billings, Montana and we are bound for Missoula, where an uncertain reception awaits us both. But that is miles on down the line; for now, it is just you and I and the bus. As the Greyhound climbs the on-ramp to the interstate and the Montana landscape scrolls past with undulating power lines and grazing antelope, we size each other up from across the aisle. I look at you and you look at me, each of us wondering who the other person could be.

This, my bus-bound friend, is Craig Lancaster's forte: conjuring the lives of others in a way that is so real that, to revive an old cliché, the characters seem to step right off the page. The fiction in *The Art of Departure* is just a razor's breadth away from reality. It's no surprise that Lancaster got his start in the writing business as a newspaper reporter. Many of these stories have the warm, homespun feel of a good human-interest feature you'd find in the pages of your local paper.

"But," you say, turning from the bus window, "I don't come to fiction for reality—I read it to escape from real life." *Just like I'm escaping my crappy marriage right now*, I imagine you silently add.

To that, I'd answer: Well then, you're in luck because Craig Lancaster can also conjure up some dramatic stories full of heartbreak and laughter. In the pages to come, you'll find a fascinating and diverse gallery of characters who have plenty of tales to tell. I think of the high school basketball coach whose newest player could either lead his team to legendary victory or end his career in a communal shaming; or, the lonely widower named Frank Abrams (no relation to me) whose bond with a neighbor's son spreads Yuletide joy to everyone involved; or, the runaway teenage girl who gets in over her head when she hits the big city; or, the grizzled old news reporter about to be downsized out of a job; or, "the only guilty man in the Montana State Prison" who's coming to terms with his crime; or, the Boy Scout troop who go all *Lord of the Flies* on their Scoutmaster; or—well, I could go on, but I want to get out of the way here, so you can meet these folks and read about their exploits for yourself.

I'll mention just two other characters before I go. They're found in one of the earliest short stories of Lancaster's I ever read: "This is Butte. You Have Ten Minutes." Here, you'll meet a man so attached to his personal electronic device he's known to us as "the man with the BlackBerry." Like the author, he is a keen observer of those around him. He's an inventor of lives, a scribe of the everyday, a chronicler of humanity. But all the notes he types to himself in his personal device are a protective shield. BlackBerry Man is a lonely guy who finds solace in imaginary lives and holds himself at arm's length from those around him...until he meets a woman he christens Darcia. Their chance encounter brings about a new awakening. It's the kind of story that encapsulates all that is good about Craig Lancaster's fiction.

Did I mention that Darcia and Blackberry Man are strangers on a bus?

Enjoy the road trip through these stories, fellow traveler.

David Abrams
Butte, Montana

*short
fiction*

somebody has to lose

From the *Burdon County Bugle*, November 4, 1997:

Longtime residents of these parts know what they were doing on this date 12 years ago—Nov. 4, 1985. They were settled in front of their television sets to watch 3-year-old Mendy Grunwald, from right here in Burdon City, as she made an appearance on "The Tonight Show with Johnny Carson."

Well, little Mendy did herself and the whole county—heck, the whole state—proud by sinking 10 shots in a row with a foam ball into a basket rigged up for the pint-sized point guard she was that evening. After this display of shooting prowess, Johnny Carson challenged her to H-O-R-S-E, and she dispatched the comedian in five shots, earning the admiration of her host and the adulation of a nationwide TV audience.

Things haven't been the same for Burdon County or Mendy Grunwald since. The hoopla lasted awhile after she and her parents returned home from California (she was even featured in People *magazine), and in the ensuing years, Mendy has gone on to be every bit the basketball star everyone expected her to be.*

This is all worth mentioning now as she is finally 15 years old, finally a high school freshman, and finally eligible to play for coach Paul

Wainwright and the Burdon County Broncos. Practice starts today, and it's sa fe to say that with Mendy Grunwald in the fold, folks around here expect the Broncos to end a 10-year state title drought and hang banner No. 9 from the rafters....

Some men trust their eyes, some their heart. That first week in November, as always, Paul Wainwright put his faith in his nose.

On the first day of practice, the particular odor in the gymnasium told him that he again had come to where he belonged. It teased his nostrils even before he pushed through the swinging double doors, beckoning him onward as he walked through the dank tunnel that connected the locker room and coaches' offices to the hardwood, past the orange-painted cinderblock walls bearing the pictures of players who were ghosts now at Burdon County High School but remained forever fifteen, sixteen, seventeen, eighteen years old in Paul's head. He next passed under those stands that held the faithful, year after year, thousands of faces that he knew together and alone. His anxious footsteps, beating out a rhythm in time and a half just this once, every year, echoed through the empty gym. First week of November. In more than half of the years of his life, Paul Wainwright had made this inaugural walk, pulled along by the pungency from generations of sweat mixed with the body heat of a thousand crowds, the leavings of leather against wood, of sneaker soles and desire and heartbreak and euphoria. The reason he kept showing up, a quarter century now, lay in the corners of the gym that never got swept, in that worn spot along the baseline where every player he'd ever coached had stood, in the peeling paint of the scorer's table, in the steel beams crossing the ceiling where now he looked and silently counted off his legacy teams—1974, 1975, 1978, 1979, 1980, 1983, 1984, 1986, state champions all. Paul Wainwright strode into the gym and saw signs, visible only to him, that marked the route he had traveled as a high school basketball coach. Down on the north end of the gym, forty-five degrees up and out from the free-throw line, lay the spot where Wendy McCaig's heave left her fingers in '74, falling through the basket at the buzzer, sending Paul's first team into the playoffs on a high. East regionals, state, home with the trophy, the start of it all. As close as Paul held the memory of that shot, and of Wendy, he remembered the setup pass even more clearly. Valerie Sneed then, Valerie Wainwright today, seeing the big center from Laurel flailing toward her, slipping a bounce pass eight feet to her right to Wendy, wide open.

Draw that line back across the lane, bisecting it, to the left block, and that's where Dana Winslow crawled through a thicket of girls for an offensive rebound and a flash layup in '83 against Dawson County, giving the Broncos an unlikely ticket to the playoffs and a state championship that astounded even Paul, that he could win with so flawed a team. He could draw lines all over this gym, perpendiculars and parallels and squiggles, and at each endpoint, a memory posted up.

Paul stood in the center circle, the whistle around his neck dangling against his black polo shirt, and went over his notes. To someone in the know, it would have seemed silly for him to have written it all down—twenty-five years into a routine that seldom changed, Paul could run his practices by rote—but he drew comfort from the exercise. In precise script, he had practice segmented perfectly, from basic dribbling drills to layup lines to the first wave of installing the offense. Paul felt fortunate that he had long ago persuaded youth league and junior high coaches in town to adopt a basic version of his set; it meant that he could quickly bring the girls up to speed every November before taking them even deeper, into the multiple options and cuts to which they had not yet been exposed. In two hours, he would know exactly who was going where—in addition to the varsity, his primary concern, he would have to fill junior varsity and C teams—and what, exactly, he'd have to work with for the next few months.

"Think fast," Susie Michener said, and the sound of the flung ball slapping against the hardwood pulled Paul's attention from his notes. He reached out a hand, and the ball stuck. It always did

"You ready, Coach?" she asked.

"Oh, yeah. They ready?" He grinned at his first-year assistant, the star of his last championship team, a group now a decade in the rearview mirror. He had persuaded Susie to come home and, he hoped, let him slide away from the job in a few years, if his nose ever told him it was time to go.

"They'll be out soon," Susie said. She slapped at the ball in his hands, stealing it. Paul dropped his notes and scrambled into a defensive stance, playfully daring his erstwhile guard to make a move. She jab-stepped at him, smiled and then slipped the ball under her arm.

"What do you think, Coach?" she asked. "Do you think we're going to be any good?"

Paul reached for the scattered sheaf of papers. He looked back to the rafters. "You're the last one in Burdon City to know what that's like," he said, his eyes guiding her to the banners. "To know what it takes. You and me, and that's it. But I tell you what: In a few months, I think we'll have ten, twelve girls who know the feeling."

Susie looked at Paul, but he kept his eyes tilted toward the ceiling. "I've never heard you talk like that before," she said. "Were you this confident when I played?"

The sound of the double doors swinging open drew their attention. Mendy Grunwald, socks flopping down her long legs like loose skin, waved.

"Start stretching, Mendy, while we wait for everybody else," Paul said. And then, to Susie, low so only she could hear: "You never played with anybody like we've got coming."

Paul started with the simple stuff: layup lines to get the kids used to the feel of the ball and their movements with it. Three or four dribbles, plant a foot, go to the basket. One line of shooters, one line of fetchers. The first girl to shoot, a freshman named Oberst, drew a clank of iron, the ball ricocheting back at her. She ducked as it flew past.

"That's a lap," Paul said, and Oberst peeled out of line and began her plodding trip around the periphery.

Mendy was next. Two dribbles and she was off her feet, laying the ball gently against the glass, underhanded. It dropped through.

Motion drills were more of the same. Mendy was quicker out of the blocks, longer, more fluid than the other girls, moving seamlessly from one drill to the next, her long, slender, sure legs carrying her across large gaps of hardwood with quickness and grace. One of the things Paul had to get used to, years earlier when he was starting out as a scared young coach, was the peculiar way many girls moved. Basketball maneuvers didn't come naturally to them; the motions were learned behaviors, and they often came across in herky-jerky fashion.

It had never occurred to Mendy to play that way. Paul had known her since she was a baby, and for most of that time, she had carried a basketball. It was almost an extension of her, a part of her body. Here she was, a six-foot, two-inch freshman, growth and muscle maturity still well ahead of her, and already she had more talent than Paul had seen in Burdon County, or anywhere else. When Mendy caught him grinning, he winked at her.

By the time the juniors and seniors reported for practice, an hour in,

Paul had seen enough. As per usual, the freshmen—Mendy excepted—and all but two sophomores would be dropped to the junior varsity and C teams, returned to the slow cooker of the lower levels for more seasoning. He sent those girls to one end of the gym with Susie and turned his focus to the ten who had made the cut. Looking at them together, he saw more possibilities than he had allowed himself to dream of in the parched decade behind him.

There was Reese Cacciola, a senior point guard. Paul didn't much like her mouth, but he loved the way "Cash" would crawl inside the jersey of an opposing player, never yielding, never stopping. He'd put Sabrina Newman, a junior, at one of the wings. He could find more talent down on the other end of the court with Susie's group, but Paul figured Sabrina's hustle would win a game, maybe two, and that could mean everything. Another junior, Victoria Ford, would start in the backcourt opposite Cash. Senior Vanessa Samples, the only black girl on the team (one of only four in the whole town), was a tree trunk anchor for the middle. Nancy Plummer, Amanda Newman, Jana Lundquist and Sandy Madsen would hold down the bench and provide depth the likes of which Paul hadn't seen in a long while.

That left Mendy.

"Mendy can play anywhere," he told Susie, sidemouthed, toward the end of practice, as the girls ran yo-yos—sprints from baseline to free-throw line, from baseline to midcourt, from baseline to the far free-throw line, from baseline to baseline.

"We knew that, right?" Susie said.

"Yeah, but knowing it and seeing it … come on, Suze, imagine the possibilities. You know what we can do with her handling the ball?"

"Pick-and-rolls up high."

"Yep. We can pick teams to death. On defense, we can double-team anywhere on the court and let her play center field. We can use her as a decoy. We can shut down half the floor and dare individual players to beat us. It opens up everything."

Susie frowned.

"What?" Paul said.

"We've gotta be careful, you know. Cash figures this is her team, her year. It could be a chemistry problem."

Paul waved her off. "Cash will be fine. She's smart enough to understand what's happening."

"Smarts aren't the question, Coach. She spent her summer at Blue

Star and AAU camps. By her thinking, it's her moment. I'm just saying, it'll be better if the team doesn't perceive that there's a star system here."

"There's not."

"No, of course …"

"We're running the same sets we always run, the same options, everything," Paul said, and he was immediately taken aback by his apparent peevishness. "Only the players have changed, and in one case, significantly. They'll understand that."

Their drill finished, the girls lingered on the baseline, lacing their hands behind their heads and gulping air.

"Grab some water and then huddle up," Paul said, and the girls stampeded toward the hallway.

"Coach?" Susie said.

"Yeah?"

"All I'm saying is, be sure you ride Mendy just as hard as you do the others, if not harder. They'll be watching you, watching us, to see how she's treated. They know how good she is. Plus, Mendy can take it."

"Hands in, Broncos," Paul said, holding his right arm up and out, his palm stretched perpendicular to the ground. The girls crowded in and reached for his hand.

"One week from today, we play Custer County," he said. "That's as much of the schedule as you need to think about. A lot of people around us seem to be interested in what's happening in February and March, but that is not our concern, so when we're here, together, I don't want to hear a word about it, OK?" He scanned the eyes looking back at him, making contact with each set. "A lot of people will talk to you about what it means to be a Bronco. They'll tell you that you have to live up to something. You do, but it's not what they're saying. You have to live up to your own duty to play as hard as you can, every minute, every step of the way. You show up to practice ready to go, out of respect to yourself and your team. You back each other up. You will never go wrong here if I have your complete effort, all the time. If you give this team less than that, you will not last. Those who play for the team will not let you stay. Do you understand?" The girls all nodded. "You pay attention, you learn, you apply what you've learned on that basketball court, and I guarantee you, the rest will take care of itself. This is our journey, together, and it belongs to us. Do you hear me?"

"Yes, sir," the girls shouted.

"OK, let's break it down. 'Team' on three. One, two, three ..."

In unison came the shout: "Team!"

The girl slung the backpack off her shoulders, opened the pickup door and dropped the bag into the rear of the cab as she settled into the seat. Dirk Grunwald patted his daughter's leg.

"What's wrong, sweetie?"

"Nothing."

"Where's the smile?"

"Taking a break."

Dirk put the truck in gear. "First day of practice, I expected a little more enthusiasm. Things not go well?"

Mendy tinkered with the truck's radio, moving the dial off Dirk's preferred country and western and finding something more palatable on the town's only FM station, a hundred-watt basement outfit anchored by a morning deejay-sidekick combination who called themselves T.J. and the Rake.

Now, by late afternoon, the morning duo was probably halfway into a case of Keystone and the station was on autopilot, pumping out tunes and commercials in monetarily pleasing proportions. Dirk, who forbade his only child from listening to T.J. and especially the overly salacious Rake, decided to tolerate the shift in tone.

"Practice went fine. I really like the girls," Mendy said. "It's just ..."

Dirk, piloting the pickup down Burdon City's main drag, looked sideways at his daughter. "Just what?"

"The other girls don't always see what I see. I hit two of them in the face with passes today. They were open, but they didn't know it. I really felt bad."

Dirk chuckled even as his girl sat quiet in her seat. Mendy's wide-eyed innocence was perhaps his favorite thing about her; he loved that she could be so astoundingly good at something and yet not recognize her own talent enough to be arrogant about it. From the very beginning, he had approached her basketball playing from divergent points of view. On one hand, he felt boundless pride in her ability and potential, knowing that the game could carry her to incredible opportunities. On the other, he braced for the day that renown would somehow fundamentally alter her, chipping away at the underlying sweetness and replacing naivete with hard jadedness. It hadn't happened yet, thank the Lord, but high school ball—at this high school in particular, for this coach in particular—would ratchet the pressure on her, he knew.

"Honey, let that go. It's the first day. They'll get used to you, and you'll get used to them. What else is going on?"

Mendy stared at the floorboard.

"Mend?"

She looked up, red-eyed.

"Cash."

"Cash what?"

"You know, Reese Cacciola."

"Oh, right. What about her?"

"Dad, I think she hates me."

Dirk looked at his daughter, who could no longer fight off the tears. "Oh, honey, nobody hates you. That's silly."

"She teased me the whole time. Asked me if I'd ever missed a shot. Said she figured no one else would have to shoot with me on the team."

Dirk reached across the bench seat and tucked his daughter's long blond hair behind her ear. "Honey, it sounds like she's just having some fun with a newbie. You knew this was coming. We talked about it."

Mendy sniffled. "I told her that she knows the offense better than I do, that there's the possibility of a shot on every pass. What a dumb thing for her to say."

"And what did she say to that?"

"She asked me if Coach told me that, and asked me if he also told me that I'd win a state championship. She said, 'He told me the same thing, and I haven't won one yet.' "

Dirk's gut tightened, as if gripping and metastasizing around a brick. The whole blessed town was going overboard with this thing, in his estimation. This basketball season had commenced in a perfect storm of amplified civic pride. It was the city's 125th anniversary, the 25th season as coach for Paul Wainwright and ten solid years since Wainwright's team had won state, and Dirk's daughter was openly expected—destined, some believed—to make it a coronation. He could see the manifestations of overhyped interest along Main Street in the banners proclaiming Bronco Pride, in the silly newspaper article that morning that relived the ancient history and put the expectations of an entire county on the shoulders of the scared girl beside him. Reese Cacciola, a senior down to one last shot at a legacy, no doubt felt the pressure, too, and it had put her at loggerheads with Mendy.

Needing a lifeline for his daughter, if only for a day, Dirk went to the well of his own considerable, and largely forgotten, athletic career as a reserve on dominant UCLA teams in the '60s.

"Baby, what did Coach Wooden always say?"

Mendy looked up and saw her father's grin, and that did it. She smiled back at him.

"Things turn out best for the people who make the best of the way things turn out," she recited.

Dirk reached out and rubbed the top of her head. "Learn it, love it, live it."

Paul glanced up from his computer screen and saw Eric Embry on the other side of his office door. The sportswriter held up his left wrist, showing Paul his watch, triggering the memory: Paul had told him to come by around five-thirty. In eighteen years of dealing with the guy, Paul had found Embry to be many things, some of them not so good. But damned if he wasn't persistently punctual.

Paul held up a hand, asking for a minute. He was done inputting the day's grades and didn't really need the time, but he enjoyed needling Embry. Sure enough, the reporter rolled his eyes and paced down the hallway. Paul counted off ten seconds, twenty, thirty, then walked to the door and opened it.

"Come on in, Eric."

The sportswriter, now at the far end of the hall, turned and came back at a half jog, a belly roll loosing the grip of his golf shirt and spilling over the waistband of his Dockers. "Thanks, Coach. I'll be quick. I've gotta get back and start laying out the section."

Paul ushered him in. "Have a seat." Settling into his own chair and rolling back from the desk, Paul put his feet up. "What can I do you for?"

"How'd the first day go?"

"Good. Real good."

"Do you have the varsity picked out yet?"

"Yep. We'll go with the Newmans, Ford, Samples, Grunwald, Plummer, Lundquist, Madsen and Cacciola, at least to start the season."

"Who'll be starting?"

"You'll find out a week from today, just like everybody else."

"Oh, come on, Paul."

Paul put his feet on the floor and leaned in. "Come on, nothing. We go through this every year, Eric. I'll pick the starters when I'm ready. We've had one practice."

"Can you at least tell me if Mendy Grunwald will start? I mean, she has to, right?"

"Says who?"

"Seriously?"

"Yeah. Is there some law about who starts that no one told me? I mean, I'm only the coach."

"Paul, Jesus. Stop busting my balls here."

Paul threw his hands up. "No, I'm serious. I read your story today, and I figured we didn't even have to play the season. I imagine they're hanging the state championship banner right now, and you're in here with me, missing it."

"Oh, come on."

Paul pulled open his desk drawer and retrieved the clipped-out article he'd stashed that morning. "Here it is right here: 'Folks around here expect the Broncos to end a 10-year state title drought and hang banner No. 9 from the rafters.' "

"Paul, you know as well as I do what people are saying and expecting. I didn't write anything that isn't true. You know everybody's been waiting for Mendy to get here. It's pretty disingenuous to act as if you don't."

Paul stood up and moved to the front edge of his desk, towering over the sportswriter.

"No, I'll tell you what's disingenuous: For anybody to elevate a girls basketball team—and a freshman kid—to a matter of civic import. They pay me a $3,200-a-year stipend to run an athletic program, and my job is to make it a positive experience for twenty-some-odd girls, not to turn one girl into a superstar. So I'm telling you the God's honest truth, Eric. I'm still evaluating the team. And if you print any of that except 'I'm still evaluating the team,' I'll never speak to you again."

"OK. Jeez. Take it easy. This is going to be thin."

Paul sat down again and shuffled some papers on his desk, trying not to break out in laughter.

"I understand the tough spot you're in, Eric. Here's something you can use: I'm really heartened by what I've seen from the team so far"— at this, Embry for the first time began scribbling in his notebook— "and I'm eager to see how we come together in the next few weeks and months. These student-athletes have been well-schooled at every level of basketball, and we have a good mix of returning kids and new talent. If we work hard and develop the way I think we can, we'll have a chance to do some really good things."

Embry wrote down the final few words, clicking his pen against the notebook when he was finished. "Great. Thanks, Paul."

When the sportswriter was halfway through the door, Paul spoke again.

"Hey, Eric, off the record?"

"Sure."

Paul gave him a look that was half smirk, half knowing grin.

"We're going to be really, really good," he whispered.

Paul reached for the handle to the front door and then pulled his hand away, his fingers tickling the air in front of his face as if he had received a shot of static electricity. Sighing, he grabbed the brass knob and turned it.

A faint hint of what must have been dinner glanced across his nose.

"I'm home," he called into the dark of the house.

No answer.

He closed the door and set his gym bag down in front of it on the tile landing.

"Let's not start this again so soon this season," Valerie said, peering at him over the railing from above. "If you leave it there, I'll trip over it tomorrow morning. Put it somewhere else." And just like that, she was gone. Paul kicked the bag two feet to the left, onto the carpet, and bounded up the stairs.

"What's for dinner?"

Valerie wielded a spatula to scrape the remnants of something out of a Pyrex dish and into the garbage. "What was for dinner was lasagna," she said. "Where were you?"

"First day of practice, Val."

"I know that. Linda Grunwald called two hours ago, asking us to dinner Sunday. She said Mendy was home."

Paul opened the refrigerator and shoved his head in. "Mendy doesn't have to log grades or talk to the guy from the *Bugle* or a lot of other things I do."

"Don't get cute with me, Paul. I'm just saying that I wish you would call if you're going to be late."

"Fine, all right? Is there any left?"

"Top shelf."

While his late dinner bubbled under the glare of the microwave, Paul fished his wallet out of his pants and stacked it, along with his school ID badge and car keys, on the edge of the breakfast nook for easy retrieval.

"Hey, Hugh, how's it going?" he said, nodding at his son. The boy had receded into the sectional in the living room, quietly wrestling with homework.

"Dad," Hugh acknowledged.

"Where's Zoe?" Paul asked.

By now, Hugh had floated back into his math text, leaving his mother to field the question.

"Where do you think?"

Paul stroked his goatee and squinted at his wife. "Well, I don't know," he said, his voice contorted into a comic impression of Inspector Clouseau. "Could it be London? No, no, no. She was there last week. How about Omaha? No? Casper, Wyoming? Gosh, dear wife, it could be so many places. Won't you help a husband out?"

Valerie closed the dishwasher, hard. "Your dinner's ready. It's been a long day. Why don't you just eat?"

Paul reached into the microwave for his plate, and then pulled back, his fingers burned. "Goddammit!"

"Come on, Dad, I'm trying to work here," Hugh said.

"Sorry, sorry."

Valerie came over, pot holders on her hands, and shooed Paul away. "Sit down," she said. "I'll bring it."

Paul skulked to the dining room and took a seat. When Valerie set the plate before him, he reached out and held her wrist and felt her flinch.

"Sit down and keep me company?"

"Paul, it's late."

"Just for a minute?"

She pulled her arm away and moved to the seat opposite him, at the other end of the table. She smoothed her skirt across her thighs as she sat.

"Don't you want to know how practice went?" he asked.

"Tell me."

"OK, I will: It was fantastic."

"That's great. How did Mendy do?"

"Fantastic! Mark my words, Val. She's going to be the best player I've ever had."

Valerie no longer looked peeved, as she had since Paul walked in, but rather hurt. "I thought I was the best player you've ever had," she said, and Paul knew that (a) she wasn't kidding around and (b) he'd stepped in it.

"Oh, baby, you're better than the best. You're my favorite."

The storm rolled across Val's face again, and now she pivoted to concern. "It's great that you're excited. Just don't get carried away."

"Who's carried away?"

Valerie smoothed the tablecloth, pressing her hands against the fabric, her arms extended at a flat angle. "You. Everybody."

"No ..."

She cut him off. "Just ... Paul, I'm tired. Let's talk about this another time."

She stood. He rose to meet her.

"What's up with you, Val? It seems like you're pissed off about more than my missing dinner."

Valerie moved to the other side of the table. Paul moved with her, cutting off the path she intended to take. "Paul, just drop it."

"No, come on. Talk to me."

"Give me your plate."

Paul picked up the dish, a way-back wedding gift, and handed it across the table to her. Valerie carried it into the kitchen, where she ran hot water over it and scrubbed at the barnacles of stubborn food. "It occurred to me just today that this happens every year, and yet I forget about it until it's upon us again," she said.

"What?"

"Basketball season. We won't see much of you. I can just about count on your not doing much of anything around this house for the next three months."

"Our father, the ghost," Hugh tossed in. Paul turned his head, annoyed, but Valerie started up again, retrieving his attention.

"You were supposed to go get Buster's nails trimmed this week. Did you do that?" Paul opened his mouth to answer, and she interrupted him again. "No, of course you didn't. Don't worry. I'll do it. If that dog has to wait for you, he'll sound like a tap dancer when he walks."

"Well," Paul said. "I had no idea I was such a disappointment around here."

"For you to be a disappointment, we'd have to have expectations," Hugh said, bobbing back into the conversation.

"Hugh, hush," his mother said.

"That's enough for me," the boy said, closing his textbook and standing. "I'll see you in the morning, Mom. See you in March, Dad."

Paul took a step toward following his son, but Valerie reached out and grabbed at his hand, shaking her head when he looked at her. Paul had never known such naked bitterness from the boy, although he also immediately conceded that they'd been headed to this patch of discontent for a while. It wasn't just that Hugh seemed to favor his mom; that had been true from the very beginning. But recent years had pushed them further away from each other, like continental drift. In eighth grade, three years earlier, the boy who came into the world as Paul Jr. opted to go by his middle name, which had wounded Paul more deeply than he had ever let on. Any common ground between father and son had long since eroded. Hugh played football, a game that Paul found to be unduly violent. The boy's nascent sense of politics and culture fell in line with that of Valerie. He had worn out her Stephen Covey books and various autobiographies of titans of industry. (The latest, a tattered copy of *Iacocca*, had sent Paul into solitary peals of laughter, imagining such obvious and uninspired titles for his preferred reading: *Jay G.!* Or maybe Hemingway's *Really Big Fish!*) His wife and son's blue-chip-stock reading left Paul to share his love of Flaubert and Nabokov with Zoe, who might have evened things up in this little domestic quarrel had she not employed the good sense to stay upstairs and out of the fray.

"Where does he get the idea he can talk to me that way?" Paul asked.

Valerie smiled slightly, causing him to wonder if it was meant to calm him or reveal her endorsement of their son's jibes. "Give him a little space on this one. He's just frustrated."

"Well, so am I, now."

"I'll just be glad when this one's over," she said. "I'm going to bed now." She leaned across, giving Paul a peck on the lips. She pulled away as he tried to slip his arms around her.

In a house gone abruptly silent, Paul caught the late news out of Billings downstairs in the den, his mind a tangle of thoughts on three fronts— work, home, basketball. As ever, it was the last one that seemed easiest to figure out. He etched X's and O's into his gray matter, moving them around as he considered the possibilities that Mendy had opened up— overloaded offensive sets, give-and-go inbound plays, defenses that he might once have considered gimmicky but now saw as viable. When he turned off the light and headed again for the stairs, it was with a self-satisfied grin splattered across his face. In a few hours, he would commit the plays to paper. In the weeks ahead, he would see them play out in practice and, if they worked there, in games.

From under Zoe's closed door, he saw light seeping into the carpet. He gave a knock.

"Go away, Hugh."

"Honey, it's me."

Next came the audible bounce of Zoe's bed as she moved, and in the several seconds that followed, Paul wondered if she might be stashing something. Just as quickly, he scolded himself. Suspicions about Zoe and what she did when she wasn't around the rest of the family (which was most of the time) had certainly found purchase, but they were owned mostly by Valerie. Paul's policy with the kids—by design with Zoe and by the boy's choice with Hugh—had been to give them latitude and remain available to talk. So far, knock wood, Zoe hadn't let him down.

The door opened. Zoe stood impassively, in a black T-shirt and a pair of gym shorts. The shorts were his, Paul noted, another manifestation of Zoe's annoying, yet somehow charming proclivity for taking whatever she wanted from the community laundry.

"What's up, Daddy-o?"

Zoe smiled as she said it, but her black fingernails thumped insistently on the other side of the door.

"Just saying hey."

"Hey!" She smiled again, wider this time, and Paul surmised that she was being playful. He hoped so, anyway. It had become increasingly difficult to tell.

He stepped through the open door, surprising his daughter, who stumbled backward a bit as she yielded the path. "Working on homework?" he asked.

"Yeah, I guess. Carlson has us reading *The Grapes of Wrath* this quarter. I'm trying to get into it."

Paul sat on the bed and flopped an arm over Buster the bulldog. "One of the greats. You'll love it."

Zoe crossed the room to the nightstand and gathered up the book. Paul looked at the walls of her room, spotting a concert poster for the Feds and the Diablotones, whatever those were. Zoe had brought it back from Oregon, where she had spent a few weeks the previous summer with her cousin on Val's side.

"You really loved it in Portland, huh?"

She tossed the book to him, hitting him in the chest. "Oh, Daddy-o, it was the best."

"I thought Seattle was the—what do you say?—the bomb."

"Not anymore. Now come on, talk to me about this book. Like, what's the deal with Chapter 3? This guy gets out of prison and tries to find his family, and then there's a freaking turtle. That's weird."

Paul patted the bed, inviting Zoe to sit. She plopped down.

"That chapter is intercalary," he said.

"What?"

"Intercalary. I-N-T-E-R-C-A-L-A-R-Y. Remember it. It'll blow Mr. Carlson's mind if you ever say the word. Basically, what it means is it's been interposed in the book to illustrate something that illuminates the theme of the story. In this case, it's a metaphor for Tom Joad and his family and the migrants in general: They keep going, no matter how hard or how slow, or how long it will take to get there. They're tough and tenacious, just like a turtle."

"And they're literally carrying their home with them," she said.

"That, too."

"Sweet! I think you just did my homework. Thanks, Daddy-o."

"Why you ..." Paul reached across the bed and looped an arm around his daughter's neck, pulling the girl into a headlock and applying a weapons-grade noogie to her amid a cacophony of giggles.

"Dad, stop it." She laughed harder, and he bore down. Buster clambered to his feet and nipped playfully at Paul's sleeves, trying to join the fun.

"Dad!"

Paul released her, and she fell back onto the bed, laughing.

After she caught her breath, she sat up again.

"How was practice?"

"Really good," he said. "I think it's going to be a fun season."

"Mendy's really good, isn't she?"

"She is. But you knew that."

"Yeah. This town's going nuts for her."

"It'll die down."

"You sure?"

Paul wasn't. "Yes."

"Dad?"

"Yeah, sweetie?"

"Can we go shoot some baskets? Like we used to?"

Paul looked at his watch. 10:45 p.m. "Now? Really?"

"Please?"

In the dreamlike glow of the sleepy gymnasium, with the yellow sodium lights illuminating half the court and darkness lapping at the corners, Paul watched and fetched as Zoe flung basketballs at the hoop. Her form, picture perfect just as he had taught it to her years earlier, ensured that more balls went in than did not. Paul couldn't help but think that had Zoe's interests not lain elsewhere, she might have been a terrific player for him.

And then, on the next shot, he was glad it had never worked out that way. In a different set of circumstances, she might never have asked to be in the gym at this moment. The vision came on like a thunderclap—Paul, seeing himself in his dotage, remembering his life not as a sequential narrative but rather as a series of snippets that whipped through his head faster than he could make out the finer details. Superimposed on the seventeen-year-old girl in front of him now was his memory of Zoe at birth, at one, at two, at three—her mind a sponge even then, her heart full of love and tenderness, her soul old, from the very beginning. He could see that girl, and he could see what she had become, and he felt the depth and fierceness of his love for her. He knew he would treasure this fast-dying day far beyond its end.

The fairway split like a broken heart. Valerie's ball dropped in for a soft landing and rolled to a spot dead center in the brown-flecked grass.

"Somebody's been practicing," Grant Lundquist said, whistling and cupping a hand over his brow as a hedge against an ambitious November sun.

"What can I say? Business has been very, very good," she replied, shaking her hips boogie-style as she ceded the tee box to her playing partner. "Lucky break to get such a nice day this late in the year. I'm glad you thought of this."

Lundquist's porterhouse hands and fencepost legs marked him as a former athlete, and the gut spilling over his belt gave away the office-bound years that had followed. After a rickety backswing—Valerie stifled a giggle at how her high school sweetie's head came up and his shoulders came off the line—he ripped through the release, launching the ball to a spot a good eighty yards ahead of Valerie's and well off target, into the rough.

"Damn."

Valerie laughed. "Come on, slugger. Let's get going. I need to hustle if we're going to get nine holes in."

"I need to talk to you about something." Grant leaned against his passenger-side door. Valerie opened her own car and hung through the window.

"It's about Paul and the team," he said.

She dug a fingernail into the seal around the window. "I figured."

"What?"

"Nothing. Just ..."

"Yeah?"

"Look, I really hate this time of year, OK?"

Grant peeled back the Velcro on his golf glove and wriggled out of it. "Well, I don't have to tell you why this year is different—for the team and the whole town."

"Mendy."

"Yes, Mendy. And what Mendy represents. She's the closest thing to a celebrity this town has ever had."

Valerie shook her head. "She's just a baby, Grant."

"Maybe so, but there's no putting this thing back in the bottle. Frankly, I'm worried that Paul's going to muck it up. You know what I'm talking about. I don't think I'm speaking out of turn."

Valerie waved a hand. "No, you're fine. I hear you. What do you want from me?"

Grant moved closer. The hairs on Valerie's arm stood at attention.

"Talk to him. Try to get him to play ball, so to speak, with the rest of the town. People are really into this thing, Val. They want to hear from him—and with the first game less than a week away, they should have heard from him by now. They want to have pep rallies and fundraisers and lots of other stuff, too. Between Mendy and this team and the town's 125th, there's a whole lot of pride in Burdon City that's looking to get out. Will you talk to him?"

Valerie expelled a heavy breath. *I've been telling him this*, she thought. *He's been on autopilot, and I told him it would bite him. Here it comes.* "I'll try. I can't promise more than that. You know Paul. He does what he wants to do."

Grant set a hand on Valerie's arm. She tingled at his touch, one she knew as a girl and found herself thinking about as a woman. "I'll be blunt, Val. He's been coasting on those eight championships for a long time, running that team like his own kingdom, but people—important peo-ple who carry a lot of water around here—are getting impatient, and when Paul acts like the town isn't a part of this thing, it only makes it worse. I saw Eric Embry at the Stockman last night, and he told me Paul wouldn't let the *Bugle* cover practice yesterday. That's nuts."

An instinct to defend seized up in Valerie, surprising her. "He's never let the paper into practice."

"That's not really the point, Val. It's different this year. This isn't just his team, not now. It belongs to everyone. I can't remember the last time I saw Paul at a Kiwanis meeting or at the Elks. He needs to share this with the town, or the town's going to turn on him. I'm saying that as respectfully as I can."

Valerie pushed her sunglasses onto her nose and started her car. "I'll talk to him," she said.

"Thank you," Grant said, backing away as she pulled out of the parking space.

On the drive to her office, Valerie thought of a summer, so long ago and yet so cinematic, even now, when two young men drew her fancy and she chose the one a few years older, the one who stoked that feeling in her—a sort of whoosh that would travel from her head straight to her crotch, dancing along her spine on the in-between. The one with a nimble, tactical mind on the court and a gentle demeanor away from it. She remembered thinking how she and Paul would be unstoppable together, their similarities converging and amplifying, and their differences fitting together like one hand into another.

But that had been long ago, before she noticed or cared that Paul could be so unbending to anything but his own sense of things. She remembered thinking once that his coaching acumen would take them somewhere, maybe to a big-time college program, and she scoffed aloud at that memory now. Their life would always be like this. He coached little girls. He taught literature to kids who didn't care, who would either end up running the family farm in Burdon County or running far, far away—Missoula or Bozeman if they were headed to college, Denver or Salt Lake or San Francisco or Seattle after that. In any case, they would leave and wouldn't be back, and most of them wouldn't give a damn about Mr. Wainwright or his notions about George Eliot once they were gone.

At a stoplight, Valerie considered all of this and slammed the heel of her hand against the steering wheel. At forty-two years old and well removed from that girl blossoming into womanhood and making snap judgments about her future with breezy surety, she wondered now, not for the first time, if she had bet on the wrong horse.

The clamor of the lunchtime crowd in the teachers lounge rippled around him, but Paul scarcely noticed as he fell in deep with a book he had dug out of the basement early that morning. Zoe's literature assignment had stirred something in his cranium, a remembrance of reading a book about the writing of a Steinbeck biography—a biography of a biography, Paul had once called it. Now, having found the book and renewed acquaintance with it, Paul was there in the house in Sag Harbor with the author, rooting through the great man's freezer and arguing with himself over whether to partake of an instant dinner. The biographer had been given the keys to the house for a weekend, a chance to reconcile with Steinbeck's ghost, and Paul felt the strum of envy at such an opportunity.

The uneasy settling of a body into the seat next to Paul broke the trance.

"Got a minute?"

Paul closed the book and pursed his lips, looking at Marvin Waddell. The rotund principal wriggled in the hard plastic chair and tugged at the bottom of his shirt, trying to smooth it over prodigious mounds of flesh.

Waddell leaned forward and clasped his hands on the table. Paul looked down at the man's knuckles. They were squeezed white.

"Marvin, you don't look so good."

The principal laughed—but it was small, tentative, as if he didn't intend for it to get out. He ran his right hand through the hair at his temples, dappled with gray, to the back of his neck. "I've got a request from some of the parents."

"Oh? Which ones?"

"Come on now, Paul. This is hard enough."

"OK. What's the request?"

"They want to form a booster club."

"So let 'em. It's a free country."

"They mean the real deal, Paul. Affiliated with the athletic department, official fundraisers, a weekly meeting with you ..."

Paul picked up his book and opened it again. "Absolutely not."

"Now, just hear me out."

Paul closed the book and dropped it to the table. The teachers at the nearest table, Matsler and Renfro, ejected from their conversation and looked at Paul and Marvin.

"I'm not doing it, Marvin."

"Why?"

"Why? A hundred reasons why. This town's already half crazy about this thing, and we've had one practice. Now, you want to endorse this madness by bringing these people into the school under the banner of the athletic department. No way. I won't do it."

"Maybe it won't be that bad."

"Not that bad? Are you kidding me? I can think of no suffering quite so profound as having to listen to those people from the stands twenty-five times a year and then run tape for them every Monday night so they can tell me to my face what I'm doing wrong."

Marvin unbuttoned the cuffs on his shirt and rolled up the sleeves.

"Look, Paul, I've stomped on this thing before when it's flared up, but … well, it's different now. It's coming from more places. I was really hoping you might—"

"I won't."

"—you might at least consider it."

Paul had a head of steam behind him, but he eased up. Marvin suddenly looked tired, old. Paul reached across the table and patted his arm. "Marvin, look, you're my friend, and I'll never forget the opportunity you gave me. I'd like to think it's worked out for both of us. But I'm telling you, as a teacher and a coach and a friend, I won't be able to accept something like this. If this is the way of the world now, I'll be happy just to be a regular old English teacher and somebody else can have the headache."

"Jesus, Paul, nobody's suggesting that."

"I'm just telling you where I'm at on this deal. Can you head it off?"

Marvin pushed his corpulent body up from the table.

"I'm going to have to, I suppose."

On his way back to the classroom for his final group of the day, Paul stopped by the mailboxes in the main office and retrieved a folded piece of paper.

The stroke-perfect cursive of Elise Langley was a dead giveaway.

Mr. Wainwright … With the season starting up again, I expect to see your lesson plans through March by next Monday. As you know, the proper instruction of those students who don't play basketball is every bit as important as it is for those who do. Thank you, Elise.

He balled up the note and banked it off the wall into the waste bin.

Deep into the early hours of the next morning, Paul would ponder the mechanics of cause and effect, wondering and worrying over whether Marvin Waddell and Elise Langley had insinuated themselves onto the practice floor, a place that he considered next to sacred and belonging only to him, Susie and the girls on the team. He chewed on his sourness.

The punishments and admonitions started with the first drill, when the same freshman as the day before, Oberst, blew a layup. In quick succession, she was joined by the next three shooters, Cash and Mendy included.

"Unacceptable," Paul shouted at them, stalking them from sideline to sideline as they made their lap around the court. "Layups and free throws, layups and free throws. Make them and you win. Miss them and you lose. You girls better get your heads into it."

Free throws turned out no better. With every miss, the girls set out in circles, at one point leaving only two C-teamers in the middle of the floor. "This team may not win a game," Paul told Susie.

As Paul ran through the offense, the whistle rarely left his mouth.

"Give me the ball," he told Cash.

She fired a chest pass at him.

"Mendy, it's like this." He squared up to the basket, squeezing the ball between his hands and planting a pivot foot. "First option: jump shot." Into the air he went, releasing the ball at the peak of his jump and watching it backspin softly into the net. Cash, her face red, gathered the ball and rifled it back to him. "Second option: drive." Paul took two dribbles into the lane and then fell back to his spot on the periphery. "Third option: make the next pass." He slung the ball to Victoria Ford, directly to his left on the wing. "You know better than to just throw the ball over without even looking."

Paul turned to the players clumped on the sideline. "Shoot, drive, pass. When you get the ball in this offense, that's the sequence. I don't want anybody not following it, you got that?"

"Yes, sir," the girls answered glumly.

"You get the ball. If the defender has collapsed into the middle, you shoot the open shot. If they're crowding you, drive around them. If you're covered, make the next pass. This is not difficult. Run it again."

Paul blew the whistle, and Cash dribbled into the middle of the floor, veered right, stopped and whipped a two-handed overhead pass to Mendy on the left wing. It soared over the girl's head and crashed loudly into the bleachers.

Paul blew the whistle again. "No! Give me the ball." A freshman tossed the ball over from the sideline.

"Cash, what was that?"

"A pass."

"That's the worst pass I've ever seen in this gym. You need to be better than that. Give me a lap."

The point guard, five and a half feet of angry muscle twitching like a tuning fork, set out running. Paul proceeded to chew on the other girls.

"I don't know where your heads are, but if you don't find them, and I mean quick, things are going to turn out very bad next Tuesday. Do you understand?"

The girls answered. "Yes, sir."

"Get a drink and then come back ready to play."

The girls fell out.

At the fountain, as Mendy slurped from the falling water, Cash said, "Catch the ball, superstar."

Mendy wiped her lips with the back of her hand. "Make the pass, Cash." They moved toward each other, ready to escalate matters.

Before it could go further, Vanessa Samples stepped between them, with enough strength and girth to make her directive stick. "Both of you just shut up and do what Coach says."

When the Reverend Grunwald made clear where he was headed with the Sunday sermon, Paul wondered how deep into the pews he could sink before it would be obvious to God and everyone that he was trying to disappear. Not far, he reckoned. The good pastor, Paul's old hunting buddy, had a clear line of sight to him and seemed to be using Paul as a fixed point on the horizon amid the choppy water he aimed to sail into. Directly behind Paul sat Mayor Dunphy. Two rows back and to the left was Grant Lundquist, to whom Valerie had sent a big smile as they were taking their seats.

No escape.

"It seems to me that our fair city is awfully stirred up these days," the Reverend Grunwald was saying now. "Awfully stirred up. And I do believe that it's not for the usual reasons, with us so close to

Thanksgiving and Christmas. No, I believe it's something else, and trust me, I am not so dumb as to be unaware that part of that reason dwells under my own roof."

A ripple of laughter—more nervous than not, as Paul assessed it—spread through the chapel. Paul could feel Dunphy's laughter on his own neck.

The Reverend Grunwald went on.

"I want to say to you now that pride in our town, pride in our school, pride in our children—these are good and worthy things. But pride, as we all know, has an ugly underbelly. It is a deadly sin, and for good reason. It kills slowly, from the inside, poisoning our hearts and minds, sometimes without our even being aware."

Paul rolled his chin back and forth against his sternum, working out a knot in his neck. Valerie reached for his hand and squeezed hard.

"We love our town because we know what it has been and what it can be. We know the sacrifice we've given, time and time again, when something larger than ourselves demanded it. We are proud of that. At one particular sport, our town has been the best ever in this state, perhaps better than any school in any state. We are proud of that."

Paul looked up now and locked eyes with his friend at the pulpit.

"We should be proud. But let us not ever forget that we are not here to cover our boys in glory on the battlefield or hold our girls above all others on the basketball court. We are here to love one another, and to love God. No matter the time on the clock. No matter the score. That's why we are here. To love God, as God surely loves us."

Paul stood on the sidewalk outside First Lutheran, waiting for Valerie to bring the car around. The previous night had brought the first good freeze of the season, and he set the toe of his wingtip onto the grass to hear it crackle underfoot. He thought of home, north Texas, and the hellacious winter storms that would crash through the region every couple of years, encasing everything—grass, hedges, oak tree leaves, slow-moving children—in perfectly thin ice.

"Good sermon, wasn't it?" Bob Dunphy, eyebrow raised, looked at Paul.

"Good sermon, indeed. If you know what to listen for."

Stormy lines moved across the mayor's pink face and then receded.

"Good one, Paul. Listen, we need to talk."

"About what?"

"The team. The town. Waddell tells me you're not too keen on a booster club."

"That's what I told him, yes."

"May I ask why?"

"No time, mayor. Practice has started. For the next few months, I'm all booked up."

Dunphy put a hand on Paul's shoulder and squeezed. "Look, Paul, now's not the time, but I think this is something worth talking about. I tell you what: Why don't you come to our Rotary meeting tomorrow morning. Six a.m.? You can meet the fellas and hear some of our ideas."

Paul stepped out from under Dunphy's grip as Valerie rolled up in the Explorer. "My wife," he said. "Listen, mayor, I can't make it tomorrow. I'm booked solid. We'll do just fine with the same bake sale we have every year. We bought new uniforms last year. We've got new shoes. We're good. Really. But thanks. Thanks for the offer."

Two quick steps carried Paul to the SUV and he climbed into the passenger seat. As Valerie pulled away from the curb, Paul looked back out the window at slackjawed Bob Dunphy.

"What was that?" Valerie asked.

Paul loosened his tie and unfastened his top button. "Fucking town."

"What?" Zoe asked from the backseat.

"Everybody's gone nuts. Dunphy wants to form a booster club for the girls basketball team. A booster club, Val."

"Yeah, I've heard about that," she said.

"From who?"

"Grant."

Paul hurled his tie to the floorboard. "Lundquist?"

"Yeah."

"When?"

"A few days ago."

"What the hell did he say?"

"He said the town is into this big time and that you ought to let people inside a little bit more. It's not a radical point of view, Paul."

Paul turned away from her and looked out the window at the passing stubble fields. "You know, I've had his kid on the team two years now. Jana? She's pretty good. Quiet. Hard worker. Gives me no guff. She's a lot more like her mom, luckily for her."

Valerie ground her hands on the steering wheel. "Janet was their whole world, Paul. Grant's raising that girl alone, has been for three years. You should cut him some slack."

"Yeah, Dad, come on," Hugh tossed in. "Mr. Lundquist is a good guy."

Paul said nothing.

"Anyway, maybe you ought to hear them out," Valerie said. "It might save you some trouble later."

"I think Daddy-o ought to do what he thinks is the right thing," Zoe said. "You know better than anybody else." She put a hand on his shoulder. Paul reached for it.

"Yeah, Dad knows best," Hugh said. "Just ask him."

Paul turned in the seat, his face gone crimson. "I've heard quite enough from you lately, Junior. Sarcasm must seem like the highest form of debate to you right now, but you're just making yourself look silly."

"Don't you call me that," Hugh said, his fists forming tight balls.

Valerie slammed on the brakes. "Enough. Everybody, just cool it. Zoe, Hugh, this isn't your conversation. And, dammit, Paul, don't egg him on."

She put the Explorer into gear and eased into the subdivision.

"It's my team," Paul said, staring out the window.

Valerie exhaled. "Yes, dear. Of course it is. It always has been."

Zoe's thoughts traveled, as they had intermittently for months, to an early July night. She and Mendy had lain on their backs in the cool grass of the Grunwalds' backyard, staring intently into the black sky as starbursts in neon colors exploded above their heads. She couldn't remember now if she had moved first or Mendy had. It didn't matter, really. What lingered, as if Zoe were feeling it today for the first time, was the electricity that pooled between them as the wispiest hairs of her own bare leg mingled with Mendy's. Zoe dared not make a move, dared not lose the connection, and eventually, she gathered the courage to turn her head to the left and look at the younger girl, who was already staring at her. They smiled simultaneously, and then turned their gazes skyward again, and inside, Zoe felt liquid and warm.

Now, as Mendy tossed in jump shots in the driveway while their folks talked inside, Zoe fetched the ball and tried to drum up the courage to speak of it.

"Are you nervous about Tuesday, Mend?"

Another shot fell through the net.

"Nope."

"Really? The town's gone a little nuts."

"I don't notice."

"Come on."

Another made shot.

"I don't."

"I envy you."

Another made shot.

"Why?"

"Well, you've got everything going for you, everybody is watching you. Don't you like it?"

"I guess."

Another made shot.

This time, Zoe fetched the ball and held it. For the first time, Mendy looked at her, annoyed.

"Do you think about the fourth of July?" Zoe asked, surprising herself with her boldness.

Mendy scratched the back of her neck. "Sometimes I do, I guess."

"I think about it all the time." Zoe passed the ball back to her.

"Why?"

The next shot hit the back iron and arced back into Mendy's hands.

"I liked it," Zoe said. The older girl decided to throw everything in now. It was just her heart and her desire. "I think I'd like to kiss you. Could I do that?"

Mendy pushed up another shot, straight and true and dead center. "No, I don't think so. Whatever you think is going to happen between us, it's not."

Zoe got the ball and passed it back to her. "OK, Mendy." She cursed herself in her head. *OK, Mendy?* That was all? Not "I've been dying inside to tell you how I feel and this is what I get"? Zoe thought of all the times she'd touched herself, imagining that her hand was Mendy's, that she was Mendy, that Mendy was her, that the feeling from that night lived on in both of them. Suddenly, she couldn't get out of there fast enough, needed air, needed to be somewhere—anywhere—else. As the tears came, she ran.

Mendy shot again.

Coffee sludge and bacon grease met Paul at the door of the Double Barrel on Monday morning, another blast of comfort for the man who trusts his nose. Most early mornings found Paul here, among the long-haul truckers and the farmers and the pensioners who had nowhere and nothing else, but on this Monday, hesitation dragged on him. Thirty-six hours from game time, he'd have preferred to be just about anywhere else, so long as it was absent of folks who wanted to jaw about Bronco basketball.

He scanned the room, nodding politely at the proliferate greetings of "hey, Coach" and "go get 'em," finally finding Dirk sitting in the back of the room, at a table that would allow for at least a semblance of privacy. *God bless the pastor*, Paul thought. *He knows when I need to talk.*

"How's your stomach, old man?" Dirk teased as Paul poured himself into the opposite chair.

"Hanging in there. Just keep those eggs on your side of the table, will you?"

Dirk stabbed at a whittled-off hunk of white and gobbled it up. He found himself in a reflective mood. His friendship with this man across from him had been easy, right from the start, twenty-five years earlier. The young pastor, a man deeply devoted to his faith, found common ground with a younger-still educator whose own politics and spirituality were so different from Dirk's. Paul, he knew, came to church because coming to church is what a man of influence does in a small town, but Dirk never got the impression that he'd reached Paul in that place where a man finally gives himself over, no restraint and no hesitation, to the Lord. It troubled Dirk sometimes to know this about Paul, and though he knew he shouldn't, he often saw it as his own failure, that he could not shepherd his best friend to that peace and joy.

And yet, the two men had shared enough hunting trips—where in the screaming silence of solitude, they had dug into penetrating conversations about love and family and ethics—that Dirk trusted Paul implicitly and completely, and never was that unshakeable faith in his friend more important than now, when Dirk's own daughter was central to the plot.

"You OK, buddy?" Dirk asked.

Paul dumped three servings of half-and-half and four sugar cubes into his coffee. "Yeah. I need to talk to you about something."

"OK."

Paul stirred his drink, clinking the spoon against the ceramic rim of the cup to get at the last drops. "It's about Mendy."

"I figured."

"I'm going to bring her off the bench tomorrow."

"OK."

"Do you want to know why?"

"Is there a reason I should?" Dirk burned with the question of why, but one of the promises he'd made to himself was that he wouldn't interfere in Mendy's coaching. He'd given her the genes and the grounding in fundamentals, and now she belonged to Paul.

"Yeah, there is." Paul rubbed his eyes. "Look, I don't have to tell you what we've got in Mendy. You played big-time basketball. You've seen it. You know."

"Yes."

"And Mendy, she will be the starter soon enough. There's nothing anybody can do to stop that. But there's something about this team that's just not right. Some of them, they don't see what you and I see, not yet. To them, she's this young kid who's coming to take something from them. So I'm going to bring her off the bench, let her find her way with these girls, let them see how unbelievably good she is, how she changes everything just by her presence. Everything will sort itself out as we go along."

Dirk considered the words and considered Paul, and for the first time, he took note of how haggard the coach looked. "You've been thinking about this a lot, I take it."

"More than anything else. And look, Dirk, I'm probably not explaining it very well. Every one of these kids, I've asked them to prove that they deserve to be on this team. I've asked the same of Mendy, but maybe this will let everyone else see that, too."

"Makes sense," Dirk said.

"I'm glad you think so. I felt like I owed you an explanation, so you'd at least know what's coming. It's going to upset some people."

"They'll get over it."

Paul chugged coffee. "I keep thinking so. I'm starting to have my doubts."

"When will you be telling Mendy?" Dirk needed to know, needed to be ready to provide comfort, if comfort were necessary. This girl, his baby, had grown up with a basketball under her arm, and in all those years, she had never been a reserve. He wondered how she would take it, and perversely, he found himself excited to learn the answer. How Mendy dealt with this would, perhaps, provide some insight into his own questions about how she would handle her growing fame.

"I'm not telling her, per se. I'll tell the team who the starters are tonight after practice. I really need to keep this focus on the team. Mendy, she's going to go places and do things most of these girls can only dream about. I'm not worried about her, you know?"

"I get it."

"Do you think she's going to be OK with it?"

A slight smile crossed Dirk's face. It was the question of the hour, and an open one at that.

"We'll see."

KBRK-FM, 7:42 a.m., Tuesday, November 11, 1997:

T.J.: "All right, that was Chumbawumba with 'Tubthumping,' right here on KBRK The Brick. This is T.J. and I'm here, as always, with the Rake. Rake, my man, we'll probably play that song eight more times today. What do you think of that?"

The Rake: "Don't care."

T.J.: "You don't care? Why not?"

The Rake: "I want to talk about something else."

T.J.: "Well, Rake, the floor is yours. This here is a democracy. What do you want to talk about?"

The Rake: "You know how we're the Brick? How we always say that, you know, KBRK The Brick?"

T.J.: "The baddest radio station in the land."

The Rake: "It just reminded me that tonight's the big night, the Burdon County girls basketball team opens the season against Dawson County, right here."

T.J.: "People are loving this team, Rake."

The Rake: "Yeah, well, anyway, I was just thinking, for a few years now, that's all we've seen from the Broncos. Bricks."

T.J.: "Ooooooh. Rake! Unkind, brother! Besides, the Broncs have a not-so-secret weapon this time around."

The Rake: "You're speaking here of the lovely and talented Mendy Grunwald."

T.J.: "The one and only."

The Rake: "You know, I'd like to show her how to put it in the hole."

T.J.: "Uh ..."

The Rake: "You know?"

T.J.: "Not cool, Rake."

The Rake: "I'm sorry, man, I'm sorry. I'm just so stoked, dude! The Broncos are going to be awesome this year, man. Awesome!"

T.J.: "That's what everybody's saying."

The Rake: "There's some fine girls on that team."

T.J.: "Rake …"

The Rake: "I mean players, man, players. And how about Coach Paul Wainwright, huh? Coaching all that prime talent. Lucky dog."

T.J.: "Easy now …"

The Rake: "Everybody knows it, man. Dude picked up his wife after she played on his team. I'm just saying, he has an eye for talent, if you know what I mean."

T.J.: "I'm pretty sure that was some years later."

The Rake: "Whatever, dude. Have you checked out Mrs. Wainwright? She's still got it going on. Props, Coach Wainwright!"

T.J.: "Let's move on. Who do you think's gonna win tonight?"

The Rake: "Burdon County, no doubt."

T.J.: "You're that sure, are you?"

The Rake: "And then The Rake will win later with one of those fine girls. Call me, ladies. You know where I am."

T.J.: "He's just kidding, of course."

The Rake: "Who's kidding? I'm telling you, top to bottom, this is the foxiest team we've ever had."

T.J.: "Rake, seriously …"

The Rake: "I'd like to dress 'em all in cheerleader outfits and …"

The dead air on KBRK lasted six days until, just after 2 a.m. on November 18, the signal crackled to life with *Dr. Mathilda's Herbal Remedy Hour*, a previously recorded talk show out of Chicago. Over the next several weeks, the station veered from simulcast all-talk to sixties country and western to a tri-county trading post show, and finally back to all-talk.

T.J. was seen later that week making deliveries for the Pizza Shack. The Rake was never spotted in Burdon City again.

On Tuesday, the town woke to a hard freeze. Paul, returning through the garage after taking Buster out for his morning pee, found his daughter lying on the cold concrete, between the two cars, wearing only a T-shirt and his mesh shorts.

"Jesus, Zoe," he said, dropping to his knees beside the girl and gathering her into his arms. He could feel the shape of her bones through her frigid, purpling skin. "What happened?"

He held her close, rubbing her back, trying to bring forth heat. He wrapped her in a hug, and her chill moved through him.

"I'm so stupid, Dad."

Enveloping her, he said, "No."

"I am."

"How long have you been out here?"

The girl broke down, burying her forehead in her father's chest, telling him all in a choked whisper, her shoulders heaving, her father rubbing her back, holding her, not knowing what else to do except whisper in return, "It's going to be OK. Everything is going to be OK," over and over.

At breakfast, Paul covered for the girl.

"Zoe's not feeling too good," he said. "I told her to stay home and get some sleep."

Buttering a slice of sourdough, Valerie said, "I think I know this ruse."

Paul slammed a carton of orange juice on the countertop. "She's sick. I saw her. It's not a ruse."

Val held up a hand, her common signal. The debate was done but not resolved. It was ever thus. Hugh looked at his father, annoyed.

"Are you coming tonight?" Paul asked.

"Not me," Hugh said.

"I didn't expect so. I'm talking to your mother."

Valerie rinsed her plate. She wanted to appropriate Hugh's answer, but she knew it wouldn't fly.

"I'll be there. Same as always. You know that."

Without another word, she went downstairs.

Paul ambled along the sideline to the BCHS bench, the most common walk of his life, and his stomach turned on him. His final words had been delivered to his girls, and he now faced the crowd alone, before his team tumbled from the locker room in perfect lines for drills he'd choreographed nearly three decades earlier.

On the Burdon County side of the gym, you couldn't have slipped a piece of paper between the wedged-in partisans. A roiling wave of black and orange, they waved fleshy arms holding hand-lettered signs of exhortation: the benign ("Go BCHS!"), the self-satisfyingly clever ("On this ranch, Broncs bust Cowgirls!"), and, something new this season that Paul entirely expected and yet felt offended by just the same, the ones that elevated individual over team ("The Great Grunwald!").

Susie waited at the bench, the one face he wanted to see. He broke into a lopsided grin as he approached, and they shook hands.

Now Paul turned to the crowd, seeking orientation points. As usual, Bob Dunphy and Grant Lundquist sat two rows behind the bench, the closest they could get, and Paul knew that those two voices, kept at bay only by his own focus, would scratch at his ear all game.

Across the way, standing to the side of the visitors' bleachers— uncharacteristically full—stood Marvin Waddell, whose duty as sentry against the excesses of his own students had ensured that he had never seen a complete game in thirty years at Burd-High

Next, Paul found Valerie, perched on the top row of the home seats in a futile effort to stay out of earshot of the criticisms against her husband that would begin their annual bloom in minutes. He winked at her, and received a tissue-thin smile in return.

"Here comes your finest season yet, eh, Paul?" Dunphy was loaded for bear, and loaded.

Paul turned his gaze to the court and said nothing.

The disappointment, the rage, didn't come in increments. As the name of each player rang out over the public-address system, it was greeted with polite applause—restrained almost, as if not to squander genuine cheers on pawns when the queen had yet to come out to play. The names and positions tumbled forth—Sabrina Newman, Victoria Ford, Vanessa Samples, Jana Lundquist and, finally, Reese Cacciola—and it took a couple of beats before everyone in the place realized that Mendy Grunwald wasn't among them.

At the scorer's table, Eric Embry sat agape. In his newspaper report that morning, he'd blithely noted Mendy among the starters, the surest bet in the world, a no-brainer to end all no-brainers.

Grant Lundquist leaned forward and poked a long finger into Paul's back. "What the hell are you doing?"

Paul tossed a reply over his shoulder: "You touch me again, and I'll have you escorted out."

Dunphy stomped to the end of the row, all *shits* and *fucks* and *assholes*, and made a straight line for Waddell.

As for the rest of them—Dirk Grunwald excluded, and maybe even Valerie Wainwright—they booed, their hunger and their lust and their human frustrations mingling and matching and raining down on their girls, and on the man who would presume to lead them.

Mendy yanked off her sweats four minutes into the first quarter, with the Broncos behind 8-2 and the stands silent save for the bubbling ire at Paul. Her appearance on the sideline turned the mood. At the next dead ball, the cheers flew to the ceiling as Jana Lundquist trudged to the sideline and Mendy bounded onto the floor.

"You did great, Jana, good pressure on Number 7," Paul said as she reached the bench. She, in turn, looked toward her father, who was staring down the coach.

"It's about time, Wainwright," he said. His daughter, at the end of the bench now, buried her head in a towel.

On the Broncos' the next possession, Cash broke the Custer County trap and streaked for the middle of the lane. The two Cowgirls planted their feet, watching three Broncos bear down, and played the angles right, cutting off the passing alleys and forcing Cash left. A too-hard shot caromed off the glass and went the other way.

"Give it to Mendy!" came the cry from the stands.

Mendy played on to the middle of the second quarter and quickly imposed her talent on the equation. At ten-all, she floated downcourt on the wing, the dribble in her possession. At the three-point line, she pulled up, straight up, and sank the shot, the Broncos' first lead.

With three minutes left to go, she had staked them to an eight-point lead, 22-14, and Paul brought her to the bench. Again, the crowd's mood turned on him.

"How do you feel?" he asked Mendy, slapping a high-five with her.

"Amazing."

At halftime, Bob Dunphy took it on himself to solve the problem with Burdon County High School basketball. His first play, to storm the locker room, was turned away by Marvin Waddell. His second idea, hatched with Lundquist in the concession area, was more direct.

"We're gonna get this fucking guy fired," Dunphy said. "He thinks we're fools. He thinks he's making fools of us."

When the Broncos started the third quarter with the same five players who began the first, Dunphy leaned in to Grant and upped the stakes. "He'll never coach another game here."

Grant turned in his seat and searched out the eyes of Valerie Wainwright. She raised an eyebrow. He shook his head slowly.

And so it came to this.

With Mendy sitting, Custer County scrapped and fought and moved the score to a tie. Mendy came in midway through the third quarter, scored six points—giving her twenty-two on the night— and never took another shot.

On a broken play, a wild chase for a loose ball, Mendy dove and jammed her right wrist, her shooting hand, into the hardwood floor, tearing tendons from bone.

You could have heard a heart drop in the silence that followed.

Mendy headed for the hospital, accepting slaps with her good hand from teammates, from Paul, from fans. The Broncos, who scored just seven points the rest of the way, headed for the loss column, a two-point defeat that was sealed when a Cash jumper from twenty-five feet fell short of the basket.

In the days that followed, as a school and a town tried to pin down exactly what happened in the frantic moments after the game, accounts varied.

Grant Lundquist said he would swear on a stack of Bibles that Paul initiated contact with Bob Dunphy in the hallway after the game and, unprovoked, punched the red-faced mayor in the nose, breaking it.

The Lundquist account would come to be the gospel according to the Burdon County school system, which presented Paul with a clear, if unsatisfying, choice: retire today or be fired for cause tomorrow.

Vanessa Samples, who was drinking from a water fountain at the moment in question, would tell teammates, her parents, and anybody who would listen that the mayor had said "your career is over, you fucking piece of shit" and that Paul had then punched him in the nose, breaking it.

Marvin Waddell came late to the scrum. All he could say with certainty is that someone had punched the mayor in the nose, breaking it, and that he saw a hell of a lot of blood.

The mayor's official word was appropriately parsed: "Let's all just move beyond this regrettable incident."

Paul Wainwright would say nothing on the record. On a Sunday, let into the building by Marvin Waddell so he could empty out his office, he came across Susie in the gym.

"It's your team now, Suze," he said.

At home, a clearer picture emerged.

Paul and Valerie turned invisible to one another. One adrift, the other ashamed.

Hugh stayed at home for a week, unable to face the mockery he was sure would be waiting for him at school.

Zoe stayed home for longer than that, all the way to Christmas break.

Valerie began meeting up with Grant Lundquist for long lunches.

Paul sat for hours in his study, finally granted time to write, with nothing to say. Dirk Grunwald called and came by. Paul never answered the phone or the doorbell.

On Christmas Eve, Paul rapped at Zoe's bedroom door.

"Go away, Hugh."

"Honey, it's me."

Paul interpreted the silence that followed as assent and entered.

"Hon," he said. "Merry almost Christmas."

Zoe sat cross-legged on the bed. "We don't even have a tree. Some Christmas."

"Did you ask Santa for what you want?"

"There is no Santa, Dad. Come on."

"I think you should hedge your bets."

"Why?"

"Maybe you'll be surprised."

"What, I'm going to magically disappear, like none of this ever happened?"

"Maybe."

"No way."

"Where do you want to go?" he asked.

"I don't care. ... Wait, no, I do. As long as it's just asking a non-existent being and I'll never get it anyway, I'll just go for it: I want to go to Portland."

Paul reached into his back pocket and tossed an envelope on the bed.

"What is this?" Zoe asked.

"Look."

She opened the envelope and shook out the contents. Plane tickets tumbled onto the bed. Paul Wainright. Zoe Wainwright. Billings to Portland. Round trip.

"No way!"

Paul sat down. "You and me, two weeks. We'll see if we can find a place and a job."

Zoe fingered the tickets. "But Mom..."

"We've talked about it. It's no good anymore, Zoe. It hasn't been good in a long while. She wants to stay. Hugh wants to stay, too. We can stay if you want, but for me, it won't be here, in this house. So let's go take a look. No commitments. OK?"

Zoe held her right hand aloft. Paul gave it a high five.

The inscription on a postcard ("Greetings from Portland") fished from the Grunwalds' mailbox on December 30th, 1997:

Hi, Mend...

Sorry about your hand. You're still the best!

Zoe (and Coach)

this is butte. you have ten minutes.

The old coot shuffled by, his white hair making curlicues like blown smoke. A cinched belt dangled from his right hand, and from the belt loop hung a pillow, a faded quilt and a battered Dan Brown paperback. The old guy's left hand held up his pants, a position that forced him to adopt a gait that was half walk, half two-step across the dirty linoleum of the depot.

The man with the BlackBerry, watching from the far side of the waiting area, turned to his keypad and punched out a message.

There's the fringe of society. And then there's the fringe of the fringe of society. Those people ride the bus.

She was no doubt asleep, unaware that he had been setting messages adrift for the past half-hour. He rubbed his forehead with the heel of his right hand. If she wasn't asleep, she was ignoring him, and that didn't fit the narrative.

He looked across the steadily filling depot—past the hard gazes of men with no reason to care, past two young mothers squeezed into tube tops like sausages, past wary immigrant eyes—and found the old guy again. The man had settled into a plastic seat and thrown his head back into a nap. His Adam's apple pushed from the inside of his leathery throat, and his ample front teeth protruded from his open mouth as he snored.

The man with the BlackBerry decided to call him Luther.

He looked down at the handheld again. 1:07 a.m. His bus—Luther's bus, too, apparently—wouldn't load for another twenty minutes or so. He pulled up his email program and began two-thumb typing.

Luther Threadgill, 82. Retired. On his way to Seattle to visit his daughter, who he hasn't seen in many years, on account of her running away back in those years when Luther drank heavily. But that was a long time ago, and she has agreed to see him now, and he has everything he needs for the trip—his pillow and blanket and book. He could use another belt. Maybe she'll buy him one.

The man with the BlackBerry hit send and watched the message ping into his queue.

It isn't so difficult for a man with a BlackBerry to end up in a dingy bus depot at a dead hour. It started with an oil change in Fargo at an insta-lube place, where an aimless young man with faraway eyes—*Mike McCann the Meth Head*, the man with the BlackBerry surreptitiously called him—failed to fully tighten the drain plug on the oil pan. From there, it was a simple matter of setting down miles and a long, thin trail of motor oil. The warning light illuminated between Miles City and Forsyth, and the man with the BlackBerry pushed on toward Billings, figuring he could make it.

Thirty-seven miles short of the mark, the Corolla belched forth a metallic grumble and died.

"Threw a rod," the tow truck driver told him nearly an hour later, when he finally arrived and crawled under the nose of the car for a look-see. "Son of a bitch went right through the pan."

"Oh, hell," the man with the BlackBerry said as he relayed the news home in a text message. "I just had the oil changed this morning."

"Yep," the tow truck driver said, "and there it is." He pointed back down I-94 a piece at the last dying cough of oil. "You get it done at one of those in-and-out joints?"

"Yeah."

"I seen this happen a lot. Those guys there don't take much care."

"Bloody hell," the man with the BlackBerry said. "How long to fix it?"

The tow truck driver whistled. "Long time. Expensive."

The man with the BlackBerry rode the rest of the way in the cab of the tow truck, batting back her electronic invective (*How could you not know you were leaking oil? How dumb are you?*) with apologies and attempts at placation. In between, he attached a name to the tow truck driver, who hadn't offered one.

Jeff Hobbs. 37 years old. On his third marriage. Works the graveyard shift at the refinery in addition to driving the tow truck. Former football star. Oh, and there's this: He's gay.

He hit send, saw the message drop safely into his inbox, tucked the handheld away and stared at the lights of Billings coming into view.

"That's insane. I'm not driving six hours to Billings to pick you up." He winced as her words crashed into his ear.

"What else can we do?" he protested. "The man here says it will be at least a week before he can fix the car. I can't just sit here."

"No. I'm not coming."

"Come on. We could spend a couple of days in Red Lodge or Chico, have a little fun."

She said nothing.

"Please?" he asked.

Nothing.

"Why are you being this way?"

"I'm not being any way. Find another way home. Your problem is not my emergency."

"What am I supposed to do, walk? Hitchhike?"

He waited. She said nothing.

"Well?" he said.

Nothing.

"Huh?" he said.

The electronic garble of her sigh came back at him. "I don't really give a shit."

The burn spread across his face as the connection went dead.

The man with the BlackBerry stared at the late-night snack options while a swarthy man (*Emile*, he would later be dubbed) drummed his fingers and waited for his customer to judge the attractiveness of egg salad on white versus corned beef on rye.

"Snickers and a Pepsi, I guess," the man with the BlackBerry said. Emile rolled his eyes and fetched the order.

A moment later, the balance of the room shifted as the waiting riders herded toward the door. The man with the BlackBerry jammed the candy bar and the soda bottle into the side compartment of his leather duffel bag and hustled to join the gathering crowd. Luther Threadgill, last seen snoozing contentedly, had beaten everyone to the head of the line.

"Do I just walk my bag over to the other side?" The man with the BlackBerry nodded at the luggage being loaded into the belly of the bus.

"You don't have a tag," the driver said. Lines folded into her forehead and the space between her eyes. Her dirty blonde hair was pulled into a strident ponytail. "No tag, you carry it on."

"I'm sorry," he said. "I didn't know. It's my first time on a bus."

She stared at him. "You could have fooled me."

Chastened, he scurried up the stairs. Most of the riders ahead of him had made tracks for the back of the bus and the window seats. Luther had found a perch up front, on the aisle. The man with the BlackBerry chose the row opposite Luther and began stuffing his duffel bag into the overhead bin, struggling to squeeze it over the taut mesh.

"You might ought to put it under the seat," came the voice from behind him. He turned to see Luther pointing at the bag.

"They don't let you put anything much bigger'n a bag of peanuts up there," Luther said. "More room under the seat."

The man with the BlackBerry plopped down, retrieved the bottle of soda and shoved the duffel under his legs. "Thanks," he said, toasting Luther.

"My pleasure."

The man with the BlackBerry drummed his fingers against his bottle. "Ride the bus a lot?" he asked.

"Yep," Luther said.

"Where you headed?"

"Bozeman."

"That where you live?"

"Nope. I live here. Sister's there. Dying. Gonna go see her."

The man with the BlackBerry dropped his eyes. "I'm sorry."

"It's not your fault."

"I know … I just … well, I'm sorry to hear about that."

"Thanks."

Luther wrenched himself away from the aisle and turned to the window. The driver stepped aboard and secured herself in the Plexiglas cage.

"We'll be traveling west tonight," she said over the intercom. "Stops in Livingston, Bozeman, Butte, Missoula, St. Regis. You'll have time for breakfast in St. Regis. We'll make brief stops everywhere else. You can smoke there. Don't smoke on this bus. If you smoke on the bus, it's zero tolerance. We stop, and you get off …"

"Can you turn up the heat?" a voice called from the back.

"It'll warm up as we get going. Put on a sweater. As I was saying, you smoke, you're off the bus. Don't ask me to make any other stops unless it's an emergency. Don't cross the yellow line up here. Don't tap on the glass. Be back on the bus on time at the stops. I will not wait on you. Any questions?"

Silence.

"OK, enjoy the ride."

The man with the BlackBerry looked over at Luther. The old man's chest heaved in slumber.

Nadine never thought she would drive a bus for a living, but ever since Rob went to prison for negligent homicide, she's had to do it to keep the family solvent. Her oldest, 17-year-old Robert Jr., just got his 15-year-old girlfriend pregnant. Maddie, 11, needs braces. Little Mace has an inner-ear infection that's been driving him, and her, nuts. Sometimes, she dreams of driving the bus off a cliff and ending the misery.

Streetlamps sent light streaming across the road as the bus chugged out of town, and the man with the BlackBerry felt his eyelids grow heavy. He took a few idle sips off his bottle of soda and then stashed the remainder back in his bag. Then, thinking better of Luther's advice, he pulled the bag onto his lap and wrapped his arms around it, linking his fingers.

His head fell forward into sleep.

A hundred and twenty miles down the road, the bus left the interstate and weaved toward Livingston.

"We'll stop at a gas station up ahead and you can get out and smoke or grab a snack," Nadine announced.

The man with the BlackBerry released his death grip on his belongings. The fingers on his right hand tingled and throbbed, and he curled them to summon relief.

He leaned to his left and pressed his face to the window, watching the sideways rain leave streaks on the outside of the glass. Ahead, Livingston glowed, pushing hard against the darkness.

As the bus edged into town, the lights softened the angular buildings and street corners, illuminating them in a way that the man with the BlackBerry found pleasing and dreamlike.

"Livingston," Luther said.

"Oh, yeah. It went by quick."

"I'm almost there," Luther said.

"Yep, twenty more miles."

"Maybe the last time I'll see her." The man with the BlackBerry looked at Luther, suddenly drawn and gaunt, and wished there were something he could do or say.

"What's your sister's name?" he asked.

"Olivia."

"Beautiful name. Is she younger or older?"

"She's my baby sister. Nine of us kids, me the oldest, her the youngest. Her and me, we're the only ones left. The bookends."

Luther looked ready to cry. The man with the BlackBerry smiled, hoping to radiate comfort. "She's fortunate to have you."

Luther's mouth opened as if to speak, but Nadine cut him off.

"Ten minutes. Not a minute more," she said as the bus rolled into the parking lot of a combination gas station-casino. Lights, alternating purple and yellow, sprayed the interior of the bus with polka dots.

"I'm gonna grab a smoke," Luther said, rising from the seat and slipping his belt, which was now freed from toting, through the loops on his trousers. "You watch my stuff?"

"Sure."

Luther goose-stepped off the bus a few paces behind the rest of the nicotine addicts. They gathered in a clump against the wall of the casino, out of the rain, and sucked on their cigarettes. Nadine, too, was getting her fix, but she stayed well away from the riders, as if maintaining the integrity of the bus castes.

The man with the BlackBerry took the census. He had accounted for Nadine and Luther, who never did blaze up but merely stood with his hands in his back pockets, his face upwind of the smokers.

Merry Andrews, 23, wearing her older sister Peg's hand-me-down jeans. Merry is following her longtime boyfriend, Paul, to Spokane, where he just took a job with the sanitation department.

Eva Lopez, 63, has finally decided to reveal that she's a lesbian, which will come as a surprise to exactly no one in her family.

Ruben Gott, 27, is breaking parole by leaving Billings to take a job with a construction company in Spokane.

Oscar Bonilla, 33, is down to his last twenty dollars and will try to find work in Butte.

Bella Anderson, 31, will win Oscar's heart before the ride ends.

He hit send and then put the BlackBerry away as the smokers trudged back to the bus.

Luther said nothing else as the bus unwound the miles to Bozeman. The man with the BlackBerry watched, entranced, as Luther removed the belt from his trousers and bound up his belongings again. The bus lurched left and right, whipsawed by wind and rain through the mountain pass. The man with the BlackBerry watched as Luther's head bobbed along.

At the Main Street exit, Nadine guided the bus off the interstate and pointed it toward town.

"This is Bozeman. We won't stay long," she announced. "A quick unload and load."

Luther stood, gripping his sagging pants and giving them a tug.

"Best wishes to your sister, Luther," the man with the BlackBerry said, extending a hand.

The old man's head whipped around. "Huh?"

"I mean … best wishes to Olivia. Sorry about that. You remind me of someone I used to know."

He extended his hand again, and Luther shook it. "Thanks."

The old man lurched off the bus with two other passengers, Merry and Bella (who was leaving Oscar's heart in his chest, apparently). Nadine, standing outside the door, wished them well. The man with the BlackBerry watched through the window opposite him as Luther ambled inside the depot.

He looked down at his handheld. 4:23 a.m. He sent a text message.

In Bozeman. Be there in a few hours.

To his surprise, the BlackBerry vibrated moments later.

Take a cab home. Or whatever.

Five minutes after Luther had vacated his spot, she claimed it. The man with the BlackBerry had been thumbing through his messages and didn't notice her until she folded into the seat, and by then she was impossible to ignore, with black hair, black nails, black pencil dress, black stockings, black flats. The man with the BlackBerry ran his eyes from her left shoulder to her fingers, and it was only there that he found a hint of color. She had been chewing at her cuticles, leaving angry, raw fingertips hanging from her porcelain hands.

She caught him staring. "Morning," he said, coaxing a smile.

She looked away.

The bus swung out of the parking lot and growled toward the interstate. He launched a new email message.

Darcia McMahon. She's 33 but looks 25. She's a high-end call girl, just off a job and headed home to Missoula. She makes six figures a year and hates her life. She chews her fingers from the stress. She would trade it all for two children, an overweight husband named Ted and a small house with a garden.

Darcia tapped the man with the BlackBerry on the arm.

"What are you doing?" she asked.

He cleared the screen. "Nothing. Just surfing around. Answering some messages."

She pointed at the gadget. "Doesn't that thing keep you boxed in?"

Her plaintive questioning—her legs swung around so they were in the aisle, her body perpendicular to his, her eyes never leaving him—made him uncomfortable.

"Not really."

"That I doubt."

He made a quarter-turn in his seat to better face her.

"I travel a lot," he said. "This is how I keep in touch. I would be much more boxed in, as you say, without it."

The corners of her mouth turned up. He now saw lines breaking through her makeup, erosions suggesting that she might be a bit older than he'd originally pegged her.

"I travel a lot, too," she said. "And yet I don't have one of those."

He laughed. "You probably don't travel as much as I do."

"You want to bet?"

Her words came out aggressive, a challenge. He smiled at her. He liked it.

"Bet?" he asked. "What are the stakes?"

She smiled in return. He felt smitten. "You tell me how much you travel—give me dates and places—and then I'll tell you how much I travel. And after I've won, I'll tell you what I want."

He started with that week, how he had left Missoula early Sunday and headed due east on I-90, swung south at Laurel and arrived in Cody.

"Four hundred and sixteen miles," he crowed. "Did it in just over six hours."

Monday morning brought meetings at the Cody hospital, and by that afternoon, two hundred and fifty-two miles later, he was in Gillette, ringing up handsome sales of his company's latest wonder drug.

"I slept that night in Belle Fourche," he said. "That's another hundred and three miles."

She listened impassively, chewing her fingers, and he took notice of just how big her eyes were. When she had first sat down, he thought her striking. Now, he could see, she was beautiful. Completely, fully, achingly beautiful.

"Go on," she said.

Tuesday delivered him to the Belle Fourche Health Care Center (commission!), the Spearfish Regional Hospital (thirteen miles and another commission!), Rapid City Regional Hospital (forty-eight miles, cha-ching!) and the long drive to Sioux Falls (three hundred and forty-seven miles, goodnight, sleep tight, don't let the bedbugs bite).

More sales flowed at three hospitals in Sioux Falls on Wednesday, and then the man with the BlackBerry turned the Corolla—fifteen months old, fifty-five thousand miles on the odometer—north toward Fargo, two hundred and forty-four miles away. Thursday, he noted smugly, he had his biggest day ever. Enough to put in that pool that she had been asking about for years.

"And then it went to shit," he said.

She sat erect. "Shit?"

The oil change. The oil loss. The breakdown. Six hundred and ten miles from Fargo to Billings, and he covered just five hundred and seventy-three of them.

"That's why I'm on this bus," he said. "I'm just trying to get home. But that was my week, nineteen hundred and ninety-six miles. It would have been more. I'm on the road forty-five weeks a year. You still sure you're going to win?"

"Yes," she said.

"Okay, tell me."

"I have a question first."

"Shoot."

She pointed at the BlackBerry. He held it like a rosary. "Why are you tethered to that thing?"

"I'm not tethered," he protested—a bit too quickly, he thought. "I need this. I'd be lost without it."

"So you're a slave."

"You don't know me." He waved his hand at her.

She turned away.

A few minutes of staring out his window at the passing darkness did nothing to soothe him. The words stung. More than that, they stuck. That he had gotten angry at her for being correct left him feeling foolish.

He turned to Darcia. "So how do you figure you win?"

She stared ahead for a few seconds before she spoke.

"Every day for one thousand, three-hundred and fifty-seven days, I've been riding a bus."

"You're putting me on."

"No, I'm not."

"Why would you do that?"

"Why not?"

"That's not an answer."

"It's the best one I have."

"Come on. Tell me."

She swung her legs back into the aisle. "My husband drove for this line. On February 23rd, 2007, in Liberal, Kansas, he was shot in the face by one of his passengers. It blew his jaw clean off. He bled out on an empty bus because all his passengers scattered. Can you even imagine what that must have looked like?"

He opened his mouth. No words came.

"I try to picture it sometimes, but I can't do it," she said. "In my head, his face is in pieces, like a puzzle. And lately I've realized that I'm forgetting what he looked like when his face was complete."

She paused after she said this, and the man with the BlackBerry lifted his downcast eyes to her. Her expression was unchanged.

"Anyway, a week later, the CEO offered me some money and lifetime bus passes. I think he thought I was going to sue. I wasn't."

"Jesus," the man with the BlackBerry said.

She raked her bottom lip with her teeth.

"So on March 7th, I boarded a bus in Tucson, where I lived, and I've been on one since."

"Jesus."

"Yeah."

"How long are you going to do this?" he asked.

"I have no idea. Until I don't feel like doing it anymore."

"Where do you go?"

"Everywhere."

"Where are you going now?"

"Where does this bus stop?"

"Seattle, I think."

"Seattle, then."

"And after that?"

"Wherever."

"Jesus."

"You keep saying that."

"I know."

She turned back to the seat in front of her. He fiddled with his handheld. She gnawed on her fingers. The rest of the riders slept, and Nadine mowed the miles.

"Don't you get lonely?" he asked.

She shrugged. "When you're lonely to begin with, there's nothing more that can touch you."

"I wish I could do what you do," he said. "I travel, but there's always a job. Always someone to see. I'd like to just get out and go for a while, maybe a month or two. But I think I'd get lonely."

"You're not lonely now?"

"No. I have a family."

"But you never see them."

"I'm not lonely," he said. "Are you?"

She shook her head. "I'm always among people. I like to watch them. I like to imagine what their lives must be like. I can do that, and I don't have to make an investment in them. Like you, for example. I've already forgotten your name."

"I never told you my name."

"That's my point."

He fingered his BlackBerry, tracing the outline of its keys, suddenly needing the tactile relief they provided. "I know what you mean about watching people," he said. "When I'm on the road, about the only thing I do for fun is people-watch. I go the mall sometimes and just sit. I like to invent names, jobs, family situations. I send little stories to myself so I can remember them later, after I'm gone."

She pointed again at the BlackBerry. "Did you name me?"

"Yes."

"What?"

"Darcia."

It was as if the moon hidden in her face lit up, and again, he felt smitten. "It fits," she said.

"Really?"

"Maybe so, maybe no. It doesn't really matter, does it?"

Nadine nosed the bus off the interstate and headed toward the lights of the mining town. The man with the BlackBerry watched the buildings pass in repose. After a couple of miles, the bus left the street and pulled into a depot adjacent to a dark shopping center.

"This is Butte," Nadine told them. "You have ten minutes."

Darcia grabbed his hand. "Come on."

He reached for the BlackBerry.

"No, leave it," she said, and he dropped it to the seat as they pushed ahead of the passengers gathering behind them.

She cut a sharp line for the depot, pulling him along.

"What are we doing," he asked.

"Not being lonely. Come on."

They stepped into the white glare of the lobby.

"Go in the restroom," she whispered. "Get in the stall. I'll be there in a second."

He did as she instructed, unable to penetrate what she had compelled him to do. He felt as though he were outside himself, watching his own movements with fascination and abject fear.

He skipped through the empty restroom to the large stall in the back, opened the door and stepped inside. His heart beat out a bass line in his chest, and sweat gathered and danced on his brow.

He heard the door open and the clip-clap of her flats on the tile. She rapped at the stall door, and he opened it.

She yielded no room to breathe, closing the distance between them and finding his mouth with hers, their tongues fighting it out.

He grabbed her by the shoulders and kissed her. He felt fierce, indomitable. Alive.

"You can't come with me, you know," she said between breaths, as he kissed her neck and chest.

"I know."

Their collision was raw, violent. He moved in again, and she pushed a hand against his face, clipping his nose and bloodying it. He threw her against the metal wall and pulled up her dress, and she gasped as he clawed at her stockings to get inside her.

"Call me by my name," she said.

"Darcia," he said, and she squeezed him tight inside her legs. He vibrated angrily, pushing into her, and they moved in rhythm.

As he finished and the sadness washed over him, he found himself saying something he hadn't been able to tell anyone, not even himself.

"I am alone. She hates me."

Nadine hit them with a disapproving stare as they returned to the bus, now several passengers lighter. Darcia headed for an empty spot in the back. Toilet paper jammed into his bleeding nostril, he reunited with his BlackBerry and took his customary seat.

"Next stop is Missoula, two hours," Nadine said as she settled in.

A few minutes later, the man with the BlackBerry stumbled into sleep, never stirring as messages from home, slathered in vitriol and covering his failures as a man, as a provider, as a husband, filled his inbox.

The morning sun sparked off the snow-dappled mountains as the man with the BlackBerry left the bus. He thanked Nadine for the ride.

He dialed the cab company and was told that the driver would pick him up in ten minutes. He exhaled and watched his frozen breath blow away. He took in his city at three-hundred and sixty degrees, pivoting slowly in place. For eight years, it had been a place to be when he wasn't somewhere else. In the cold light of a new day, he saw possibilities.

Still on the bus, Darcia slept.

He caught his reflection in the rearview mirror of the cab and saw the blood crusted under his nose, now bulbous and inflamed. The splashes of red on the front of his shirt had turned dark. His hair looked like hell. When the driver glanced up and met his eyes, the man with the BlackBerry looked away.

The cab weaved through the morning traffic, and the man with the BlackBerry double-thumbed a message to the angry woman waiting at home:

This is Neil Hansen. I'm 42 years old, I've been on the road nearly half my life, and I've been gone too long. When I get there, we're going to settle this once and for all.

alyssa alights

The girl pushed her back into the wall, straining against the mortar as if believing that it would relent and let her wriggle out of the raindrops falling into puddles around her. She didn't actually believe any such thing; a break like that never comes your way, not when you really need it. But what were her choices? She could sit in the rain or try to get out of it, if only by increments. She dug in again, pushing the heels of her worn sneakers against the asphalt and shoving backward, and she could feel the rough edge of the brick pierce first her steadily soaking T-shirt and then the skin on the small of her back. She pushed till it hurt too much to push further, and then she looked skyward and took a raindrop in the eye, a just reward for seeking answers there.

The alley she had chosen wasn't much of a shelter, but she figured it would have to do. She hadn't seen any better options since walking out of the Greyhound station hours earlier. She had tried a few downtown doorways, but soon enough, the rent-a-cops had come around and moved her along. She had considered—and then quickly abandoned consideration of—finding a bench in a city park. Too out in the open. Here, sandwiched between a parking garage and a hair salon and partially hidden by a trash bin, she figured she could at least close her eyes and rest. If someone came along, she would surely hear him (*and it's always a him*, she thought) and she could hunker down or, if she had to, make a run in either direction to the street.

She thought of that scenario again, and now it was suddenly alive and dangerous. She cursed under her breath and tried to assure herself that she was as safe as a girl sleeping in an alley could be. Still, she had long since learned that she was the sort of girl who needed a contingency plan. Running to the street—screaming if necessary—was hers. She hoped it wouldn't come to that, but she had hoped before and been disappointed.

"Just let me close my eyes," she said softly. She let her legs go slack, straight out from her, and the rain, falling sideways now, found and pelted them. The drops soaked through the denim, and she grew chilly. She tucked her chin and squeezed rain out of her auburn hair. The jagged teeth of the Billings skyline swallowed her in darkness, and her eyes grew heavy. It wasn't long before sleep came for her. So, too, did the stardust memories of what had led her to such a place.

The departure, while abrupt, could hardly be called a flight of whimsy. She knew precisely what she was doing, and why, and that she hadn't told anyone the what or the why was her own decision. It had felt good to actually make one; decisions were all she had that truly belonged to her. A new town, a new name, a new start—she figured she was owed that, but because she had never known the universe to make a concession to the likes of her, she hedged her bets and forced the issue.

On the day she left, she awoke at four in the morning and quietly filled her backpack with what it could hold—clothes, mostly, and her journal, but also a couple of granola bars and a small bottle of water. She crept past her mother's closed door and stuck close to the baseboards, where the floor was less likely to betray her. In Patty's room, she lingered, though she knew she shouldn't. Every moment she waited increased her odds of being found out. She stared at Patty's skin, the color of cream, and she stroked the girl's hair, pulling back only when Patty stirred. She held her breath and waited for the girl to roll back into slumber. When Patty did, the girl stepped out of the room and continued her creep on little cat paws toward the door.

Finally outside the house, she cut a path out of Sidney on side streets, staying well off the main drag, with its restaurants and gas stations. Even at such an early hour, the eyes that would surely see her leaving would give way to the tongues that would surely tell on her. It wasn't until she neared the intersection of Highway 200 and Highway 16 that she dared skip over to the main road. She settled onto the shoulder and began walking southwest, toward Glendive, where a bus to Billings awaited.

She patted the right front pocket of her jeans, which held a wallet. That, in turn, contained eighty-three dollars, all the money she had managed to save from her job at the M&M. The wallet, she knew, was the most important thing she was carrying. Every few steps, her right hand found its way to the front of her pants, and she traced its outline, verifying again its existence.

A mile out of town, the first semi of the day rumbled behind her, coming from Williston. She turned and thrust her right thumb skyward and smiled. Just as she figured he would, the trucker eased his rig onto the shoulder. When she caught up to him, he reached across and opened the passenger door.

"Where you headed?"

"Glendive," she said.

"What's there?"

"My grandma."

"I'm headed for Spokane. You want to go?"

"Glendive's fine. My grandma's there."

"Sure," the trucker said. His creased face and black eyes bore in on her, and she sensed wildness and unpredictability behind them. That scared her, but the idea of not getting the ride scared her more. Her mother would be awake soon, and maybe she would call the cops. Maybe not. Someone she knew would see her out here, and that made her an easy mark. She clambered up, and the trucker kept her at bay with a raised hand.

"You got any money for fuel? I'm not supposed to pick people up. I could lose my job."

"I don't," she lied.

His eyes flickered, and her guts did flips. She looked at the ground.

"Well, get in. We'll figure something out."

That he expected to be topped off could not have surprised the girl any less, and though she found him repugnant, she ciphered out the equation and found that it balanced. Blowjob equals ride equals Glendive equals bus ticket equals escape. She closed her eyes and went down, and when she sensed that he was set to go, she squirmed free of the hand pressed at the back of her head.

"It's a goddamned mess," he said.

She said nothing.

"I ought to put you out right here."

She watched the unfolding asphalt.

"Goddamned stupid girl," he said, and he turned his attention back to the road. The truck lurched up a rise on the two-lane highway, and when it crested, she looked left at the watery ribbon of the Yellowstone River below and the painted buttes in the hazy distance. It looked like freedom to her, or the next nearest thing.

She asked him to pull over at the gas station abutting Interstate 94.

"Your grandmother work here?" he asked.

"No, but this is where she picks me up." She released the door handle and clambered down to the concrete.

"You sure you don't wanna come to Spokane with me? We could have a real good time." The way he smiled and unfurled the word "real"— *reeeeeaaal*—gave her insides another hard twist.

"I can't," she said.

"Your loss," he said, and he reached across the vacated seat and pulled the door shut.

She watched until the truck crossed back under the interstate and made the wide left turn onto the westbound ramp. Once it was out of sight, she ran for the restroom on the side of the gas station. She almost made it to the toilet before the previous night's dinner and the bile she had been swallowing for a week turned on her.

When her eyes fluttered open, she caught and held her breath.

Something was out there.

She craned her neck left and right and scanned the alley. Nothing.

The rain had passed. As her senses rallied into form, she heard the ping of water falling from the eaves into pools that had gathered in the alleyway.

The storm clouds that had been rolling in on her all night had peeled back, revealing a mottled, blue-gray sky backlit by a quarter-moon. Even through the glow of the street lamp, she saw stars, and she silently thrilled at the vision. Her mind opened, and she stepped through her memories just a couple of months earlier, to the Fourth of July, when she and Patty had lain on the trampoline in her grandparents' backyard and watched the fireworks cascade through the sky from the fairgrounds. With each burst of red and blue and green, she had turned and watched her sister in profile, the little girl's wonderment stitched across her face. Afterward, they had counted stars, and the older girl had pointed out the Little Dipper and the Big Dipper and Orion's belt. Such a simple thing it was, but she had known that it was a touchstone memory, something she could cling to as Patty grew older and more independent. She had learned to keep such things close to her heart. And now, in the darkness, she held on for dear life.

She pulled the fraying winter coat tighter around her shoulders. She had outgrown it a year earlier, but there hadn't been time to get another before she departed. As the chill set in, she offered silent thanks that she had remembered to grab it from the front closet. She could find a bigger coat later. Tonight, she needed this one.

Her eyelids sagged again, and she faded away.

Forty feet above, at the top level of the parking garage, the silent sentry crept back to the ledge and looked down.

He had very nearly missed her. The rounds brought him to this place nightly. Tonight, there was no work—no stinking punchdrunk bums to chase out, no oversexed teenagers going at it in a parked car. He had made a final sweep along the periphery of the lot, collecting a few bottles and cans that he could use, picking up scraps of paper that he would throw away later. He was about to glance away when the girl wriggled into view beside the trash bin. He had stepped back lest she look up and spot him. Then he had pressed forward again—slowly, slowly—to take another look.

That had been three hours ago. His bicycle sat a few feet away, propped on its kickstand. The cart attached to the back axle held the treasures of a night's scrounging—a few magazines, bottles and cans, a couple of blankets he had found earlier in the evening behind the men's shelter. He kept the police scanner pressed to his ear, but it had been a quiet night, with no malfeasance that required him. *It's just as well*, he thought. He wasn't sure he could leave, not with that girl down there.

The scanner crackled, and he turned the volume knob down and pressed the speaker tight against his head. Some bums breaking beer bottles in North Park. Patrol car on the way. North Park was his beat, but it could wait.

I'll do a sweep tomorrow, he thought. *If they're still in North Park tomorrow, they'll be sorry.*

He twisted the knob on the scanner to the off position and looked down again to the concrete below.

She had gone still.

The man soft-shoed to his bicycle, his deft movements belying his size. He made sure everything was in order, and then he threw his right leg over the crossbar and started pedaling, down, down, down in a tight circle to the bottom of the garage.

The big man crept like a stalking cat. He walked toward the girl at an angle so as not to cast a shadow across her eyes and rouse her. When he was close enough to see that she was, perhaps, even younger than he expected, he brought the blanket out from behind his back and gingerly set it across her.

The girl flopped her head to the left, and he froze. The knotty muscles in his legs, honed by days on the bike, twitched with the impulse to run, and the big man grimaced at the effort required to resist. After a few agonizing seconds, the girl's breathing kicked in again, and so did his.

He stepped backward, ever so slowly, and mounted his bicycle.

When he had pushed back silently to the street, he turned and pointed his nose east, toward the coming dawn.

The jab from the broom caught the girl under the rib cage and launched her, yelling, out of a pleasant dream. Eyes wide, she looked up to see a short woman with black hair and frantic eyes. The woman held the broom like a vaulting pole.

"This isn't your house," the woman spat out, and when the girl pushed herself off the concrete, her tormentor backpedaled but kept the broom aloft and rigid.

"That really hurt, bitch," the girl said. "Put that thing down."

"Go on," the woman said, signaling the desired direction with the business end of the broom. "I'm so sick of finding people like you back here. This isn't your home. Get out."

The girl stooped over to collect her things, keeping an eye on the woman with the broom.

"I was just sleeping," she said. "I didn't do anything to you."

"Sleep somewhere else."

The girl patted the familiar spot on the front of her jeans and found the wallet. She shimmied into her too-small coat and then did a double take at the sight of the blanket.

"Get out," the woman said.

"All right. Jesus." She quickly folded and packed the patterned blue-gray Indian blanket whose better days had been spent wrapped around someone else, and then she turned to the woman and offered a saccharine smile. "Thank you kindly for the hospitality," she said.

"Go." The woman bristled.

With an exaggerated waggle, she sashayed past the woman, moving uncomfortably close and fixing her with a downward stare. The blessings of being a tall, gangly girl were few—most of them confined to basketball, which she despised—but intimidating short people was one of her favorites. Sure enough, the woman took a step back as the girl passed.

Halfway down the alley, she raised her arms triumphantly, as if she had gone twelve rounds and won.

The bewildered woman found her voice and called after her: "Don't ever come back."

Arms aloft, the girl turned right at the end of the alley and disappeared.

At a corner, she stood and took in the bustling cityscape. Her face twisted as she made note of her surroundings. Looking south toward the railroad tracks, she saw possibilities: boutiques and small restaurants and the like, all going concerns, many perhaps in need of someone to sweep floors or take food and drink orders. She could do those things and many others. She resolved to come back as soon as she was ready.

Her first stop, though, lay several blocks away, and she walked toward the tracks to find it. She kept her eyes forward and didn't meet the stares that migrated to her. It wasn't difficult for her to imagine how shocking she must have looked. She had slept outside, in a steady rain, and she had emerged from sleep facing a mad woman with a broom. She'd had no time or opportunity for primping. As another passerby stared a moment too long, she pawed at her brittle hair, dropped her head and kept moving.

The railroad tracks cleaved Billings in two. Behind her lay the workaday part of town, the one that filled every weekday morning and emptied at night. Ahead, the part of town that scratched out its existence daily came into view. The girl crossed the rails and stepped into Old Town, into the province of grown-over lots and buildings bullied by weather and neglect, an area of many decades' decline now pockmarked by small signs of gentrification, mostly old buildings retrofitted for new offices. A block ahead, she saw the men's shelter, and she knew from her surreptitious Internet surfing at school, as she plotted her leave, that her destination lay just beyond, in the thrift shop that helped support the shelter. She patted the wallet in her jeans pocket. After the bus ticket and some food, she had thirty-seven dollars and change, and she hoped that would be enough for some decent work clothes and enough cosmetics to make her passable for employment.

The morning action frothed around the shelter, with the previous night's guests hitting the streets to while away another day before coming back for a hot meal and a cot. Her intrusion— "Here comes the sausagefest," she said to herself as she approached—drew a few predictable wolf whistles, but mostly, the men let her pass without a word. She dodged a few gappy grins, neither returning nor encouraging them. As she walked on to the thrift store, she felt a tightening in her stomach, something she recognized as a fear that their fate—to be turned out daily, without a real home and without real love—might someday be hers. Soon, if she couldn't make her plan work.

The girl lingered a moment before going in and tried to shake the doubt from her head. She couldn't afford to lose confidence before she even started.

If that's all you've got, she said inside her own head, *just go buy a ticket home.*

She pulled open the door and stepped inside.

The fashions were wrong—everything that fit seemed a decade out of date—but the prices were right. She collected five pairs of women's slacks, in an assortment of fabrics, and five blouses and sweaters for twenty-two dollars and fifty cents. When she told the woman behind the counter that she would use the garments as work clothes, the clerk asked softly, "You staying someplace?"

"Not yet," the girl said.

The clerk threw in a beaten-up duffel bag, bigger and more sensible than the girl's backpack, free of charge. When she inquired about makeup, the clerk dug around in her own purse and scared up lipstick, foundation and eyeliner.

"Thank you," the girl said. The kindness awed her.

The clerk smiled, patting the girl's arm. "Good luck, kiddo."

Facing herself in the mirror, she wondered if she should be thankful or horrified that she had only a single 40-watt bulb to reveal her dishevelment. The reason for the stares seemed clear enough now; shocks of her red hair flared out from her head at ridiculous angles, and her face was smudged with grime, relegating her freckles to the background.

She cleaned her face and hair as best as she could, then slipped out of the clothes she had been wearing for two days. Standing there, naked and clean, she felt good for the first time in a long while. Her body—hard right angles for so long—had begun to fill out in all the proper places, and the rangy limbs that she tried hard to love, as they came from her father, were giving way to the soft edges of a woman. She turned ninety degrees to the right and took in her profile in the mirror. She broke into a toothy smile as she looked at the outline of her breasts. God, she loved her boobs. They were perfect—big enough to attract attention (sometimes unwanted, but still) and shapely enough to ensure that she wasn't top-heavy. She liked that she could move men's eyes with her chest, and so long as her not-so-secret admirers looked discreetly and didn't move aggressively toward her, she took no offense at being watched in that way, like some girls do. She was certain that she didn't want to live in a world where breasts couldn't be admired.

She cupped her bosom in her hands and admired her endowment once more, and then she dressed.

At most of the businesses, the proprietors simply shook their heads when asked about a job. Hard times, most of them said. Some intimated that they were barely staying afloat and that an addition to the payroll— even someone as eager to work and as inexpensive as a girl like her— would sink the works.

At the hamburger place on Twenty-Ninth Street, she sat in agony as the manager went over her application. The smell of french fries and grilling meat teased her nose, and she squirmed when her stomach rumbled.

"This looks good, Alyssa," the young man said as he thumped the eraser end of his pencil against the form. "We might be able to throw you a few hours to start, and we'll see how it works out."

"Great," she said, coaxing a cautious smile. She resisted the urge to tell him that she preferred to be called "Tomato"; this wasn't the time to go wrecking things with a moniker she would have to explain. Instead, she thought about the remaining cash in her wallet—reaching down yet again to feel the outline of it—and then she thought how irresponsible it would be to spend it here.

"You didn't put anything here for an address," he said, pointing to the empty lines on the sheet of paper.

"I'm just getting established, you know?" she said. A tight smile laced her face.

The manager pursed his lips. "Of course. We will need some ID and your Social Security card."

"Why?"

"It's the law. Tax purposes."

"I don't have those things."

"Can you get them?"

"Maybe. Are they really necessary?"

He creased the application. "Without them, Alyssa, I'm afraid we can't go further."

Alyssa looked into his eyes and searched for a bit of softness, some indication that he could grant her mercy. "Isn't there any way around it? I really need this bad."

He unfolded the application and spread it on the table in front of him. He looked it over for a few moments, repeatedly clicking the pen in his right hand. Click, click, click.

"How long have you been on the street?" he finally asked.

Her eyes found the floor again. "Not long."

"Where's home?"

"Sidney."

"You're so young," he said. It sounded odd to her; he couldn't have been much more than a few years older than she was. "You're not really nineteen, are you?"

"No."

"Is it really that bad, then? Maybe it would be better to go home until you're ready for this."

She looked up. "Mister, I'll never go home. That's not happening."

Before she left, he gave her a double cheeseburger, fries and a small cola, and he wished her luck. She didn't cry until she was out of sight, a couple of blocks away.

She couldn't find it inside to call on any more businesses; the exchange with the hamburger joint manager had drained her. She disappeared into her own head and wondered and worried that maybe he was right. Perhaps it would be easier to just go home. Her mother, she was sure, would take her back. Pam Tomassio, so inept at finding the balance between necessary tough love and merciful slack, would no doubt consider this all some wonderful journey of self for her elder daughter, and she would be oblivious to what had sent the girl away in the first place. Her mother's latest boyfriend would no doubt be happy to see her, too, and the idea brought her lunch closer to the surface.

The biggest draw was Patty. Her heart yearned for the little girl. If she were to go home and bear down on her studies, she might have a shot at catching up to her class and graduating on schedule, and then her life would be hers to make of it what she could, without skulking around and lying so poorly that even a fast-food manager could pick her apart.

The only problem with that reasoning was the same problem that had existed all along, the very one that had chased her to Billings in the first place. She closed her eyes in the desperate hope that she could block the image, but it was no use. *Alyssa, Alyssa, Alyssa, Alyssa*, he said again, whispering in the recesses of her head. She smelled the whisky stink of his hot breath on her neck again.

She rose from the bench. She felt like throwing up.

"How old are you?" the shelter manager asked.

"Twenty-one."

"Don't lie to me."

"I'm not."

The woman sighed and peered through bifocals at the girl, who shifted her weight to her right foot and tried to match the woman's gaze.

"How old are you really? I'm not going to ask again."

"Seventeen."

"Unaccompanied minor."

"What's that?"

"You're an unaccompanied minor. We can't take you without a guardian. Would you like to call someone?"

"No."

"We can't take you."

"So what am I supposed to do?"

"I can call Youth Services."

"What happens then?"

"They'll call your guardian."

The shelter manager picked up the phone, and at that, the girl turned and ran out the door and back onto First Avenue. She crossed the busy street without looking, her heart thumping hard at her breastbone, the sound of squealing rubber as a pickup slammed on its brakes.

She kept running, the duffel bag in her right hand whipsawing the air. At Second and Third and Fourth, she slowed down just long enough to look for oncoming traffic, and once on the other side, she again fell into a long stride that gobbled pavement. At Sixth, she cut diagonally across the three lanes of traffic stopped at a light and turned east. Finally, she pulled up, aware that no one was chasing her and that the heart of downtown had fallen behind her. She walked on the sidewalk and tried to rein in her breath.

Ahead, she saw a park. She glanced left and found the rimrock that held Billings in a perpetual embrace. In the fast-approaching dark, she watched in wonder as the clouds swirled in the sky.

Awash in a vivid dream, the girl broke out in a smile. In the version of herself that she saw, she did nothing particularly exotic or noteworthy, but she had an audience, and in her head, she wore nice clothes and flitted along happily, tending to paperwork coming in and efficiently sending it back out.

She's so pretty, a voice said, and Dream Alyssa preened.

Like a doll, someone else said, and Dream Alyssa's cheeks went as red as her hair.

The brush of a hand against her bosom vaulted the girl into consciousness. Scrambling to her feet, she hit her head against the long bench seat of the picnic table she slept under.

"What the hell?" she squalled. She was on her feet now, and what she saw draped her in fear. Three men stared back at her.

"Leave me alone," she yelled.

"We were just looking at you," said the one at her far left. A split second behind the words came the sickly odor of malt liquor. Her eyes darted left and right, looking for something she could use as a weapon. She saw only the smudged-ink haze of night and the park's expanse.

"Yeah, we were just looking," another said, advancing on her.

"I'm serious. I'll scream," she said, and the last word came out shrill.

"Be nice," the first one said. Alyssa backed up.

Just as she figured her best move would be to run—she was confident she could get away, but she didn't want to leave her belongings behind—something flashed between her and the advancing admirers. A bottle of beer hit the ground in its wake and drained out.

"Fucking Alleycat," the third one said. The man next to him—the one with the hulking shoulders and huge hands whom the girl had instantly sized up as the biggest threat—threw a bottle at the figure who had interceded, only to take a fist to the back of the head for his trouble.

"What'd you do that for, idiot? We've lost another beer," said the first, the clear leader of the confederacy.

Alyssa watched the men jostle each other, and she finally grasped that it had been a man on a bicycle who had coasted through. The one they called Alleycat cackled and spun around, pedaling back toward the men. As he bore down on them, they scattered.

"You owe us two beers, Alleycat," the first one called back even as he lit out. Unaccustomed to such exertion, his body thumped and bobbed, like a car with a flat tire.

Alleycat, who had skidded to a halt in front of Alyssa, cupped his hands around his mouth and answered: "Alleycat don't owe. Alleycat only take."

He watched as the men rambled through the park. They stopped only after they reached the other end, a hundred or so yards away. They were pixilated figures illuminated by the glow of the street lamp now, and from a safe distance, they yelled at Alleycat and jabbed their fingers into the night air.

Alleycat turned to Alyssa, who just stared back at him.

"Girl," he said, "what are you doing here?"

Alyssa kept her distance. This man on the bike had rescued her, but from the looks of him, she wondered whether she had traded three problems for one that was much larger. He was massive; she, nearly six feet tall, pegged him at six and a half feet, easy. What surely had once been an impressive Afro was now thinning and gone gray, and it clung to his head in a malformed horseshoe of nappy hair. Alyssa looked at him, bewildered, as he extended a meaty hand.

"I'm Marvin," he said.

"Those guys called you Alleycat," she said.

"People who know me call me that. You don't know me."

She took another long look at the extended hand, which Alleycat—Marvin—now waggled insistently. She offered hers in return.

"I'm Tomato."

Alleycat giggled. She pulled her hand back.

"What the hell kind of name is that?"

"Mine," she growled at him, shoving her hand into her jeans pocket.

"What name did your folks give you?"

"It doesn't matter."

Still chuckling, Alleycat said, "Okay, then. Tomato it is."

"What the hell kind of name is Alleycat?" she asked.

He just grinned at her.

Tomato and Alleycat sat opposite each other at the picnic table. Alleycat left his bike and the attached cart standing nearby and kept his police scanner close.

"What's that?" she asked.

"I listen in on the cops. Tells me where to go on my rounds."

"Rounds?"

Alleycat smiled and tugged at the front of his windbreaker. The metallic buttons disengaged, revealing a yellow T-shirt underneath. The silkscreen message: North Park is my beat.

"You're a cop?"

"Nah. I just help them guys keep things clean."

"Is that why you rescued me?"

Alleycat looked down and picked at his fingernails. "I guess."

"Thank you."

He looked up and smiled. "So why are you here, girl?"

"I left home. I'm trying to get settled, you know?"

"Where's home?"

"I'd rather not say."

"How old are you?"

"Seventeen."

Alleycat whistled. "Young."

"It doesn't matter, OK? There's nothing for me at home." Her eyes dug into him, angry.

He tried to soothe her with a smile. Her jumpiness spooked him.

"It's dangerous out here," he said.

"It's dangerous back there."

"See those guys down there," he said, pointing to the other end of the park at the three who had harassed her. "They're decent guys when they don't drink. I don't like them drinking in my park. I catch them, I take their beer away. If they're just sitting, that's OK by me. People's got to have a place to sit down."

The scanner crackled, and he reached over to turn the volume up. He listened intently.

"Car wreck on Division," he said. "I gotta go."

Halfway to his bicycle, he turned back to Tomato.

"Stay here. You'll be safe. I'll be back."

"What about those …" Tomato said, motioning to the other end of the park.

"You'll be safe."

Alleycat straddled his bike and set off through the park, setting a course to the men, who had slid into a picnic table of their own. Tomato watched him come to a stop and call over the ringleader. Alleycat gestured aggressively as he spoke, and the other man nodded. When the chat was over, Alleycat looked back and waved, and Tomato responded in kind.

Three times, Alleycat came by the park and checked on the girl, only to be drawn away each time by another scanner call. By the third pass, she was asleep again under the picnic table, wrapped in the blanket she had found in the alley the previous night.

It was four in the morning when he shook her.

"Girl," he said. "Can you wake up and walk?"

Tomato rubbed her eyes. "Where were you?"

"Rounds."

"What do you mean, walk? Where?"

"It's over tonight. I gotta sleep."

Tomato pushed herself up and out from under the table.

"You have a home?" she said.

"Sort of. You can come if you want."

Tomato choked down the uneasiness inside her. She had two options, neither of which thrilled her. There was trust, or there was cold, hard ground under a picnic table.

She gathered up her things and followed Alleycat, who pedaled slowly.

Their shadows cast long images against the downtown buildings as they sliced through the heart of Billings. It was just the two of them, the sound of Tomato's feet and the metallic whirr of Alleycat's twelve-speed. Tomato was thankful for the company. A walk in the pre-dawn darkness would have been spooky alone.

As they cut across Montana Avenue, the arms dropped on the railroad crossing. Tomato looked left and saw nothing, then looked right and saw the yellow light of the coming train a couple of hundred yards away.

"We can make it," she said, but Alleycat's thick arm stopped her. "We wait."

The train bore down, the metal-on-metal glide of wheels on the rails emitting a high-pitched wail. Tomato counted the cars rushing past and remembered a time when she and her father would chase trains across the badlands on the edge of Montana. "Count the cars, Alyssa," he would say. "Count the cars." She marveled again at how the memories of him would jump on her so quickly and with such random triggers. She found comfort and grief in that, with the two emotions often fighting it out to an unsatisfying draw.

Finally, the last car spooled past, and the arms lifted to clear the way.

"Train's dangerous," Alleycat said.

At Minnesota Avenue, they turned right, toward the men's shelter. A few lost souls who didn't get beds for the night huddled in doorways and took no notice of Alleycat and Tomato passing through.

At the corner, they came upon a man hunkered down by a bent parking meter, a beer in his hand and two more, unopened, at his feet. Alleycat dismounted his bike—"Hold this," he said to Tomato— and snapped the can from the old man's hand and shook its contents onto the street. In a singular motion, his right foot crashed onto the two uninitiated beers, spraying foam. Tomato flinched.

"What the fuck, man?" the old guy said as he scrambled to his feet and careened away from Alleycat.

Alleycat climbed back on the bike and pedaled on, with Tomato skittering along behind. By the time the old man found the voice to start yelling, they were around the corner and across the next street, where they disappeared into the checkerboard of houses on the South Side.

Tomato hung back on the crumbling sidewalk as Alleycat made his way to the boarded-up door of the house. Weeds, ankle high and beaten brown by the heat of August and September, filled the yard.

Alleycat turned around. "Come on, girl."

She inched up the walkway.

"This is your house?"

"Ain't mine," he said as he tugged at the corner of the plywood. "It'll do OK for a sleep, though."

He gave the wood a mighty pull, and the nails groaned as they broke free from the door jamb. A blast of mildew hit them square in the face.

Alleycat pushed his bicycle through the door, and then he rolled his shoulders and slipped inside.

"Come on," he said, and Tomato followed.

Inside, Alleycat fired up a camp lantern, and light tumbled into the dark space. The walls of the place had gone yellow with age and neglect, and flooring had been ripped away. In the middle of the room lay an old mattress, a chair whose cloth upholstery had been pressed smooth by wear, and an ancient boom box encased by stacks of CDs.

"Home," Alleycat said, grinning.

Tomato opened her mouth, ready to protest the apparent sleeping arrangements, but Alleycat cut her off.

"You take the bed," he said, giving the mattress a name far more dignified than it deserved. He pointed to the chair. "I sleep over there."

Wordlessly, Tomato walked to the mattress and set down her duffel bag. She opened the zipper and began unpacking. Alleycat pressed play on the stereo, and the Isley Brothers drifted into the room.

"'This Old Heart of Mine,'" Alleycat said with satisfaction, and he began softly singing along. Tomato smiled. He knew it note-perfect.

"You like that blanket?" Alleycat asked, pointing at the item she had just pulled from the bag.

"Yeah, I do," she said. "This blanket was the first thing that told me everything's going to be OK."

Alleycat's smile turned electric at that, and he sang louder.

"Marvin," Tomato said.

"You can call me Alleycat."

"Marvin," she said again. "How long have you lived here?"

He stopped smiling and singing. "You're out of the cold, right? This ain't so bad."

"No, no," she said, fumbling for the words that might take away the insult she had unwittingly set upon him. "I'm just wondering. You know, I … well, I guess I wonder how hard this is going to be, me being out here."

Alleycat's face softened. His eyes grew large.

"I've been out here a long time," he said, "but in this house only a few days. I like to stay moving. There's lots of places to hide around here, if you know where to look. I know. I've been out here a long time."

"How long?" she asked.

"It ain't important, girl. Get some sleep now. Tomorrow'll be coming soon."

He sat in the chair and watched through slits in his eyelids as Tomato curled up under her blanket. A couple of times, she looked back at him, and he feigned sleep.

"Marvin?"

He said nothing.

"Marvin?"

"What, girl?"

"Why did you bring me here?"

"You don't need to be out there."

Silence moved in again as she considered the answer.

"You're not going to do anything to me, are you?" Her voice was small.

"No, girl."

"Why are you here, Marvin?"

"Ain't important, girl."

Tomato flipped onto her side and said nothing else. Soon enough, exhaustion took her down for good.

Just as he had done the night before, Alleycat kept vigil over the sleeping girl.

cruelty to animals

We were done for when I bought the dog.

That's what I'm thinking somewhere over Idaho, on a twin-prop sputtering toward Seattle, where I'm going to hunker down and try to figure out what to do next, now that my last next thing has fallen apart.

Look, we had problems. Who doesn't? I might even be willing to concede that we had more problems than most people do, although you'd have to satisfy me that such a thing can be quantified before I'll cop to it. In any case, I'm not going to fight the basic premise: We were a mess. We were two people living in two cities in two states in two houses, and we kept pretending that maybe someday those circumstances would change and we'd be together. You know what? I'm going to say now that maybe that was a lie. I don't know. It didn't feel like a lie, at least not always. I do know that we were making it work, even if it was dysfunctional as all hell.

Then I bought the dog, and now nothing works.

But, look, I'm leaving a bunch of stuff out.

If I'm going to be truthful, and now seems about as good a time as any to start, I knew what I was doing when I sent her that first email. My marriage was skidding off the runway, and if you think that I should have been in a counselor's chair working on a solution to my troubles at home, I'm not going to disagree with you. But I didn't do that. No, I wrote a note to the kid sister of the first girl I ever loved. I hadn't seen her in nearly twenty years, when she was a fourteen-year-old, all arms and legs and orthodontia. I had added her as a Facebook friend the previous spring, along with a good chunk of the four hundred or so people I'd graduated with at Billings West High, a few co-workers and a handful of people I didn't even know but who seemed to know me. The more the merrier, as they say.

Most of those people quickly receded into the background. Facebook, like so many things these days, is all surface and no depth. You see somebody you once knew, say hello, exchange a few pleasantries, realize you can't possibly bridge twenty years, and you move on.

But Diane, she was different. For one thing, she wasn't a gangly little girl anymore. She was thirty-four years old, one hundred percent woman if her online pictures were to be believed, and beautiful in a way that moved me in all the right places. Her sister, Rachel, lurked somewhere in my little online universe, but I rarely heard from her and spoke with her even less frequently. But Diane. Oh, man, Diane. I took advantage of any chance I had to swap notes with her, stay up late chatting online or whatever. I even played that stupid farm game, just because she did. Even if I grant you that online communication is two-dimensional in a way that makes it a poor substitute and a dangerous stand-in for genuine human interaction, I couldn't help myself from falling in deep with Diane. She got me. She could tell when I wasn't eating well or sleeping well, just from my demeanor in the little electronic box where we talked. I began sharing my frustrations about work, and she helped me there, too. When I told my creative partner, Jonathan, that his bigfooting of me during pitches was damaging our relationship, he was properly chastened. "I owe you an apology, Doug," he said. "It was weird to hear you say it so directly. I don't know. Usually, you just go into your office and break something when you're frustrated." That was a gift from Diane, the ability to confront Jonathan. She was changing me.

Anyway, a few months later, I'm heading for D-I-V-O-R-C-E, and beyond my most immediate thought, which is that I'm glad we don't have any kids, I'm thinking this: Who do I know who can tell me what I'm getting into here? And just as quickly, I'm thinking: *Diane. Diane. If she can't do it, no one can.* Diane's been married and divorced twice. Now, you're probably thinking that someone who's thirty-four and has been divorced twice maybe knows more about the subject than is healthy. I might have thought of that, too, if I hadn't been thinking about what Diane would look like with her clothes off.

So I shoot Diane an email: *Hey, looks like I'm getting divorced. You have any advice?*

I'm sitting there browsing through some fantasy-football website when the reply comes not three minutes later: *I have tons of advice, but the best thing I can do is pray for you. Would that be OK?*

I'm thinking, well, it's not really what I had in mind, babe, but yeah. Pray for me. It can't hurt.

I came to find out that Diane probably isn't the praying type, which is just as well, because neither am I. What she was, though, was a text-messaging fiend. I started getting them by the score—when I woke up in the morning; on my commute to work, when I was fighting half of Seattle up I-5; in the middle of brainstorm meetings, where I was trying to figure out another way to sell cat food. (*Your cat will die if you don't feed it. Buy Little Friskies!*) I was digging the attention. The messages came so fast that I eventually turned my BlackBerry to vibrate-only so my co-workers didn't kill me, and in time, I came to associate that little double-buzz in my pants—no double entendre intended—with the pure pleasure of seeing her words.

Diane wanted me to come home to Billings, to spend some time with her, to make love to her. She started sending me pictures to let me know exactly what was waiting for me, pictures that didn't leave anything to my imagination, which was in hyperdrive anyway. It's all yours if you come, she said.

I blocked out a week's vacation, booked a flight, and hoped that people could keep their cats alive until I got back to Seattle.

(I'm going to say this for the benefit of anybody who thinks I've got a good thing going to this point: When you buy that snazzy new phone— and you will, my friend, or I'm not doing my job correctly—and you sign up for that unlimited data plan, it's important to note that data and text messaging are not the same thing. Had I known this, I'd have not come home to a woman who still lived in my house, who stood in the living room quaking with fury, holding a thirteen-page-thick cell phone bill and screaming, "Who in the hell do you know in Billings, Montana, who you send 5,314 text messages to in a month?" What can you say to that?

I said, "Well, we weren't talking about the weather, that's for sure." I want you to learn from my mistakes. Paying the unexpected $800 bill is the least of the indignities. That night, I was living in a pay-by-the-week motel and my friends—Facebook and otherwise—had begun to flee the Good Ship Moron.)

After a few months, things had begun settling out, at least a little. The divorce decree came in and Bree moved on nicely, as I knew she would. She got the house and the better car. I got the goldfish, which died the first week I was in my new condo in downtown Tacoma, where I'd run off to because I didn't know anyone there. Everything else, we split.

I saw Bree back in February at the Experience Music Whatchamacallit—you know, that thing over by the Space Needle that looks like a giant loogie? She was holding hands with someone, a guy taller and thinner than me, and that socked me in the gut in a way that I couldn't have anticipated. I don't think she saw me; I started working backward through the exhibits and left. I don't think I could have taken actually speaking to her.

Funny thing about seeing someone I know in a metro area of three-point-three million people: When I was in much smaller Billings—I flew there once a month, and once a month Diane came out to see me—I never saw anybody I knew, except Diane. That's odd, right? I mean, I grew up there, in a little house on Lyndale, next to a stretch of pasture that's now jammed between a McDonald's and a strip mall. Man, if that's not quintessential Billings, I don't know what is. *Welcome to Billings. Oil Changes and Unwanted Lip Hair Removal in the Same Building.*

It's not like I was going to see my people. My folks are dead, and my brother and sister scattered with the wind. Jeff was in Concord, New Hampshire, the last I heard, some kind of professor or something. We don't talk much. Laurie, she's an Army wife down in Tennessee. But Diane's connections were still strong. Her parents lived there. So did Rachel and her family. Diane and I hit our fifth month of being an item, whatever that is, and I hadn't seen any of these people. It started to bug me, and I told her so.

"Don't pressure me about this," Diane said.

"I don't mean for it to be pressure. I'm just asking what the deal is. We've been together a while. Do they even know about us?"

"I'm not sure what together means."

"Well, look, we're something, aren't we? I don't normally make a dozen trips a year to Billings. Something's going on."

"Yeah, well, you're not here. Once you're here, we'll be together. Otherwise, I don't really see the point in getting them involved. You know that's going to be awkward, especially with Rachel."

I spilled the Coke I was pouring into my Jack Daniel's. "I stopped dating Rachel in 1990. I think we can move past that pretty quickly, don't you?"

She didn't say anything to that, but she moved in close and she kissed me, and soon enough, I was chasing her down the hall into the bedroom. I knew she was trying to divert my attention. It worked.

By midsummer, doubt hadn't just crept in; it was sleeping on my couch and eating me out of house and home. It wasn't just the hiding me from her family. In retrospect, I should have confronted the "once you're here, we'll be together" bit the first time it flared up. I'm convinced now that a proactive course would have stopped things before they got out of hand.

Why should I have been expected to move? I was the creative director at one of the best ad agencies on the West Coast, in a city that fed us as much work as we could handle. Damned if I could find something similar in Billings, the 169th-ranked media market in the United States. Advantage: Seattle.

And Diane, she was a nurse. Billings has fine hospitals, some of the best in the region, but they can't really compare with Harborview or Swedish or Virginia Mason or Seattle Children's. Advantage: Seattle.

I'd put these things in front of her, implore her to come join me, and she would say, every time, "If you loved me, you'd come here, where I need you."

I loved her, OK? I still do, when you get right down to it. A million pop songs can be wrong, because I'm here to tell you this: Love isn't enough.

On a mid-July evening, after Jonathan and I had sold a concept to a chain of coffee kiosks, we sat on the roof of my condo building and watched the setting sun glittering off Commencement Bay.

"How's it going with Diane?" he asked.

"Stuck in neutral."

"How so?"

"There's the whole won't-move-to-Seattle thing, for starters."

"Yeah, I don't get that at all."

"That's just the tip of it. You know, that way she could see through me and my problems when we first started out, I loved that. But now it's like she's turned that power against me."

"What do you mean?"

"Conversations are full of land mines. She seizes on individual words and beats me over the head with them. The other day, I'm fumbling my words pretty badly as we're going around and around again on being couple publicly. And I say, 'Look, I'm trying to articulate some-thing here.' And she says, 'No, you're trying to formulate it. If you were articulating it, you'd be saying it.' Who says something like that?"

Jonathan chuckled. "That's actually pretty funny."

"In isolation, yeah. It gets old when it comes at you continually. And I'll tell you something else: There's a lack of empathy there. Last night, she asked how I was doing, and I told her, 'Well, I'm nervous about this pitch tomorrow. I'm not sleeping well. I feel like crap.' And she said, 'Well, I have to go to bed.' "

"That's cold."

"Yeah, and it happens all the time. I don't know, man. In many ways, she's everything I ever wanted. Drop-dead gorgeous, smart, funny. But more and more, I feel like garbage when I talk to her."

Jonathan took a long sip off his beer. "Sounds like she's ninety percent perfect and ten percent battery acid."

"Apt description."

"And it's the ten percent that will eat you alive."

As recently as last month, I was hanging in there with Diane. We'd had a few good visits, and I was thinking that maybe we still had a shot. One day, she sent me an email with a picture of a chihuahua, one of those little yappy, chalupa-defending dogs.

"I want him," she wrote.

This smacked of opportunity. I set aside my work, figuring I'd just stay late to catch up, and I started searching for breeders in Billings. It didn't take long. I found one out in Shepherd, called the lady up, found out that she had a litter born four weeks earlier that would be ready to go in the next month or so. That was cool by me. I agreed to send her a check for five hundred dollars, and then I hung up and called Diane and told her the news, and I could hear her jumping and clapping like a little girl. She said she would name him "Guido," because little dogs with gangster names are genius, and I was thinking that this was the best five hundred dollars I'd ever spent.

A few days ago, I landed in Billings. David Sedaris was playing the Alberta Bair, and while there's a limit to how much oh-so-cleverness I can take, Diane really likes him, and I was on a Greatest Boyfriend in the World roll because I bought the tickets without her asking me to. We got a room in the Crowne Plaza and made a reservation for steaks at Jake's. After that, the plan called for hitting the show and then coming back to the room and wearing out the bed and anything else we could scale without clothes on. A good plan.

We were dressing for dinner when Diane said, "I wish I didn't have to wait for Guido."

I fumbled with the buttons on my sleeve. "It's just a couple more weeks. He's going to have a great home with you. Way better than that cage in the closet."

She stopped. "What?"

"You know, the closet. I saw her take him out of it when we visited him yesterday."

"He lives in a closet?"

"You didn't know that?"

"How could I know that? I was sitting on the couch. I didn't see where he was. How could you let him live in a closet?"

"I'm sorry. I didn't think anything of it."

"That's terrible."

"I don't know. I guess it didn't seem like a big deal."

"Didn't seem like a big deal? Of course it's a big deal. That's animal abuse. You call that woman. You call her right now and tell her we're coming to get him."

"Come on. That's silly. He's not ready yet. And we have plans."

She stamped her foot. "Call her now."

We didn't have steaks at Jake's. We didn't see oh-so-clever David Sedaris. We damn sure didn't have sex. We sat in our hotel room and played nursemaid to a quivering, big-eared, long-legged rat. Diane talked to Guido in a singsong voice that amused me for about ten minutes and then had me wishing the windows could be opened from the inside so I could leap to my death. Guido sat on my chest and peed on my shirt. Daddy was not pleased.

This morning, Diane took me to the airport. I rode up the Rims in the passenger seat, rigidly holding Guido away from me, because if he started to evacuate his little bladder again, down to the floorboard he was going to go.

"Idn't he da tweetest widdle ting," said Diane-cum-Tweety-Bird.

"Oh, yeah. He's the best."

She looked at me and grinned wide. "We're a happy widdle famiwy."

As we said our goodbyes, I got a quick peck from Diane and was told to kiss Guido on the mouth. I didn't want to do it, but in the interest of famiwy harmony, I acquiesced. Neither Guido nor I seemed pleased with the encounter.

At the TSA counter, I turned back and Diane was holding the little guy up and waving one of his paws at me. I waved back and felt a flush of stupidity for doing so.

After I'd run my shoes and my belt and my carry-on through the X-ray and suffered the indignity of the wand, I turned around again for my customary blown kiss from Diane, but she was gone.

The captain just said that we're making our final descent into Seattle, and here's what I'm thinking: When I bought that dog, I punched my own ticket out of Diane's life. She doesn't want me, not really. She wants a companion who won't challenge her, who won't make her deal with his moods or feelings, and she wants someone who thinks everything that tumbles out of her mouth is golden. She wants someone who's cool with living in Billings. Guido's her man, on all counts. I can't possibly compare.

I'm going to miss her. I'm going to miss those moments, increasingly rare, when she makes me laugh uncontrollably, like the story she told about a patient who was carping to go home. She told him that soon enough he'd be playing footsie with his wife, remembering a moment too late that he was a double amputee. I'm going to miss sidling up to her on a cold night and sleeping in a warm embrace till morning. I'm going to miss the way she could make me feel like the sexiest man on earth, which I most assuredly am not.

It's going to be lonely for a while. Maybe for longer than that.

I think I'll get a cat.

quantum physics
and the art of departure

The second round came, and soon after the third followed, and his anxiety grew. He stirred the Jack and Coke with his forefinger and stared across the table at her.

"We love our house," she said, her head swiveling between the friends flanking her. "But it will be too small soon."

She looked at him and greeted his gaze with a sneer only he saw. "Isn't that right, hon?"

His jaw dropped as if to speak, but his words found no room.

"Oh, Laura," said the friend on her left, the brunette. "That's so exciting."

He dropped his finger back into the drink and stirred it again, and she talked some more.

She hooked her arm in his as they walked to the car. He clenched his elbow tight to his ribs, and she let go.

"Kiss me," she said after they were inside. Her breath vaporized in the cold, and the liquor stink of it blended with the smell of leather from the seats.

He gave her a quick peck on the lips.

"No," she said. "Really kiss me."

He leaned in again, and she cupped his cheeks in her hands and pulled his mouth to hers. Her tongue slipped between his lips, pressing insistently at his teeth, until finally he opened them. He tasted the vodka on her breath and smelled the smoke in her hair.

"We need to go," he said, pulling away.

"We will," she said, and she moved in again.

"Later," he said. His hand pressed against her shoulder to guide her into the bucket seat.

After a few blocks, she said, "Do you want me to come over there with you?"

"It's slick out tonight."

"I could, you know."

"I know."

"Do you want me to?"

"I need to watch the road."

Her drunken lovemaking was, by turns, fierce and haphazard. She licked his face and slithered her tongue in his ear. When she moved to the other side, he reached up and swabbed her spit away. She lay back and invited his mouth to find her, and he did so by rote. The most preposterous memory stepped to the front of his mind. Sam Kinison, the manic comic, had a routine about oral. "Lick the alphabet," Sam the Man said. So he did. She writhed and grasped at his head, and then, as the moment neared, she turned him on his back and rode him until it was done.

As she draped across him, he looked for patterns in the ceiling.

"It was good?" she asked.

"Yes."

"It's been a while."

"Yes."

"I think we should do it again."

He said nothing.

She reached for him and found him flaccid. "Oh."

"Tomorrow," he said.

She turned away and ground her backside into him. He patted her shoulder and waited for her snores.

The exchanges began as a lark. He'd been surprised to hear from her, and after the catching up and the back-and-forth bragging about this and that, they started trading richly detailed imaginations of how things might have gone had other choices been made.

It began with her telling about some reading she had done in the area of quantum physics. He knew nothing of quantum physics, but she made it sound interesting. She said that for every option taken, the consequences of the opposite choice emerged in another universe. Somewhere, she wrote, she had turned back on the Jetway fifteen years earlier and stayed with him. Somewhere, they were having coffee, talking about books and making passionate love in the afternoon.

As each new message built upon the one previous, it came with a caveat: *This is just for fun. It's not real. It's just us inside the computer.* For a while, maybe they had believed it, or tried to. He wasn't trying very hard anymore.

While his wife slept upstairs, he sat at the computer, the electronic glow illuminating him in the darkness of the basement. He coaxed the browser to life and pulled up the email account that she didn't know about.

New messages (0).

"Damn," he said.

He rapped out a note.

Somewhere, Alternate Ross didn't go to a bar tonight with his wife's friends, who he doesn't know and doesn't like. I hope he was in bed, keeping Alternate Lisa's feet warm.

He hit send. He waited a while. Maybe she would see it and write back.

He punched in the address for the sports news site and scanned headlines. A few minutes later, he returned to his email.

New messages (0).

He signed out, logged off and went up the stairs, taking care to walk on the edges lest they give him away.

The light brushed across his face, rousing him. He opened one eye and saw her robe on the bed. He pushed himself off the mattress, his muscles barking at the imposition.

In the living room, he looked out the window at the morning. Her car sat in the driveway. The kitchen and dining room, filled with the muted pastels she had chosen, stood empty and quiet.

He went to the basement. She was at the computer. Warm water filled his veins.

"What's up?"

She swiveled around in the chair. "Hi, hon. Just balancing the checkbook."

"Industrious, aren't you?"

"No, just bored."

"I'll leave you to it." He turned to go upstairs.

"Hon?" she said.

He stopped.

"Yeah?"

"Your last five paychecks."

"Yeah?"

"They're smaller."

His jaw tightened. "Insurance premiums rose again. And I bumped the 401(k)."

She looked at him.

"Oh, and I'm giving a bit more to the United Way. Seemed like the right thing to do, with us having so much ..."

She smiled.

"You're a good man, Ross Newbry," she said. "But we don't have *that* much."

"We have enough."

"Don't worry, hon," she said. "Things will pick up again soon. I'm sure of it."

She turned to the computer. He went upstairs to a breakfast he no longer wanted.

For a long time after the messages commenced, he felt guilty about the way they would distract him. It wasn't really cheating (was it?). He wasn't stepping out on her, and he knew two guys just in their circle of friends who were carrying on brazen affairs. So what if he had a little text-based entertainment on the side? He was a good husband (wasn't he?), and she was fortunate to have him (wasn't she?).

He still loved her. He was sure of it. Pretty sure. He had moments when he thought his heart would spring a leak, he felt such adoration for her. A toss of her head would remind him of that first year together, of passion that sent them speeding into bed, onto the couch, atop the kitchen table in frenetic lovemaking. It had been a while, though. The past year, in particular among the decade they shared, had been rough. Her career—*if you can call selling catalog jewelry a career*, he often thought—had taken off just as his stalled. The bonuses had dried up.

He moved from a corner office to a glass cube in the middle of the room. No more views of downtown Billings from a fourth-floor perch. Now, he had only a boss—a twenty-six-year-old, climbing-the-ladder punk he had trained and whose hot breath he increasingly felt on his collar.

She had the leverage. It's not something they talked about; nobody who has leverage talks about it. Nobody has to. Leverage insidiously changes the balance of things when you're not even looking, and even when you are.

She wasn't a naïf. She knew what she wanted, and she aimed to have it. His desires, he increasingly worried, weren't part of the equation.

After dinner, he crept back down the stairs and called up his email program. He had long since abandoned fear. She couldn't sneak up on him. The floor above his head had a hundred, maybe a thousand, spots that groaned under foot. And if he didn't hear that, surely he would hear her on the stairs before she could see what he was doing.

"What are you doing down there?" she called down from the kitchen.

"Checking my team," he said. He'd never played fantasy football, but he had concocted and maintained an elaborate lie about his nonexistent squad, which was having a hell of a year with Brett Favre at quarterback.

New messages (1).

Thank you for warming my feet. I bet Alternate Ross and Alternate Lisa did more than just warm up, though. Why don't you tell me about it?

Through his sweatpants, he grasped his present erection between his thumb and forefinger and gave it a few quick rubs, and then he started typing.

"I've marked a few I think we should look at," she said the next morning as she pushed the real estate section across the table to him.

"Isn't this premature? This is a great house."

"I think we need to start looking. If we find the right one, maybe we can move in the spring."

"The spring?"

"Yes. I want to get this done."

"I don't understand the big hurry," he said.

"It's not hurrying, Ross. It's just planning."

"Planning for what?"

"Don't be obtuse."

"I'm not."

"We can't live here forever. It's too small."

"I love this house."

"Ross, you silly man. You can love another house, too."

He found her online, a rarity given the time difference.

He typed out a message: *Hey beautiful. Can you chat?*

Hey right back at you. How are you?

Frazzled.

Frazzled how?

The same old.

You hang in there. I'm here, whenever you need me.

I need you always.

That's not what I mean, silly.

I know. I'm sorry. I shouldn't be needy.

Be what you need to be.

I need to be with you.

You are.

No, I mean for real.

For real, for real?

Yes.

The next message was slow in coming.

You know I would love that, but that's ... that's a hard thing. For you. For me. For reasons we both know.

I know.

I know too. Damn.

Maybe someday.

Maybe.

I love you.

I love you too.

The snow went away by March, and so did they. He stood among their boxed-up life in the living room of the new place under the Rims, slicing through tape with his car key.

"It's beautiful," she said.

"It is."

"Do you love it?"

"I will."

She moved close, slipping into his arms. He kissed her forehead.

"I'm going to run back to the other place real quick," he said. "I think I left something down in the basement."

"What?"

"Just some old CDs I had squirreled away. Nothing big. I won't be long."

"Hurry back. Lots of boxes to unpack."

In the basement closet, he dug out an old T-shirt, a box of photos from the Cayman trip a few years earlier, and a couple of old Squeeze CDs, holdovers from his college days. *Jesus*, he thought. *I'm ten years gone from there, and what can I show for it?*

He trudged back upstairs, again sticking to the edges, mostly out of habit. No stairs or wooden floors in the new place. He would have to scope out new ways of posting a sentry.

He slipped into the bathroom. He stood at the toilet and attended to business, all the while scanning along the counter and the tub to make sure nothing had been left behind. In the wastebasket, something caught his eye.

After zipping up, he knelt down for a closer look.

He reached into the basket and pulled the white plastic stick out and turned it over in his hand. The blue plus sign told the story.

The car carried him in wide loops around his new neighborhood, buying him time to think, even as thinking gave him no good answers. Twice, he reached for the cell phone, to call her and demand to know what was what. Twice, he set it back down. There was nothing she could say that he didn't know, or that would change his mind.

He glanced at the digital clock in the dashboard. 2:24 p.m.

He pointed the car toward downtown, toward the bank he lined up for this day, toward the cash he had been setting aside for this reason. He could get to Denver with the clothes on his back. A parking lot somewhere could hold the car for a long time before anybody would figure it out. And by then, it wouldn't matter.

And in Sydney, many hours away but really not so far at all, Alternate Lisa would take him in. He just knew it.

the paper weight

Gilchrist suspected it would be bad when The Drone called him at home before nine in the morning. The eggs burned while The Drone ripped through half of the OED just to tell Gilchrist that he should clear his schedule for a meeting at eleven. Gilchrist's long experience with the guy suggested there wasn't a detour or digression he wouldn't take, especially if he were somehow, probably by accident, in the general vicinity of a point.

An hour later, when The Diploma didn't even say hello at the coffee pot, the picture became clearer. Kevin Gilchrist hadn't honed his bullshit detector just to ferret out the lies of politicians and other professional windbags. Something big was going down, and from the pallid looks on the faces of The Drone and The Diploma, Gilchrist guessed that whatever it was would land on him.

Just before eleven, The Drone came out of his glass office and signaled Gilchrist to step into The Diploma's much larger adjacent office, also glass. Gilchrist had been the one who coined the term "the glassholes" as a collective for The Drone and The Diploma, a moniker so enthusiastically embraced by his colleagues that the name—and Gilchrist's role in promulgating it—inevitably made it back to the two people who were supposed to be out of the loop. The transgression hadn't come with punishment, per se, but Gilchrist didn't think it was an illusion that his ass, and his copy, had been hurting a lot more lately.

"Kevin, come on in and have a seat," The Diploma said. The Drone closed the door and sat down in the chair nearest The Diploma's desk.

Gilchrist looked along the wall behind The Diploma and found the reason for the nickname. There, framing twenty-eight-year-old William Pennington's head, hung his undergraduate and master's diplomas. He had graduated summa in 2003 from the University of Kansas with a major in journalism, and then he went on to the University of Missouri and picked up a master's, also in journalism, two years later.

These facts about The Diploma caused Gilchrist to despise him on several levels.

First, he had only four years of honest-to-goodness, in-a-real-newsroom experience. And in those four years, he had kissed enough of the right asses to be running the whole shooting match at the *Herald-Gleaner*, which, back in the days when people actually read newspapers, had been a pretty damned good one.

Second, the guy went to Kansas and Missouri, for Christ's sake. If one were to equate collegiate sports with politics, it would be a little like defining oneself as an abortion-rights Republican from Alabama. (Gilchrist had begun to suspect that The Diploma didn't care much for sports. On the odd occasions when he would join a newsroom bull session, uniformly uncomfortable moments for everyone, The Diploma would put on a serpentine smile and slink away when talk turned to whatever game was in season.)

Third, The Diploma had a master's degree in journalism, which Gilchrist figured to be about as useful as a screen door on a battleship. Journalism—real journalism, the kind practiced by Gilchrist and those who had come before him at the *Herald-Gleaner*—didn't happen in a laboratory. It wasn't theoretical. It was real. It happened outside the glass walls, on the street, among people whose stories demanded to be told and among people who, as a matter of course, would lie, equivocate, prevaricate and falsify to keep somebody like Gilchrist from discovering the truth. The Diploma came out of Missouri with big ideas about databases and web hits and social media, none of which meant a damned thing to Gilchrist.

And then there was The Drone, Mike Lindell. A decade older than The Diploma, he didn't have any fancy sheepskins. He was a Montana boy, born and raised in Billings, schooled first at Northwest College in Wyoming and then later at Eastern Montana College. Gilchrist had shared a newsroom with Lindell for more than a decade and more or less tolerated him, but it was only in the past year that their stations had changed, to Gilchrist's considerable dismay.

The Diploma arrived the previous spring and immediately set about finding a managing editor, a right-hand man. A few people in-house put in for it—some of them damned good, like the region editor and Gilchrist's boss, Ann Benjamin. But one by one, as they came to figure out what the job would entail, they bowed out. So, too, did the handful of candidates who emerged from outside the office.

Lindell, in Gilchrist's estimation the weakest link on the *Herald-Gleaner* copy desk, was the last man standing and got the job. The Drone's talent, aside from taking any piece of writing and strangling the life right out of it, lay in a willingness to carry water for The Diploma. (Gilchrist, in a pique a few months earlier, had told a colleague within earshot of The Drone that Lindell would be the one who someday showed up at work with a bucket of Flavor Aid. Gilchrist then had to explain the reference to Lindell before he was written up for conduct unbecoming.)

Now, Gilchrist looked warily at the glassholes and waited to hear what was on their collective mind.

"Kevin, thanks for coming in on such short notice," The Diploma said, rocking back in his chair and cupping his hands behind his head. "As you know, we're still looking for a night cops reporter."

"Yeah," Gilchrist said. "Tough break, losing Dodson to the *Denver Post*. Good kid. Smart. He'll do well down there."

"Yes, well," The Diploma said. "At any rate, we're still looking. But we think we have an idea."

Discomfort—more discomfort—hit Gilchrist.

"Go on."

"We want you to do the job," The Drone broke in. "But we want to do it in a new way, a way that might be more efficient."

Discomfort gave way to nausea. Gilchrist swallowed hard. He hated words like "efficient."

"What we mean is that we want cops news to be much more web-driven," The Diploma said. "For years, we've been writing long, involved crime stories. Readers don't care. They don't have time. They like car crashes and civic mayhem in small, easy-to-digest pieces. You should see our web traffic when we post a—"

"So, rip-and-read stuff," Gilchrist cut in.

"Yes," The Diploma lit up at Gilchrist's quick grasp of the situation. "Yes, precisely. Get it on the web quick. We want you to be our clearinghouse of short, accessible crime items."

Gilchrist also hated words like "accessible."

Gilchrist set his hands on the edge of The Diploma's desk to steady himself. He was sixty-two years old, nearly broke, just coming out of his third marriage, and now he was being steered toward a job that most newspapers turned over to a freshly scrubbed grad who was thankful for the shitty hours and shittier pay.

He flashed on the resignation letter, written but undelivered, sitting in the bottom of his desk drawer. He was particularly proud of the closing line—"The irony is, the word 'news' surrounds us – 'news'paper, 'news'room, 'news'print – and yet I can't remember the last time we printed anything that even resembles it"—even as he knew he didn't have the guts to show it to anyone, even someone as contemptible as The Diploma.

"What about the job I already have?" Gilchrist asked. In the coming days, he was to hit Williston to do legwork on a story about the slowdown in the oil patch, pick up an agricultural feature in Jordan on the way home and, perhaps, to touch base with the woman in Baker who lived to tell the tale after her husband blew off her lower jaw with a shotgun.

"That's the thing," The Diploma said. "Given the financial realities of our situation right now, I think we're going to have to make a choice here. Frankly, in this environment, the cops job is more important to us than covering the region. A story reported from an oil rig in North Dakota doesn't sell tire ads here in town. You write some really interesting stories, Kevin, but they just don't make much dent online. That's where the future is, you know."

Gilchrist's temples throbbed. "But out in the rest of the world that doesn't live in front of a computer, those stories get read, goddammit," he protested.

"Let's rein in the vulgarities, shall we?" The Diploma said. "Yes, your stories do well in print, but frankly, we're ratcheting down our offerings there and making a bigger play online. You want to be a part of that, don't you?"

Gilchrist stared at The Diploma, who picked idly at a loose thread on his cuff.

"Kevin, you're a smart man, and I expect that you'll do the smart thing here," The Diploma said. "We're giving you a chance to be on the ground floor of something very interesting as our business model evolves. Let's give it a try, shall we?"

Gilchrist turned to The Drone, who nodded like a bobblehead doll. Gilchrist shifted his eyes back to The Diploma. He breathed deeply, considered his words, and plunged in.

"I don't need the likes of you to tell me how smart I am, OK? If I had been smart, I would have gotten out when I saw you coming. But I'm not smart, and I didn't get out, and you apparently don't have enough string to convince HR that I can be fired, so here we stand. I'll take the job, because I like to eat and to pay my bills, and I will do what I have to do."

The Diploma smiled, and for the first time, Gilchrist seized on a way to describe that peculiar look on Pennington's face. My God, he thought. The man is a lizard.

"But first, I'm going to tell you something," Gilchrist said. "A newspaper used to mean something to people. It kicked them in the ass when they needed it, it told them what they wanted to know and what they had to know, and every once in a while, it got a hold of a story so good and told it so well that it moved entire towns to act in the common good. I've never heard you talk about things like that, and maybe that's not your fault. You're just a kid. I've seen two generations of guys like you, guys who think that progress is made by changing the typefaces or making the pictures bigger or writing for people who don't give a damn about reading. Maybe you don't have any recollection of the time I'm talking about. Well, I remember, and while I'm not stupid enough to think that it's coming back, I'll be right here as a reminder of it. Because you're dangerous, Bill. What you don't know is dangerous, and what you do know is dangerous."

The Diploma's smile faded at the edges.

"You can make me the devil if you want, Kevin, but times are changing. And we're changing with them."

Gilchrist stood up and headed for the door.

"Not for the better, it seems to me," he said.

In the alley behind the Lutheran church, where Gilchrist had run after The Drone had intercepted him in the newsroom and used two hundred and fifty-seven words to say "your new job starts tonight," he tried to catch his breath and tamp down his emotions. "Jesus, Kev, it's not that you didn't see this one coming," he growled. "You're lucky you're not out on your ass."

He cupped his hands behind his head and gulped air. A sequential string of images bombarded his head—his first day at the pre-merger *Herald* in '71, glue pots and fistfights in the composing room. The teachers' strike in '75. Passing around the flask on New Year's. That crazy shit with Elizabeth Clare Prophet and the Church Universal and Triumphant. The hellacious fire season in '88 and the damn near torching of Yellowstone. The Freemen standoff. Ted Kaczynski. He had seen it all.

"You're being sentimental and stupid," he said, again out loud, which startled him. He grew angry with himself for glossing over thirty-eight years. Yeah, there had been good times, but there had been shitty times, too. Those occasions had been arriving with greater frequency over the past ten, twelve years as the newsroom began to resemble a bank more than a saloon, as idiosyncrasies were increasingly marginalized and employee handbooks began to have a greater say in things. In Kevin Gilchrist's darkest nights of the soul, he would ask himself if he had simply become a relic. These questions had been going on long before The Diploma and The Drone put the chain saw up his ass. With each new boss—he counted four, including The Diploma, in the past decade—Gilchrist had marched into the office and said, "I've outlasted every editor at this place since 1971, and I'll outlast you, too." In every case, he had been correct, and in most cases, he had eventually won the boss over with tenacity and beautiful writing.

Not so with The Diploma on the second part, and probably not on the first, either.

At once, a compulsion to dial up someone and vent swept over Gilchrist, and it did him no favors to realize that he didn't have the slightest idea whom he should call. Were it in his power, he would talk to Nanette. He felt certain that she would know how to put it into a perspective he could live with. But Nanette was sixteen years dead and gone now. Gilchrist packed himself away in saltiness and sarcasm, all the better to face an unfriendly world, but he was a believer, too. God had his reasons for taking her; the answers were simply beyond the man she'd left behind.

The two imitations of marital bliss who followed the love of Gilchrist's life would be surprised to hear from him, of that he could be sure. He didn't need surprise. He needed solace, and he wouldn't find it with two women who probably wouldn't cross the street to spit on him if he were ablaze.

I could call Carla, he thought. And then, just as quickly, came the counterpoint: *No. Not today. Maybe not ever.*

Gilchrist let out a tonsil-rattling yell and plowed a right cross into the side of the church. The pain shot back through his hand and up his arm, and he nearly passed out. When finally he gathered his equilibrium, he staggered away, his arm limp at his side. He tried to flex his fingers; they wouldn't move. He looked down at his hand, at the blood dripping off his knuckles.

He put the back of his hand up to his mouth and sucked the blood from each knuckle, then slowly lowered his arm again.

On the other side of the alley sat the police headquarters.

"I might as well say hello," Gilchrist said, to no one.

The next morning—after a night's work that entailed six hundred and twenty-three words, total, on two stabbings and a DUI, plus enduring the guffaws of every dispatcher in a three-county area after he introduced himself—Gilchrist dialed Carla's number.

He waited out four rings and nearly bailed before she answered.

"Hello?"

"Carla, it's Kevin, your dad."

A pause. "Hi." She clipped off the single syllable.

"I've been thinking about you," he said.

"Oh? That's new."

"Carla—"

"What do you want? I'm busy."

"I just want to talk. It's been a while."

"It has. Do you know how long?"

"I—"

"Three years."

Gilchrist felt his dander rise. "Well, look, it's not as if a bunch of your calls have been coming over the transom here."

"No, that's true. I lived there for eighteen years waiting for you to give me your time. It took a while, but I figured it out."

"Listen, honey—"

"Don't call me that. You gave up the right to call me that a long time ago, so don't."

"Something bad happened. I've been busted down to a cub reporter. They're trying to force me to leave."

"Someone should tell them that's impossible."

"Dammit, Carla, why does everything out of your mouth have to be so tart?"

"I learned from the best, Dad."

"I'm in a real mess here, you know? I've been thinking about things, things I did wrong, things I could have done better. I just want to talk, that's all."

Carla laughed.

"What?" he asked.

"I just think it's funny. God, for the first time, you're finding out that your stupid job won't love you back and now you're hoping I will."

"No," he said.

"Well, I love you, Dad. I wish I didn't, but I do. But you can't just come back into my life with a free pass once things go badly for you. It's not going to work that way."

"Don't you get it?" he said. "I have nothing else."

"Why don't you retire? It's about that time anyway, isn't it?"

"I can't."

"Why not?"

"Everything's gone. Jane took half the savings. Ginny took half of what was left. I've got a second mortgage on the house. I need to work."

"Ah, yes, Jane and Ginny. Things you did wrong, things you could have done better, I suppose."

"Carla—"

"I'm sorry, Dad. No. Not now."

Long after it had all played out—after Gilchrist did what he had to do, and after the consequences had been rendered—he remembered the catalyst.

The fucking Drone with his fucking juvenile sense of what constituted the news.

"Kevin, you hearing that?" Lindell called across the newsroom. "You ought to roll on that."

Gilchrist looked up from his notes. He'd exacted a promise from The Diploma that he could work on some meatier stories if he could fit them in alongside his new duties. Gilchrist had hooked a good one about chronic underpayment of overtime at the fire department.

"It's two kids rutting in a car," he said. "It's nothing."

"Go ahead and check it out. It might make a fun web story. People love stuff like that."

Gilchrist stood, walking over to The Drone's desk. "Mike, it's two teenagers fucking. It's a pointless story."

The Drone looked up and looked through Gilchrist. "Go out there. Or go home."

Gilchrist wrote the item, about the sixteen-year-old boy and his fifteen-year-old girl and their scantily clad walk to the cop car. It immediately went live on the website under the headline "TEENAGE TRYST: BUSTED!" Over the next two days, it became the most-commented-on of all the stories on the *Herald-Gleaner* site, emailed more than thirty-five thousand times. It became the episode on which people cast their fears about the direction of the country or their belief that the fucking pigs should just leave those kids alone. In any case, Gilchrist learned well the meaning of "viral." Two nights later, the insufferable late-show host was cracking wise on it on television: "Now there's crime prevention. Just fill the parking spaces at Makeout Point with cop cars. Problem solved! And doughnuts!"

The Diploma gave Gilchrist a twenty-five-dollar coffee card and a note: "Thanks for buying in to the concept."

That's when Gilchrist decided to go upper deck on the place.

He waited until nearly one in the morning, until The Drone was gone and he was alone in the newsroom. He went into the men's room, into the first stall and removed the lid from the tank. Then, ever so gingerly, he climbed above the throne, wedging his feet into the handrails, and squatted his ass over the water.

His bowels released, dropping chunks of excrement. The cold splash of tank water struck behind his knees, and he threw his head back. *Damn*, he thought. *This is the best idea I've ever had.*

He clambered down and put the lid back in place.

Over the next week, Gilchrist wrote several items that drew online interest and huzzahs from The Drone and The Diploma. A post-graduation street brawl. A robber who hit the adult bookstore, grabbed the cash register and left a trail of ticker tape for the cops to follow to the park where he'd succumbed to drink. A home invasion that left a burglar with scrambled brains when the homeowner hit him with a seven-iron.

With each bit of supervisory praise, Gilchrist would drop another load into the toilet tank. As his esteem in the newsroom grew, so did the stench.

"Good lord, what is that smell?" an ad rep asked one day.

"Something's wrong with the pipes," The Diploma said. "We've got somebody coming out tomorrow to take a look."

Gilchrist, walking by, said, "That's the smell of journalism, baby."

At shift's end, The Drone stopped at Gilchrist's desk.

"I looked at your fire department story," he said. "It's good stuff. Really."

"Thanks, Mike."

"Kev, I want to tell you how much I appreciate what you've done. You've really owned this assignment. I didn't think you had it in you."

The Drone extended a hand. Gilchrist smiled at him and shook it.

"You have no idea what's in me, Mike."

A half-hour later, Gilchrist closed the stall door and removed the tank's lid. *They'll figure out what's happened tomorrow and probably install video cameras or a even card lock*, he thought. *Better give them one more as a token of my esteem.*

He set a foot on the handrail and started up, same as he'd done before. As he turned and began to hang his ass over the tank, his left foot gave way, sliding off the handrail. His legs flew out in front of him, and his head and shoulders crashed against the upright tank. He heard the crack, like dead wood baked in the sun, and he knew, even as he headed for the floor.

On his back, Gilchrist remained alert. It didn't even hurt. His arms and legs, though, wouldn't move. The smell of his own watery waste, pouring onto the floor around him from the busted tank, enveloped him. He would be stuck here until morning, until someone arrived and discovered him—his pants down around his useless legs, the toilet tank lid set across the seat, the tank obliterated and his feces carried across the floor by the water. They would find him, and they would know what he'd done, and that would be that. He would be the story they always told at the *Herald-Gleaner*. He might even end up with his own place in a police report after all these years.

And Kevin Gilchrist's only thought was how much he wished he could write this story.

star of the north

The only guilty man in the Montana State Prison squatted down and grabbed a handful of bone-dry earth when he heard the question. He'd anticipated it when the new meat's face registered recognition of him. Even so, he always found himself at a loss to give an answer that he knew by heart. The years had gone by, and people's fascination had moved on to other things, but still the question returned, again and again. The last time he'd heard it had to have been two years back, on the twentieth anniversary of the thing. A reporter had asked him then, just as another reporter asked five years before that, and five years before that, and five years before that. In a few more years, he figured, another reporter would realize that the story hadn't been told in a while and would show up to ask the question again. And the only guilty man in the Montana State Prison would think about it some before answering, as he was doing with the punk standing over him now.

"I don't regret what I did," he said, standing and facing his questioner, a boy of around eighteen, about the age his own son might be if he'd managed to stay outside the walls long enough to father one. He hardened his gaze, precluding sentimentality. He'd learned long ago that looking like he'd take no shit went a long way toward keeping it away. For all other occasions, he had other ways of staying safe. He wasn't yet certain if he'd have to employ them with this guy.

"Oh, man, Ray Bingham, I didn't believe it was really you," the young guy said. "I heard about that all the time when I was a little kid. Everybody in Billings knows about that—hell, probably everybody in the whole damned state. My pops, he said he was there and saw the whole thing. He said it was a real bloodbath."

A nice story, it was one Ray doubted. Over the years, it seemed as though everybody who was in Billings on September 16, 1988, eventually claimed to have seen what Ray did, but his own recollection was that Jeff Fielding had been well on his way to dead before anybody showed up behind Rimrock Mall and tried to stop it. Still, Ray saw little upside in contradicting the young man. Instead, he pressed on, giving the guy what he'd come to hear.

"I saw Jeff Fielding on the sidewalk back there, and I wrestled him to the ground," Ray said. This part he recited by heart, a word-perfect rendition of what he had first told the cops and later the judge and jury twenty-two years earlier and, these days, the occasional interloping reporter.

"I held his shoulders with my knees and I punched him in the face. I punched him again and again, until I felt his bones breaking. I caved in his eye sockets. I smashed his nose until it looked like a purple piece of tenderized meat. I hit him, and I didn't stop hitting him when his blood sprayed across my face. I hit him until they pulled me off. And by then, there was no reason to hit him anymore."

When Ray finished talking, his chest rolled like a wave at sea. He remembered feeling a similar breathlessness after he'd been yanked off dead Jeff Fielding. That day, he sat on his knees and clasped his hands behind his back so the cops didn't have to do anything but slap on the cuffs. Now, he looked back at his young questioner, who hadn't yet lifted his eyes from his shoes.

"Jesus Christ," the young guy said.

After lights-out, Ray kept his eyes open and chewed on the question of regret. To his recollection, Judge Mabry had been the first to ask about it, at the sentencing. The old jurist had spent much of the trial either polishing his glasses or idly spinning them by the temples. But at the final hearing, Mabry had pulled the glasses on and peered over them at Ray and asked if he wished to acknowledge the pain of Jeff's family, if he had come to terms with the horrible thing he had done.

"Hell, no, I don't regret a thing," Ray had said. "Jeff deserved what he got, and I gave it to him. That's about the size of it."

"Young man," Judge Mabry had answered, "you will find prison a cold and lonely place with that approach."

In the intervening years, Ray had come to agree with Mabry about cold and lonely, but he didn't figure it had anything to do with his attitude. That's just the way prison was, for everyone.

Ray flopped over onto his left side, facing the wall, and doubled up his pillow.

I'll never see a day outside this place, he thought. *I know that now. But if the price of being free is remorse about something I'm glad I did, something I'd do a hundred times out of a hundred if given another chance at it, I'd rather stay here.*

Ray slipped down off the top bunk at first light and stretched. He could feel the years piling on, and he'd taken to silent calisthenics each morning to stay limber. On the outside, he figured, people assimilated time's erosion of their youth bit by bit, day by day, never really grasping what was happening to them. Inside, it was different. Mirrors were polished steel, and the face that gazed back at him blurred, offering little detail. The previous December, he'd received a Christmas card from his mom and Rick, a picture of the three of them together in the visitation room, and Ray had been flabbergasted at the gray weaving through his thinning hair, the creases in his face, the crinkling at the corner of his eyes. Almost immediately, he realized that he shouldn't have been surprised. He could see the years chewing on his mom and Rick on their once-a-year visits. Why wouldn't they chew on him, too?

At forty-three years old, Ray had spent more time in prison than out. Out there, in the world, he might be considered a relatively young man. In here, age accelerated as the years passed and new generations arrived, riding the bus.

"What's your name?" Ray sat next to the young man in the dining hall, and every eye in the place followed him. It would mean something to the guys in stir, Ray's sitting and talking with this new kid. Ray had respect in the pen, as much respect as one could get from a pack of thieves, rapists and murderers, and he'd had to do ugly things to get it. He was inclined to be generous with the kid, who had shown some respect—and some balls—by approaching him the way he did.

Maybe Ray could save him some trouble by befriending him. He had the latitude to be magnanimous. If the kid crossed him, he could take everything away, and the young guy would find out about the cold and lonely Judge Mabry spoke of.

"Jack," the kid said. "Jackson Reed. My friends call me Jack."

Ray scooped some hash browns between his thumb and forefinger and shoved them in his mouth. "What are you in for, Jack? I know you didn't do it, but what did they say you did?"

"Oh, I did it. Second-degree murder. Guy tried to screw me on a deal. He had a knife. I had a Glock."

Jack jabbed at his scrambled eggs with the plastic fork, breaking them into segregated chunks of overcooked whites and yellows.

"How old are you?" Ray asked.

"Nineteen."

"Any people back home?"

"Mom and pops. My girlfriend. My daughter. She's eighteen months old. They say she could be in high school before I'm out of here." The kid's voice wavered.

"Best not to think of the day you get out," Ray said. "Makes it too hard to handle the days that you're in, you know what I mean?"

Ray was nineteen the day he moved out of the house. He'd come back to Billings after a year of working down in Kit Carson, Colorado, doing cathodic work on the oil wells for his Uncle Bob. For a year solid, he put away nearly every buck he earned. On the job, Bob picked up the cost of lodging and meals, meaning Ray had only to resist the siren song of the pool hall and bars to keep from blowing his stash. He spent that year reading a lot—Kerouac and Mailer and Bukowski, paperbacks he found in the general store—and screwing the pretty waitress at the Wagon Wheel. Amber was her name. She was twenty-four, a few years older than Ray, and she had shown him a few things. When he up and left in September, she had seemed surprised that he didn't ask her to come with him. Instead, he ran away with Caroline, the '64 skylight-blue Mustang he had bought at a lot in Arvada.

In Billings, he had asked his mom if he could move back into his old room, just for a couple of weeks until he found a job and a place. His brother, Ben, cleared out a couple of dresser drawers and made room for Ray. His mom had seemed pleased to have him back, and Rick had tolerated him, which was about the most Ray could expect. Still, it was just too uncomfortable, being there again, all of them—mom, Rick, Ben, and his fourteen-year-old sister, Kim—awkwardly trying to talk with him over dinner. Six days after Ray had moved in, he found a job at the sugar beet plant and moved right back out, this time into a one-bedroom place downtown. Everybody seemed relieved to see him go.

Ray and Jack worked side by side in the metal shop, punching signposts in the benders. Acutely aware of the watchful stares of the guards—inmates and steel could be a dangerous combination—the men stuck to their tasks and spoke in sideways mumbles.

Everybody in maximum had seen the bloom on their friendship, and the bulls who had taken a liking to Jack when he came off the bus kept a seething distance out of deference to Ray, and they even wondered if maybe he was grooming the youngster for himself. Ray couldn't bring himself to feel fatherly toward his young counterpart—to admit such a thing would be a concession that time was winning—but he felt something akin to being an older brother. Jack despaired of the sentence he was facing and still grappled with the crushing realization of what he'd brought on himself, but Ray knew that soon enough, time wouldn't be such a hurdle for him. At least Jack would get out, if he kept his nose clean.

"What did you do when you were on the outside?" Jack asked him.

Ray laid his weight into the bender bar. "You know the sugar beet factory on the South Side?"

"Yeah."

"I ran the boiler there. Grew those sugar crystals."

"You could take the smell? Man, I hate it when that place fires up."

"After a while, sure. I came to enjoy it, actually. It smelled like cash money." He smiled. "What about you? What sort of work were you into?"

"Some welding, construction. I didn't really have a career."

Ray mopped his brow with the back of his hand and wiped it on his pants leg. "I wouldn't call what I did a career. I know more about this we're doing here than I ever knew about sugar beets. It was just a way to pay the bills and keep Caroline in high-test. It drove my mom's husband crazy. He always told me I had a good head but no ambition. Shit, maybe he was right. Look where I am."

Jack laughed, and a guard ambled over and tapped the machinery with his baton. The men set back to work.

During a break, they leaned against the wall in the yard. They were pecker-deep into November, and the wind bit through their work shirts and into the flesh underneath.

"Can I ask you something?" Jack said.

"Shoot."

"One thing about … well, what happened that day. I never heard anybody say why you killed that guy."

A half-smile crossed Ray's face. The reporters who tromped into Deer Lodge on five-year cycles always asked this one, too, and he never gave them the satisfaction of a decent answer. "I never told anybody. I admitted it, didn't try to hide behind any bullshit excuse my lawyer tried to think up, and it made everybody a little nuts that I never said anything," Ray said.

"Why didn't you?"

"Because it made no difference. I did what I had to do, and nothing was going to bring him back."

"Why did you have to do it?"

Ray kicked the dirt and sent a spray of pebbles flying.

"Look, I'll say this: Jeff Fielding was a bad guy. That whole family was real bad news, man. I'd known him for a long time. He used to live a couple of doors down from us back in the seventies, and that place his family lived in was out of control from the get-go, man. I never saw his mom or dad around. Just Jeff, his brother Benji and an older sister, Tonya. Jeff was five or six years older than me, and Benji was a couple years older than him. As bad as Jeff was, Benji was ten times worse. By the time they moved into our neighborhood, that guy had been in and out of this place a couple of times. Sleeved-out in prison tats, which was a pretty amazing thing to see back then. I was plenty scared of him."

"Bad guy, how?"

Ray flashed on a memory he had replayed a thousand times, in the years before he beat the life out of Jeff Fielding and in the many days since. "Jeff took a neighbor girl, a little seven-year-old who lived across the street, into his house and undressed her. He was fourteen, maybe fifteen. He didn't, you know, violate her or anything, but he beat her up pretty good. He bit her nose, if you can believe that shit."

"Jesus, man."

"I was the one who found her. He'd kicked her out of the house, bloody, no clothes, middle of winter. She was hiding behind our shed, afraid to go home and say anything." The memory landed on Ray, a punch across the years, the shivering girl begging him not to tell anybody, her nostril shredded, the blood dotting the snow she stood in. Ray coaxed her into the house, and his mom wrapped her in a blanket. And then all hell rained down.

"Yeah. Anyway, when people found out, everybody went a little nuts about it. My stepdad, the girl's father and some of the other men in the neighborhood went over there and talked to Jeff's parents. Threatened them, if you want to know the truth. The cops showed up. A day or two later, they were all gone. Cleared out, moved across town. I'd see Jeff from time to time here or there, and he'd try to bait me into something, just because he was that kind of asshole, and maybe he knew I had something to do with how he was found out. Anyway, I just steered clear, you know? He was trouble."

"Wait, so it was about what happened to this girl?" Jack said.

Ray shook his head. "No, but he was probably lucky that somebody else didn't get to him first."

Ray lay awake again that night, replaying for the first time in many months those last few days of freedom.

Everything had started while he waited for Caroline at the detailing shop as she got one last bit of primping before the snow flew. Ray thumbed through a news magazine, sitting up and taking notice only when he came to a piece about homesteading in Alaska. The practice, which had pretty much gone by the wayside in most of America by the sixties, was still getting play up north, although not too successfully, according to the article. But if someone were willing to bust ass in the unforgiving outdoors, in a place where there were no decent roads or supermarkets, the article said, there was land to be had.

The plans were already churning in Ray's head.

"You're going to do what?" Rick Duley asked his stepson later that week. "Alaska? This sounds like a flight of fancy to me."

Ray was none too surprised by his stepfather's skepticism, so he turned to his mother.

"You're just going to up and leave?" she asked.

"Well, yeah. I mean, I'll have to sell Caroline"—he shocked even himself by saying such a thing, and yet he also knew that his willingness proved his resolve—"and get everything squared away. But, yeah, I've got a line on a pipeline job up on the North Slope, and once I've been there for a year, I can put in for a homestead."

Rick shook his head. "Honestly, Ray, I just don't think you have much appreciation for what you're getting into here. This sounds like another one of those things where you go off half-cocked, and in a few months, we'll end up sending you airfare so you can come home."

Ray folded his arms across his chest. It wouldn't be right to say he hated his mother's husband, but he didn't respect the man. Rick spent his life with his head jammed up the ass of academia. He didn't—couldn't—understand what somebody like Ray wanted from life.

"Look, man, I'm not asking for permission. I'm asking if I can stay here for a few days before I go."

Rick looked at his wife, who would be making the call. She always did.

"Of course, dear," she said. "There's always room for you here."

In the week that followed, Ray sold everything he owned save for his clothes. He found a good home for Caroline, only after exacting a promise that if the guy—a well-heeled baby boomer who lived on the West End—ever decided to sell her that Ray could have first dibs. The cash from that deal put him at about ten thousand bucks, which he figured would get him where he was headed and give him a decent stake.

On the eve of Ray's departure, he sat in the kitchen taking sips off a can of Pabst when Ben came in.

"Jesus," Ray said, scrambling to his feet. "What the hell happened?"

A purple welt ballooned around the boy's left eye. The skin looked sickly and thin, as if it might burst and spill blood and pus on the linoleum. Under the eye, a deep cut had split open.

"Me and my friends were just horsing around in a parking lot," Ben said. "I slipped and hit the bumper of a car."

"Come on. How stupid do you think I am?"

"It's true."

Ray palmed the top of Ben's head like a basketball, turning it so he could get a better look. Seeing the boy battered like that turned Ray's stomach. Given the difference in their ages, he didn't have much in common with Ben, but he loved the boy and thought he was just about sweetest kid he'd ever been around. His mind flashed on memory just a few years old, when the family had made a pilgrimage down to South Padre Island for a vacation. On the way, they'd stopped to visit Uncle Bob in Casper. Bob was the opposite of warm and kindly, even to kin, and yet Ray remembered that while everybody else had said their goodbyes by shaking Bob's hand, Ben had walked through the handshake and given the bear of a man a hug that had surprised everybody, most of all Bob.

"Who did this to you, Ben?"

"Nobody."

"Bullshit. Tell me."

The boy hung his head. "Jeff Fielding."

Jesus. Jeff Fielding had to be twenty-five, twenty-six years old. Ray was surprised that Ben even knew who he was. The boy had been only four or five when the Fieldings got run off.

"Why?"

"I don't know."

"Did he say anything, or did he just beat the shit out of you?"

Ben wouldn't look at him. "He said you're a pussy."

"Where was this?"

"At the mall."

Ray fetched a steak from the freezer and told the boy to put it on his eye and keep it there. "When mom and Rick get home, just tell them you got in a fight," he told Ben. "Don't say anything about anything. I'll be back."

On his way out the door for the last time, Ray grabbed the keys to his mother's Monte Carlo.

Ray and Jack loped around the prison yard, jawboning, same as they did damn near every day.

"You asked me a while ago about why I did it," Ray said, flinging a pebble across the splotchy ground.

Jack waited. He dared not speak. If Ray had any hesitation about talking, Jack didn't want to provide an excuse to clam up.

"I never told anybody this, but Jeff, he beat the shit out of my little brother that day. A little kid, ten, twelve years younger than him, and he just brutalized him, busted up his face and his eye."

"Jesus," Jack said. "Why?"

"He was a goddamned animal, that's why. You meet guys like that in here, guys who don't have any honor or soul at all. They'd cut you to ribbons as sure as they'd look at you. Nothing there."

"Wow. So you just went after him—"

"—and found him and made certain he'd never do anything like that again, to anybody," Ray said. "Christ, it feels ... damn, it feels like confession to say it to somebody. You know, I was a day away from

117

leaving Billings for good. I was gonna go up to Alaska, make some bucks there on the pipeline, build me a little place in the woods and read and chop wood, live off the fatta the land, like in the book. Be alone. That's all I ever wanted to do. I was so close. Another day, and I was gone."

Jack tried to lick the words he wanted to say, the solace he wanted to offer, off his tongue. Ray kept going. "And I guess I'm gone anyway. The day I met you, you asked if I have regrets. Not about Jeff, I don't. If you'd seen what he did to that little kid, you'd have wanted to kill him, too. But I am sorry I never saw Alaska. I've been there a million times in my head, and then I always wake up here, you know?"

"That's rough."

"I'll tell you something else, Jack, and it's something I've never told anybody," Ray said. "I know in my heart I did the right thing. My conscience is clear. But here's the part that gives me a little trouble sometimes: when I felt Jeff's bones breaking in his face and saw everything caving in and knew he was gonna die, I liked it. It felt … God, it felt like the best drug I ever took."

"I don't know how you do it," Jack said. "All I think about is the time I have left until I can get out of here. You don't seem bothered by it."

Ray looked skyward for several seconds. Jack picked at his fingernails and waited.

"Well, here's the thing. I know I did what I did for the right reason. The time in here is hard for everybody. If you think I'm not bothered, it's only because I've had more practice faking it. But I rid the world of a worthless son of a bitch. I can sleep at night."

The year turned and pushed through spring to the precipice of summer. Ray persuaded Jack to pursue his general equivalency diploma, telling him that as far away as it seemed, he should be thinking about giving himself the best possible chance once he got out. They shot the bull in the prison yard. They did their part in keeping the state's roadside signage up to snuff.

On the solstice, Ray received a postcard.

"Jesus," he said, turning it over and reading it again.

"What?" Jack said.

"My brother. He's coming to see me."

"No kidding."

Ray tucked the card into his waistband. "I haven't seen Ben since I was sentenced."

"Are you shitting me?"

"Damn near twenty-three years. I've seen pictures. He drops me a Christmas card every few years, depending on how things are going for him. But I haven't looked in his face since I went away."

"Why?"

Ray's heart beat fast. "He's ashamed, I guess. Of me, probably. Of being the reason, indirectly, that I'm here, maybe."

He sat down. Jack followed him.

"What are you going to say?"

Ray considered the question a while. "I just don't know. Hello, I guess."

Ben had known trouble. Ray gathered that much just from the occasional visits from his mom and Rick. They usually brought pictures, gurgling happily about Kim and her perfect family, replaying in excruciating detail all their university junkets around the world. London. Bordeaux. Athens. Ray always found it curious that they seemed not to grasp how tales of living without a tether could taunt a man who needed permission to take a piss. The joy of seeing his mother made the discomfort worth enduring. Rick was a simple matter of toleration, the same as marking time inside the prison walls. Ray had done it for years. An afternoon was nothing.

In the pen, a man notices details; he has all the time in the world to do so. Ray learned as much about Ben from what his mom and Rick didn't say as from what they did. The little boy had grown into a man, and Ray had some concept of the burden he labored under. Ray had done what he could to lighten the load, but he couldn't do it all.

He had seen it so many times in other men inside, the way entire branches of their family trees withered and died once they went to prison. For every dedicated mother, wife or girlfriend who arrived on visitation day without fail, a score of brothers and sisters and aunts and uncles and cousins excised the inmate from their lives, the way a surgeon might cut out a mole. It was as if they didn't care, or didn't think their disappearance would be noticed.

The man on the inside always notices. He has nothing else to do.

On visitation day, Ray looked deep into the murky image he projected onto polished steel, patting down the incorrigible shocks of hair that kept trying to bolt away from his head. He brushed his teeth twice. He'd bartered for some cheap cologne out in the yard, and he doused himself in it. He chuckled gently at the vanity, and then he redefined it. This was more anticipation than anything else. His palms repeatedly grew sweaty, and he wiped them down on the ass of his cotton pants.

When Ben came into the waiting area, Ray pegged him immediately. The cherubic face held its ground, even as the rounded corners of the obese man his brother had grown into threatened to swallow it up. Ray stood and rubbed his hands on his hips and tossed a smile to his kid brother, who walked toward him with a small woman a half-step behind.

"Jesus, Ben, look at you," Ray said, breaking into a wide smile and walking a few steps toward his brother.

Ben met Ray's outstretched hand and shook it vigorously. "Ray, so good to see you. You look … well, you look pretty much the same. A little less hair."

"But more than you," Ray said, pointing at the hairline that had beaten a hasty retreat to the back of Ben's head.

Ben pawed the skin up top. "Yeah, well. … Darn, Ray, I'm sorry. This here is my wife, Kara," he said, ushering the woman forward.

Her eyes, small and intense and unblinking, set Ray ill at ease, so he looked at Ben while shaking hands with her. "Wife? I had no idea, man. Congratulations."

"Just a matter of waiting for the right one," Ben said. "Kara has been a godsend to me. I mean that literally."

"Well, sit down here and tell me all about it," Ray said. "Damn, it's good to see you, man."

Ben clasped his hands, lacing his fingers, and set his chin on them. "Ray, did you ever wonder why I never came around here to see you?"

"Sure. It didn't surprise me. I'd have liked to have seen you, but it's a tough deal, how all that went down."

"Ray, I'm thirty-five years old, and in many ways, I feel like I'm just trying to live. I'm fourteen months sober after being a drunk for nearly twenty years. I've been in bankruptcy twice. I've been homeless, Ray. When you killed Jeff Fielding, you did a number on me, too. I don't blame you, Ray, but that's the truth."

Ben's continual invoking of his name agitated Ray, and he wasn't sure he liked the direction his kid brother was aiming things. He swallowed the urge to protest and waited for what Ben might say next.

"Kara has brought me to God, Ray. I was powerless before, but now God is with me, and I can do things I never thought possible. I can stay sober. I can be a husband. If it is his will, I will be a father. And God has also shown me that I must forgive you for what your vicious act did to me."

"Damn generous of you and God," Ray said, "considering—"

"Let him finish," Kara interrupted. "This is hard for him."

Ray drummed his fingertips on the table and looked at his brother, who gobbled some air and started in again.

"Here's what I've come to find out, Ray. I forgive you. But the burden on me will not be lifted until you forgive me, too. Will you, Ray? Will you forgive me for what I've done to you?"

"Ben, I don't follow you."

Ben grabbed his wife's hand, and she squeezed his fingers tight. "When I came home that day, I told you I'd fallen against a car bumper. Do you remember that?"

Ray searched the man's corpulent face and found the trace of a scar under his eye. "Yeah, I do."

"You didn't believe me."

"Nope."

"Ray, it was the God's honest truth."

The room went hazy on Ray, and he flattened his palms on the table as Ben bore in.

"I'd seen Jeff Fielding that day at the mall, that much is true, and he'd taunted me some and called you names, and he told me to tell you that he would be coming for you when he had a chance. When you asked me who did it, I blurted out his name. I figured the worst that would happen is you'd beat him up, or he'd beat you up. But you killed him, Ray. Good God Almighty. You killed him."

Ben dropped his head to the table and sobbed. Kara draped herself over him and consoled him, whispering in his ear. Ray held on as the room threatened to spin again.

"I couldn't say anything, Ray. I couldn't," Ben said. His voice became shrill, small. "I was a little boy. I didn't even know where to start. Please forgive me, Ray, please, please forgive me."

Ray stood up, and the blood assaulted his temples. He intertwined his fingers behind his head and closed his eyes. "I forgive you, Ben."

The younger man's whimpering morphed into full-on blubbering. "Thank you. Thank you." Tears streamed down his face. "Thank you for giving me my life back. I feel like I can finally live now."

Ray turned and walked away.

That afternoon, Ray sat apart from everyone in the prison yard, his back to the milling crowd of cons. Jack approached his friend slowly.

"The days are growing shorter now," Ray said, startling Jack as he came near. "Up in Alaska, on the North Slope, it's still almost twenty-four hours of daylight, but every day, they lose a little more sun. In six months, they'll be in a long stretch of twenty-four hours of dark-ness, but the days will be growing a little longer. It comes and it goes."

Jack sat down next to him.

"I'd be in my twenty-third year of that cycle. Twenty-three years! I bet I'd have never grown tired of it."

"I bet not," Jack said.

They sat quietly a while longer. Jack swept dust off his chest. Ray stared straight ahead, rigid.

"Jack, I want you to listen to me. Listen, and accept it, and don't say a word. Do you understand?"

Jack swallowed hard. "Whatever you say, Ray."

"Things are different for me now. I can't help you through your time in here. You did what you did, and you have to live with it on your own. I want you to stand up and walk away from me. I don't want you to speak to me ever again. I want you to act like you've never known me. Just leave. I like you, Jack, but I can't be your friend, and I can't carry you anymore."

"Carry me? What the fuck are you—"

Ray turned, and Jack saw steel in the older man's eyes that stopped him cold.

"Jack, if you say another word, I will cut your heart straight out of your chest."

The young man stood and stepped backward, slowly. Ray turned his eyes back to that faraway place. Jack headed for the other side of the yard, looking back once to see if his friend would look at him, but it was no use.

For the rest of the afternoon, Ray Bingham's eyes saw only the northern horizon that he had once come so close to catching.

she's gone

Ross watched his father step through the scrubby brush, the man's calloused leather palms gripping a willow branch with both hands turned up as if he were curling dumbbells. After fifteen, maybe twenty yards, the branch, cut to the shape of an outsized wishbone, began to quiver. After a few steps more, the single point up top swung hard toward the ground.

Dwight Newbry turned to his observers with a gap-toothed smile and pointed at the spot.

"That it?" shouted the man standing to the left of Ross. Then, under his breath so only the boy could hear, he added, "Jesus, I hope not."

"Think so," Dwight called back. "Lemme walk it out a little bit."

"That's a long damn way from where we're putting the house," said the man on Ross's right, the property owner. He retrieved a hanky from his back pocket and mopped his corpulent, sunburned neck.

Dwight pivoted and clomped away from the spot at a forty-five-degree angle and turned again, raised the willow branch and traced his steps. Again, the branch shuddered before violently marking the spot. Three more runs from other angles confirmed it, and Dwight took a stake out of his back pocket and pounded it into the earth.

The man on Ross's left tugged off his mesh JQ Drilling Co. hat and wiped it across his face. "Well, hell," he said. "That's it, then." He kicked at the dirt, diffusing a sandy cloud. "A long stretch, and it's gonna be a son of a bitch digging through this."

Dwight loped back to them, his lopsided grin exposing every ground-down tooth, looking for all the world like it would break his face in half.

"I told you, guys," he shouted at them. "I told you. That there is the place."

"I don't get it," Ross said on the ride back to town. "A piece of wood tells you where the water is?"

Dwight held the '68 Ford tight to the yellow line as the truck bore down on Miles City. "Yep. That's about the size of it."

"How?"

"It just does."

"It's just piece of wood. What's so special about a piece of wood?"

Dwight chuckled at the boy's exasperation. He hadn't known what to expect when April had called a few weeks earlier. *He's not listening to me anymore*, she'd said. *It's time to see what you can do with him. Past time, I'd say.* When the boy stepped off the plane a couple of weeks earlier in Billings, he'd come packing two bags and silence. Dwight tried for a few days to draw him out, to get him to talk, and that hadn't worked. It was only after he started bringing Ross along on the occasional job that the youngster opened up, if only a little. The well witching seemed to have inspired more interest than the posthole digging and the calf branding.

"Nothing special about the wood, boy," Dwight said. "A wire coat hanger'd work, too. I just prefer the willow."

The kid balled his fists. "Don't call me boy."

Dwight gave him a sly grin and reached over to tousle his hair, but Ross slapped at his father's hand. *Stupid*, Dwight silently scolded himself. *Too fast.*

"What do you want me to call you, then?" he asked.

"How about Ross? That's my name after all."

They were almost to Miles City now, the street lights twinkling at the bottom of the hill as dusk ceded to night.

"It is, at that," Dwight said. "Your momma ever tell you how we came up with it?"

"No."

"You want to hear the story?"

Ross squirmed in his seat. Every movement the boy made dripped with aggression, Dwight noted. "Yeah, I guess. I don't care."

"It's way too good a story to waste on that attitude," Dwight said. "You think about it, and if you decide you want to know, you ask me proper."

Ross spoke little through dinner. Only after Dwight put a bowl of ice cream in front of the boy—vanilla, with a hard chocolate shell—did he relent.

"Tell me the story about my name," he said.

Dwight slipped the boy's dinner plate under the table and swept crumbs onto it. "You're sure now?"

"I said I was."

"I'm just checking. I—" Dwight choked off the rest of what he was tempted to say. In the two weeks Ross had been bunking with him, he'd noticed a creeping tendency in himself to tease the kid, to try to get under his skin, just because the boy was so damned prickly. Dwight took perverse thrill in puncturing the protective layer. He hadn't seen Ross in four years, and back then he had been a nine-year-old who was a damn sight easier to entertain than the sullen teenager with whom he now shared nearly every hour. The teasing allowed Dwight to blow off some frustration he might otherwise unload in a more destructive way, but he knew it wasn't closing the gap between them.

"Your momma and me, we were living on the Fort Ord Army base in California, right there on the coast," Dwight said, sitting down with his own ice cream. "I was just a buck private, nothing too special, but when we had a chance, we liked to go exploring. Growing up here, we hadn't ever seen a place like that. God, on a clear day, the water looked blue, just like in the movies, and it went on forever."

"I've seen it," the boy said. "Mom took me there last summer."

Dwight cut to it. "Anyways, this one day, we went up north of San Francisco, across the Golden Gate Bridge, in this little town. It was a beautiful day—sunny, warm, even though it must have been late September, early October. We were in a park. Set out a blanket, had some wine, fell asleep. A great day. Anyways, the name of that town was Ross. It was one of our best memories there, so when you came along not too long after that, we figured we had the right name for you."

Dwight looked at his son, waiting. Ross didn't look up.

"That's not much of a story," the boy said, scooping the last bite of ice cream into his mouth.

"I just figured you'd want to hear it," Dwight said, and he winced as he realized that he'd let the boy know he'd been wounded.

"No, you said it was too good a story to waste," Ross said, staring at him. "It wasn't good at all. It sucked."

Dwight tugged at the napkin on the table, straightening it.

"What are you so angry about, Ross?"

"I'm not angry. I'm really glad you and Mom had a great day. That's so awesome. Didn't really stop you from leaving us, though, did it? You're here, she's at home, she doesn't want me, I'm here, I don't want to be with you. It really worked out for me, didn't it?"

Dwight clasped his hands in front of him. "Ross—"

"Shut up."

"Listen—"

"Shut up."

"Ross, about me and your momma—"

"Shut up!" The boy threw back his chair, crashing it against the stained-wood wall of Dwight's trailer. He ran to his room, shaking the doublewide again with a slammed door.

For a long time, Dwight stared into his bowl, waiting for his heart to thump with less urgency. When he finally scooped out some of the melted vanilla, the sound of his spoon clinking against the bowl reverberated in a house that had gone silent.

Quillen gave them a brisk wave the next morning as they pulled up at the ranch. Behind him, the mast on the drilling rig stood at attention, ready to seek the water Dwight had zeroed in on a day earlier.

"Thanks for coming," Quillen said, shaking hands with both of them. Ross pulled back from the man's grip; it felt like the mouth of a vise closing on his hand.

"I tell you, this is gonna be a son of a bitch, trying to dig this out. This ground doesn't hold up for shit." Quillen kicked at the dirt.

"Happy to help. A day's pay is a day's pay," Dwight said.

"Might be more than that, if I have to take another run at it. Hope not."

Ross watched the men in bemusement. Both spread their legs slightly, supporting their torsos with the widened base, like a couple of old football linemen who couldn't stand up straight anymore. Quillen—Jim was his name, Ross remembered—frowned with nearly every word, as if it caused him pain to speak. Ross's father reached back and slipped his hand down the back of his jeans, his palm out. A couple of cocks on the walk, they were.

"Kid," Quillen said.

Ross, startled, looked up. "Me?"

"No, the other kid. Yeah, you. Know how to use a shovel?"

"Yeah."

"I'll give you ten bucks if you keep that hole clear of dirt."

Four hours into the dig, Dwight's divining paid off. Water surged through the pipe and sprayed down onto them. The fat splashes of muddy water tingled on Ross's skin, baked pink by the midday sun.

"Hot damn!" Quillen said, leaping from his drilling perch. "Newbry, you're a goddamned well-witchin' fool. Look at her go!" The gusher burbled out of the top of the mast, stripping caked-on mud from the back of the rig.

Dwight looked skyward in an open-mouthed grin.

"That's it?" Ross asked.

"Well, no, not yet," Quillen said. "Gotta run a pump down into her, but that's sure as shit a water well."

He clapped Dwight on the shoulder, and for the first time, Ross looked at his father with something approaching respect.

Ross and the men sat under the awning outside the trailer. Even as dusk galloped hard across the sky, the embers of the day broiled anything that dared venture into the light. A bucket of ice holding a six-pack of Pabst and a few root beers for Ross stood sweating on the ground.

"You need a woman's touch around here, Newbry," Quillen said, waving his hand at the junked-out cars scattered across what passed for a front yard.

"Had one," Dwight said.

Quillen tapped his bottle against Dwight's, and then against Ross's root beer. "I hear you, partner. I've had my own troubles there, too. Still, if you love pussy, what else are you gonna do?"

"Good point."

"I got a cow or two, I guess," Quillen said, chuckling. "I'll have to give it some more thought before it comes to that."

Ross tried to conjure a memory of Jill's face. It was no use. He'd met his father's wife only a couple of times, and she hadn't made much of an impression on him.

Before he left Fargo, his mom had suggested that things had gone badly out here for Dwight and Jill, and so he hadn't pushed that line of questioning. Truth was, he figured he had trouble enough on his own without worrying about the two of them. Now it was a moot point as Dwight, unbidden, revealed all.

"I knew it was bad from the start, but I stayed in. I kept thinking if I just hung in there, she'd come around, but she never did."

"What do you mean?" Quillen said.

"I couldn't make her happy. She would say, 'Dwight, you're just a good ol' boy, you'll never amount to anything.' Well, hell, I'm the guy I was the day she met me. I never told her I'd be anything different than that. So she started going to night school, wanted to become a travel agent. So I went with that. Started going to Billings all the damn time for seminars and stuff. Fine, I said. I went to bed alone a lot of nights. I never complained. And then she comes home one day and says, 'I'm leaving.' Just like that. It's over."

"When was that?" Ross asked.

Dwight traced a thumb along the lip of the bottle. "Nine weeks ago."

"Bitch," Quillen said. "At least she didn't clean you out, the way my second wife did. Three years ago, and I'm barely holding on. Job's gone to shit. Drilling these wells, trying to stay afloat."

"Mine didn't do it only because there was nothing to take."

Quillen took a swig, emptying his bottle. "I should have never gotten divorced the first time. I let the best woman I ever had get away."

Ross looked at his father, wanting him to say it and bracing himself for the competing emotions—pride and anger—he knew would come if Dwight did. "Yeah," Dwight said. "Me, too."

Word quickly got around about the jackpot well up Jordan way, and the next morning, calls started hitting the Newbry house as soon the sun peeked above the eastern horizon.

"Hell, yeah, we're interested," Dwight said, fielding the first one. "Nah, I'm almost certain he can do it. I know I can." On the couch, across the room, Quillen sat scratching his belly and nodding his head vigorously at the rumor of work.

By midmorning, Dwight had lined up nine well-digging jobs—nine witching jobs for him—and Quillen had ciphered out the math and figured that if things broke right, he could get them done inside of a month and be home by September.

"You got room for me on that couch a few weeks?" Quillen asked.

"You got room for me on the back of that rig?"

There in the living room, both in their underwear, they shook on it.

"What grade are you in, sport?" Quillen asked Ross as they watched the rig make easy work on a segment of pipe. They were on their fourth well in a little more than a week and a half, right on schedule.

Ross, a head taller than the leathery man beside him, glanced at him and said, "I'll be in eighth."

"So you're, what, twelve, thirteen?"

"Thirteen."

"I've got a boy about your age."

"What's his name?"

"Mitch." Quillen pointed at the pipe's point of entry. "Better go sweep that out, huh?"

Ross did as he was told, approaching the back of the rig and slipping the blade of the shovel alongside the pipe and raking away the churned-up earth. The job done, he loped back alongside Quillen.

"Where's your son now?" Ross asked.

"He lives with his mom out in Washington."

"My mom lives in Fargo. She made me come here."

Quillen nodded at the back of the rig. Dwight had climbed behind the mast and was lubing some of the mechanical joints. "Adults play a lot of games, kid," he said. "Might as well get used to that now, but that dad of yours, he's true blue. I've known him for a long time. I trust him. I don't say that about many people."

"I don't know him," Ross said.

Quillen gave Ross a tiny shove, prompting the boy to look him in the eye. "Hey. Listen. He doesn't know you, either, but he's willing to try. I'd give anything to see my boy again. Give him a chance."

They dragged into Miles City at sundown. A brown sedan sat in the driveway.

"Shit," Dwight said. "It's Jill."

"Maybe she's come back," Quillen said. "Maybe she misses you."

Dwight scoffed. "Yeah, maybe."

"Well, listen," Quillen said, "I'm gonna leave you to it. I'll head into town and get a bite to eat and stay out of your way up here."

Quillen whipped a U-turn in front of the trailer, and Dwight and Ross scooted out. Ross walked behind his father as they headed to the door, and he was sure he saw his old man's shoulders droop with each step.

They found Jill in the living room, on the couch that had become Quillen's bed.

"Ross … wow … I didn't expect to see you," she said, standing and pulling the boy in for a hug he stiffly endured. "You're so big. What are you doing here?"

"Never mind, Jill," Dwight said, slipping an arm between them and pulling Ross back. "What do you want?"

She sat down again. "I was wondering if you'd talked to anybody about the, you know, the divorce."

"I haven't talked to anyone. You're the one who left, not me."

"I was just thinking," she said, and then she stopped short. "Listen, Ross, would you mind going to your room or outside while me and your dad talk?"

"Stay here, Ross," Dwight said. "Don't you tell this boy what to do. It's his house. He lives here. You don't, not anymore. Got that?"

"Actually—" Ross said.

"Don't be like that, Dwight," she said.

"Actually, I have some stuff to do in my bedroom," Ross said. He bolted down the hall but couldn't outrun the voices that were already beginning to boil over as he breached his door and slammed it shut.

Later that evening, Dwight and Ross settled into the seat opposite Quillen at the diner. Ross stifled a giggle at their houseguest, who had a clump of mashed potatoes drying fast in his mustache.

"What'd she want?" Quillen asked.

"Don't want to talk about it," Dwight said.

The waitress breezed past, and Dwight reached out and tugged on her apron. "Cup of coffee."

"What about you?" she said, fixing an eye on Ross.

"Root beer."

"So it was that bad?" Quillen said.

Dwight rubbed his eyes.

"Real bad," Ross said.

Dwight crashed a heavy elbow into his son's bicep. "Zip it up, Ross."

"Well, it was."

"I said, clam up."

The rising voices drew the eyes of folks at neighboring tables. "Guys," Quillen said. "Take it easy."

Ross kept going, loudly. "Yeah, you warned her, too, and then you gave her everything you had in your wallet. Why'd you let her push you around? What's wrong with you?"

"Ross, so help me—"

"Big talker."

Quillen stood and wrapped a hand around the boy's wrist, yanking him to his feet. Ross tried to hold him off by digging his feet into the carpeted floor of the restaurant, but Quillen pulled him past the cash register and out the door, twirling him until his back crashed into the grille of the pickup.

"That's your father," Quillen yelled, his face inches from the boy's. "You don't embarrass him like that."

"He embarrassed himself."

"He's your father!"

Ross stuck out his chin and jabbed a finger toward Quillen. "Just like that? No way. He doesn't get to decide that now."

Quillen palmed his forehead and ran a hand down his face. "Look, kid, you just spilled a man's business in there. He has to live in this town, he has to face these people, and you've just put a target on him. What do you think people are going to say?"

Ross stood defiant. "If they say what they heard, it'll be the truth."

"Truth's got nothing to do with it, son. People believe what they want to believe, hear what they want to hear and pass along gossip like it's a hot potato. You understand what I'm saying?"

"I guess."

"Don't give me that. You better know."

Behind them, a line of big rigs rumbled into the adjacent truck stop, joining a fleet idling behind the building. Diesel hung in the air, flicking at Ross's nose.

"All right," the boy said. "I'm sorry."

"Don't tell me. Tell him."

"OK, I will."

Quillen paced back and forth in short sweeps, like a target in a penny arcade. He rubbed the back of his neck with his hand. "Did he really give her money?"

"Everything he had on him."

"Shit, we've done, what, five wells? That had to have been four-fifty, five hundred bucks. Why would he do that?"

Ross glanced past Quillen through the front window of the diner. He could see the back of his father's head. The guy couldn't even muster energy for his own fight. "Because he's an idiot."

"Come on, Ross, cut it out."

"She said she was nearly done with travel-agent class but just needed some money to get by. Said she was thinking about moving back. Said she missed him. Said she thought she still loved him."

Quillen shook his head. "That whore. She's not coming back. She's gone."

"Yeah," Ross said. "Her and the money."

Digging went poorly in Ekalaka, leaving them stuck on their sixth well when late August came and Ross traded morning rides with Quillen and Dwight for a seat on the school bus to Washington Middle School.

His mother called midmonth and asked if he wanted to come home. Ross surprised everyone—her, Dwight and especially himself—by saying he'd stick with it awhile.

The new routine wedged more distance between father and son. Quillen and Dwight left the trailer at daybreak, forcing Ross to get up with them and eat breakfast. After that, he tried to concentrate on homework for a couple of hours while waiting for the bus. In the afternoons, he returned to an empty trailer, waiting two, sometimes three hours for the men's arrival, with no company but a TV that had bad reception. After that came dinner downtown and, generally, beer on the porch.

Dwight struggled at fatherhood, a condition he'd never had to confront before and one that left him out of his depth. Each morning, he put a handful of change on the kitchen counter for the boy, which Ross was to use to get through lunch at school. In the evenings, after the late news signed off, he'd order the boy to bed on those rare nights when he hadn't succumbed to his own slumber long before. Beyond that, structure didn't exist. Ross grew lazy in his work, and his grades—never worth crowing about—faltered ever more. Having no friends, and being a stranger who'd been dropped into a new school in a new town without any introduction, the boy descended into loneliness. Homework gave way to brief, intense crying jags in the morning, after Dwight and Quillen cleared out, as he braced himself for the bus.

And then the beatings started.

The jocks who Ross delighted in taunting in the classroom—a surreptitious flipoff here, a profane putdown there—caught him behind the gymnasium the first time. The biggest kid, Mike Perry, the son of the football coach, bloodied his nose. Ross made it home ahead of his father that afternoon and washed the stained clothes before he was found out.

Other things he couldn't hide. The black eye. The lip split so badly that Dwight took him to the emergency clinic and had it stitched up. Ross told his father that he'd just been inattentive, walking into open lockers and such, but Dwight knew.

"I'm gonna talk to your principal," he said.

"Dad, don't do that."

"This here's bullshit, Ross. It can't go on."

Ross came uncorked. He threw his math textbook across the room, crashing it into picture frames festooned on an end table. "If you do that, it'll be a hundred times worse than this. I'll never live that down. You might as well put a target on me."

"I'm not gonna let you get beat on every day."

Quillen, heretofore having watched the debate in silence, waded in.

"He's right, you know," he told Dwight. "The easiest way for this boy to solve this kind of problem is to learn to fight back."

Quillen and Ross faced each other, hands wrapped in dish towels that Dwight had cut lengthwise into ribbons after an ineffective protest. "Fighting ain't gonna solve anything," he said to Quillen. To that, Quillen replied, "If it stops the beatings, it sure as hell will." The debate ended there.

"You got a couple of things going for you," Quillen told Ross. "You're a tall kid, which will give you leverage, and you've got long arms, which'll let you hit somebody from a distance without being hit yourself. Now, are you right-handed or left-handed?"

"Right," Ross said.

"OK, fine." Quillen positioned the boy in a classic boxing stance, his left foot forward, shoulders square, his left hand tucked into a fist and held level with his left eye, his right hand also in a fist, held parallel to his right jaw. "Tuck your chin down into your chest. No targets," he said.

"This feels weird," Ross said.

"It will, for a little while. Then it'll feel natural. Now, stay just like that, watch me and do what I do."

Quillen faced the boy and struck the same pose, a mirror image of Ross.

"I'm gonna show you four punches, and it'll probably be three more than you'll ever need. Now, this is a left jab." Quillen shot out his left hand, making a quarter turn with the fist as his arm reached full extension. Lickety-split, the hand whipped back into its starting position.

"See that?" he said. "There's not much body movement. Just the arm and your shoulders as you turn that fist over. Then it pops into place, guarding your face. Now try it."

Ross pushed his arm out tentatively, and it dropped to his side as he reeled it back in.

"Get your hands up. Remember your defense. Now, really throw it."

The boy jabbed with more urgency.

"Again. Your power should come from your feet."

Ross threw his hand harder.

"Again."

He threw.

"Again."

He threw.

"Real good."

And so it went the rest of the afternoon, past dinner time, into the dark. With Dwight watching, not saying a word, Quillen showed the boy how to throw a right cross, a taut left hook, an uppercut. He showed him how to move laterally and forward, cutting down an opponent's space. They finished with Quillen, in his cowboy boots, scruffing side to side in the front yard, holding his palms up and giving Ross a moving target. The boy zeroed in, learned to judge distance, began landing clean punches with a heavy thwap against Quillen's hands. When Ross got lazy and dropped his hands, Quillen would pattycake him on the cheek and the chin, letting him know that his defenses were down. Ross learned fast.

"Shouldn't I be hitting these guys in the body, too?" Ross said when they ended the lesson, both drenched in sweat. Ross's T-shirt clung to his back and his ribs.

"If you were in a boxing ring, sure. You'd have to. But in a street fight, you want to end it fast. Fastest way is to punch a man in the face. Ain't too many guys who can take that, and a bully gets religion real fast when you hit him hard enough. I'll tell you another thing. You probably won't need more than that long left jab. A guy gets in a street fight, he's liable to load up for bear, come swinging his arm way out wide with a haymaker. You can hit a guy in the nose three times before that fist'll come around. You do that, and he won't throw a second punch. Guaranteed."

The next day, Ross had his chance to test Quillen's theory. The coach's kid cornered him on the far end of the football field and squared off. The bigger boy reared back a right hand, like an arrow in a bow, and Ross let loose a left that crashed into the kid's nose with a sickening sound, like a hammer pounding a sausage. The right hand that followed knocked out a tooth and put Mike Perry on his ass, and that's where he stayed.

Quillen and Dwight finished the wells a few days later, late September, and the old driller packed up and left. The sudden emptiness in the house rattled Ross and left him wishing he could have followed his newfound friend.

When Quillen moved out, Dwight withdrew into his own sadness. Ross heard his father's side of the occasional phone call with Jill—the pleading, the cajoling her to come home, which she never did. Ross could read the score, and he wondered why his father could not.

When Jill caught word of the drilling windfall—Quillen had put a grand in Dwight's hands on his way out, for services rendered and for room and board—she came back to town, and the three of them had a dinner out, prime rib. Ross couldn't remember the last time he'd seen his father happy like that, chatting and smiling and stopping old friends for a handshake and a clap on the shoulder. The boy was thankful for that moment and fearful of the next one.

The next morning, he found his father at the kitchen table, in his underwear, his eyes red.

"Where's Jill?" Ross asked.

Dwight gripped his coffee cup with both hands, white-knuckled. "She's gone."

"Are you OK?"

"I just want an answer," Dwight said, looking up at his boy. "If it's over, tell me it's over. If it's not, come home." He looked down at the table.

"Dad, you should tell her how it is."

"I did."

"What did you say?"

"I told her to come home."

"What did she say?"

"She said she needed some money."

"You didn't."

Dwight's shoulders slumped.

"Jesus. You gave her the money?"

"Not all of it."

"How much?"

"Not all of it."

Outside, the school bus beckoned with a honk. Ross gathered up his books.

"Are you all right?" he asked his father.

Dwight didn't look up. "Have a good day at school, son."

Nine hours later, Ross returned home to a different man. Dwight met him at the door wearing a pressed shirt and tie, western slacks and cowboy boots. He was cleanshaven and smelled of cheap drugstore cologne.

"Whoa," the boy said. "What's this?"

"Jill's coming home."

"When will she be here?"

"Any minute."

Ross unloaded his backpack on the kitchen table and headed for the refrigerator.

"Ross, I'll be in the bathroom," his father told him. "When she gets here, just let her in, OK?"

The boy sank his teeth into an apple. He mumbled in the affirmative.

Ross dallied at the fridge, considering all and finding nothing. He wondered if there was enough money left to go to the grocery store. Two of them had enough trouble finding a decent meal now that Quillen was gone, but they made it work. He wondered how having three people in the house was going to go.

As Ross cut back across the house to the couch, the impossibility of it all sorted itself out in his mind, and the questions landed in sickening succession. *Why's she coming back? What's changed? Why now?* Ross detoured for the bathroom door.

"Dad—"

The response came in a concussive pop, and the boy, shot through with adrenaline, flung his weight into the door. It gave a little and then threw him off, but in that instant, he could see the bathroom mirror and the reflected splash of red on the wall. Tears gathered in his eyes as he again battered the door, yelping, and this time the cheap, hollow-cored door ripped away from the locking mechanism.

Dwight lay slumped against the wall, head askew, face engorged, eyes dead. All of him, dead. Blood poured from his nose and mouth and ears, onto his shirt, pooling on the linoleum. The pistol he'd placed in his mouth lay now at his side, in his blood.

The boy picked up the gun. His father's warm plasma ran along his fingers, into his palm.

He backed out of the bathroom. He heard the car's tires on the gravel driveway. Jill honked to let them know she'd arrived.

Ross cocked the gun and headed for the front door.

sad tomato: a love story

The first time he cut her, she felt the endorphins rush her head and she thought, just for a moment, that she was going to die. It felt so fucking good. The blade sliced a clean, straight line above her ankle, and the blood held back until her heart beat again. It came first in a trickle and then a pour. He handled the knife like he was born to do it, the tip of his wet tongue hanging from his mouth as his eyes, immovable, focused on the target and the line. She looked at him and she wanted him so bad, and after he cut himself, too, she had him. She rode him until they collapsed together into the drying blood that stained the sheets. She didn't wake up until after noon, and then the metallic smell of what they had done with the knife turned her on all over again, so she woke him.

The second time he cut her, she wanted it to be the same as before, and she acted as though it was, but something had gone missing. The rapt attention that had turned her cotton underwear wet the first time couldn't be found on his face this time. He cut a jagged edge into the fleshy area near the turn of her elbow, and it hurt. She suppressed the whimper, because she feared that he wouldn't love her anymore if he didn't think she was tough, and if he didn't love her anymore, then he should just keep cutting until there was nothing left. After he was done, she opened herself to him again, but he fell asleep without finishing. She lay awake, his snoring head on her chest, and she licked away the blood.

The third time he cut her, she was asleep, and when the knife's edge slipped below the surface of her calf, she bolted from bed. "What are you doing?" she screamed. He looked back at her with empty eyes and said, "You like this."

"Not this way," she said. He told her that she was a bitch and a whore, and he left into the night and the cold. She cried off and on until morning, when exhaustion finally overtook her, because she was sure he didn't love her anymore. When she awoke, she cut both calves and prayed that he might accept her sacrifice.

The fourth time he cut her, she no longer cared. People she had never met came in and out of their place at all hours, and she was sampling the goods they carried, though that was mostly to please him. She didn't like the stuff, and sometimes she would fool him by feigning as if she were going to partake, and then she would stop when he looked away. All the while, he was falling further and further from her. She could see him, if she focused hard, but he wasn't really there. She offered an arm and hoped that he might find his way back. He nicked her with the knife and left with a friend, and she hardly bled at all.

The fifth time he cut her, she had something she needed to say. He hadn't noticed that she was gone during the day now, that she had gotten her hair fixed, that she was putting on makeup, that she was staying out of the contraband moving through their tenement. He hadn't noticed that she was eating healthily—which is to say that she was eating at all—or that she was working and putting money away.

He didn't know about the letter she had written to herself and to the one who was growing inside her. She promised herself, and her still-gestating child, that she would be a better, happier person. She would be a mother. A real one.

So when she told him that he was to be a father and he came apart and said she would have to end it, she cut him. She pulled a steak knife from the kitchen drawer and plunged it into his chest, and though it broke her heart to see him writhe and fall to the floor, it was the only way. In his final moments, his throes receding now, a bloody bubble emerged from his nostrils and popped, and she winced. His chest poured forth in a gusher, spreading through his shirt and cascading to the floor, and she just watched. If he wasn't going to love her, and the one who was growing inside of her, he couldn't stay.

When his fight ended—he was valiant, she thought, and that only made her sad because it reminded her of why she loved him—a pale face and sunken eyes stared back at her. Those glassy eyes spooked her, and she felt herself go cold to see him there without seeing him at all. She curled up on the couch and snuggled her head into the cushions, and she could smell him, the man she loved. She closed her eyes, smiled and went to sleep.

Two dreams came to her.

In the first, she walked hand in hand with a child across a snowy plain. The boy was small and took small steps, and her own movements through the stubble field were brief and light, as she stepped in rhythm with him. Finally, the boy looked up, and she saw his father in his face.

"How far, Mommy?"

She smiled at the boy.

"We're almost there."

In the second, the field remained, but the boy was gone. Ahead of her, a hundred yards or more, her mother walked. She called out to the woman, who walked without turning back.

"Mother, please," she yelled.

Nothing.

She woke up.

In the night, a crevasse had opened in the floor, taking him farther away, but she could still see him. He was drained of color. The dried blood on his shirt had turned black.

"I love you," she said.

He said nothing. She wondered if, wherever he had gone, he understood why it had to be this way.

The coming and going of night and day seemed trivial. She slept when sleep called for her, and in her waking hours, she sat on the floor, her back against the couch, and she watched him. The clock on the wall kept time, but she never knew what side of the day she was on. That first night, she had pulled the blinds and turned off the lights. A 40-watt bulb in her reading lamp cut through the darkness and found a way to him. The glint in his eye was gone for good now, as was he. She held the knife, his blood gone dry on the blade.

Always she held the knife.

The knock on the door folded itself into her dream at first, and then, more insistently, it pulled her from sleep.

"Alyssa. Alyssa, please!"

Her mother.

She held her breath, and she looked across the canyon to her love. *Please be quiet*, she wished. *Please don't let her in.*

The knocks came again, frantic.

She closed her eyes.

"Alyssa!"

She prayed.

She heard her mother turn and scurry down the outside stairs.

She opened her eyes and looked at him.

"Thank you," she said.

When the next knock came, some time later, she didn't flinch. Their love had gone sour, and the stench filled the room and the canyon between them. Cajolery didn't draw her out, and neither did threats. When she was sure they would be coming through the door and would find him there, she walked to the edge of the canyon that had split across the floor between them and dropped the knife to the bottom of it. It would be their secret. Nobody had to know that he didn't love her anymore.

comfort and joy

Through a sliver in the blinds, Frank watched as the crowd gathered on his neighbors' lawn. The numbers had been swelling since that morning, when the newspaper hit the streets. The story was so breathtaking, so sad, so redeeming that people from all over town felt compelled to drive, pedal and walk to the sturdy Craftsman-style bungalow to pay their respects.

Bouquets of roses dotted the yard, put there in multiple, spontaneous gestures of awe and thanks to a man who had left home two days earlier and would never be back. Frank figured the crowd at close to two hundred people now. They lined the sidewalk and stood on the perfectly manicured Kentucky bluegrass of a man who had lived among them for years and had never drawn so much as a second glance. Now, the newspaper called him a hero. Everyone did.

Frank scoffed aloud when he saw the TV news van pull up. The driver rolled the passenger-side wheels onto the curb and into the boulevard, leaving the van to sink into the grass while the cameraman and reporter grabbed their things and scurried into the throng. Had the guy pulled that stunt on Frank's side of the street, leaving ruts in his grass, the old man might have gone out there and ripped him a new one.

Agitated as Frank was, he felt relief at not having to leave the house.

That the neighbor he scarcely knew, Kevin Elam, had done a heroic thing was not in question, and Frank resolved to pay his respects in his own time and his own way. When he had read the story that morning, he had marveled at the young pilot's wherewithal in bringing a crippled MD-80 down in a way that saved most of the people aboard. Just thirty-two of the one hundred and thirty passengers aboard perished, among them Captain Kevin Elam, a man Frank had talked to only a couple of times and one for whom he now wished he could buy a beer.

Frank knew the final government report wouldn't be out for months, but he also knew enough about such things to understand how unlikely it was that Kevin Elam could have accomplished what he did. The jet had lost control and come in well short of the runway in Denver, and the pilot—adrenaline surging, knowing that a crash was inevitable and, in all probability, lethal—had put it down about as gently as was humanly possible. Even so, the twisted fuselage and gnarled metal that could be seen in the color newspaper photographs nearly caused Frank to break down. Kevin Elam was a hero. Frank knew it. The people outside knew it, too. They knew that he had saved a mother going home to her own father's funeral, an anxious new graduate headed to Dallas for a job interview, a son who had brought his first guitar as a carry-on and planned to play at a program at church, and dozens of others, including sixteen of seventeen members of the Billings Senior High cheerleading squad on their way to Orlando for a national competition. They would never make it to Florida; a chartered bus would bring them back to Billings in a few days. But they would come home alive, and that's why people stood in Kevin Elam's yard.

The crowds will go away, Frank thought. *Then I'll walk over and pay my respects to his wife and that boy. Away from the hullaballoo, I'll be able to say what needs to be said.*

He closed the blinds and headed upstairs to see if she was awake, to find out if the pain today would be better than it was yesterday. That was all Frank ever asked for when he found himself on his knees and talking to God.

Not all of the dying on Miles Avenue would bring out the news vans and the public's adulation. Some of it was happening bit by bit, moment by moment, with few people looking and even fewer caring. In his head and in his heart, Frank had been saying goodbye for two years, silently steeling himself for the day when Lucy would slip away and he would no longer carry her regimen of pills in his shirt pocket and a napkin in his back pocket to wipe her mouth after she swallowed them.

Frank knew that day was coming, and it scared him.

The crowds did go away. It took a while. For weeks, flowers and stuffed animals and notes piled up, despite the best efforts of Kevin Elam's wife and son to keep up with them. In the month that followed the crash, Kevin's face appeared on the covers of news magazines, every headline including the same word: hero. The city of Billings declared Kevin Elam Day. The mayor smiled big and gave his wife a key to the city. Frank saw that in the newspaper and thought she looked uncomfortable, and that night, he included with his prayer a new request: peace for the woman and child next door.

As spring melted toward summer, an answer to that prayer arrived. Life next door to Frank went back to some semblance of what it had been before. The woman went to work and came home. The boy went to school and then, as June rolled around and the summer break took hold, he and his friends often hung around the house, tossing a football in the yard or playing basketball in the driveway. Frank caught snippets of these things through the window. He would watch and sip his coffee, and then he would return to her.

Frank's other prayer, that Lucy's pain would subside, was a tougher sell with God. She barely moved some days, and Frank would have to pick her up and carry her to the bathroom. The small act of sitting on the toilet would aggravate the cancer that had metastasized in her bones, and in her agony she could barely make a sound, depleted as her lungs were. Frank would hold her close, careful not to hurt her further, and blink back the tears.

When he found the compression sores, he gave in and called for help from hospice, finally admitting that he couldn't tend to her alone anymore. The nurses came in, and there wasn't much they could do, either. They dressed her wounds and tried to make her comfortable.

Lucy died in the early hours of a Wednesday in late July. Nobody left flowers in her yard.

The first week of November brought a prodigious snowfall to Billings, the biggest one in eighty years, according to the TV weatherman. Frank, unshaven for a week, wearing clothes he'd put on two days earlier, stood at his kitchen sink and watched as the boy next door fought with a snowblower. The old man caught his reflection in the glass. His thinning hair had gone fully gray in two years of fighting with Lucy against her cancer, and deep lines dug into his gaunt face. He could smell his own stink. He didn't bathe or shower much these days. He didn't see the point.

His thoughts migrated, again, to the day in 1948 when he married Lucy Andriesen. *Till death do us part* were words that came by rote back then, when he was twenty-one and she was nineteen and they were invincible. Utterly devoted to one another, they never brought children into the world, never imagining that one day, one of them might have to soldier on alone. At eighty-three years old, Frank had drawn that sad duty. He still couldn't believe it, and he surprised himself sometimes when he realized how angry it left him.

The lanky child next door—Frank figured him for twelve, maybe thirteen—was having trouble keeping the machine on a line and keeping the blower chute lined up to send the snow in the proper direction. Hurtled powder hit the boy's house, then Frank's house. And then it hit the window Frank peered through, cracking the thin pane of glass.

"Dammit," Frank said, hustling into the living room in his long johns and jamming his feet into slippers. He ran out the front door and high-stepped through his blanketed front lawn, shouting at the boy. The kid couldn't hear him above the din of the motor, and just as Frank drew near, the boy turned the machine and sent a blast of snow into Frank's face.

Stung by the barrage, Frank drew back a hand and struck the boy, catching him in the left ear and dropping him.

The boy looked at Frank, wide-eyed and chin trembling. Frank stared back in disbelief at what he'd done.

Both ran for their respective front doors.

Frank spent a half-hour walking the floor, castigating himself. He talked to Lucy and told her how stupid he was, how idiotic. He said she should be happy she didn't see it. Immediately, he felt bad about saying that, and he apologized.

He knew the knock would be coming, and when it did, he still jumped. The rapid beat of his heart moved into his neck and throat, which he cleared again and again as he approached the door and opened it to find the boy's mother, her anger bubbling under her lip.

"You hit my son," she said.

"Please come in," Frank said. "Let's talk."

She stomped past him into the living room.

"I'd be happy to pour you some tea," he said.

She stopped. "This isn't a social call, Mr. —"

"Abrams. Frank Abrams."

"This isn't a social call, Mr. Abrams."

"No, of course it's not," Frank said. He gestured to the sofa. "Please, won't you sit down?"

Her eyes never leaving him, she lowered herself to the couch. Frank sat in a chair opposite her. In different circumstances, he might have been impressed by her bearing. A small woman, she filled the room with her intensity and focus. Now, she intimidated him, and he wasn't a man who was easily cowed.

"How's the boy?" he asked.

"Andy. His name is Andy. He'll be fine. He's scared. He's confused. He doesn't know why a grown man would come out and hit him, and frankly, I don't, either. Can you explain that, or should I just call the police and let them sort it out?"

Frank, who had looked at his feet as the woman's words grew sharper, glanced upward and met her eyes. "I don't know what happened," he said. "I'm appalled, absolutely appalled, at what I did. I ran out to stop him because all the snow he was blowing around out there, it shot right up and cracked my window. So I went down there and that snow, it comes out of the machine so fast and hard, you know? It hurts like hell when it smacks you in the face. I just snapped. Honestly, it just happened so fast, I couldn't believe what I'd done."

She stared at him and said nothing.

"Obviously, if you wish to call the police, I will tell them exactly what I did. And of course I apologize to you, and I hope you'll let me apologize to Andy. I'm just sick about this."

The hard lines of her face fell away slightly, and she chewed on her bottom lip.

"You say your window broke. Can I see it?"

Frank stood and led her into the kitchen. He pointed at the pane, which was crossed by a jagged crack.

"How much do you think it will cost to replace?" she asked.

"Not much. It's not a big job."

"Let me know."

"Mrs. Elam," he said, "I wouldn't dream of asking you to pay for it. I owe you and your son amends, not the other way around."

"OK," she said, "let's talk about that."

Back in the living room, she said, "I'm not going to involve the police."

"Thank you."

"I'm going to send Andy over here tomorrow. He broke your window, and if you won't accept payment, he can do something else for you."

"That's quite unnecessary."

"No, it's not. It's important that he learn responsibility. Besides, you're going to do something for him, too."

"What?"

"I haven't decided. But I'll let you know. He's a good kid, Mr. Abrams. He's had an awful year—we both have—and he doesn't deserve what happened to him today, and you're going to make it right."

"I'm sorry about your husband," Frank said, words that didn't come close to capturing what he had intended to say months earlier.

"Thank you." She stood up. "I'll send Andy over in the morning. Put him to work."

"I don't have anything for the boy to do here," Frank said.

She glanced around the living room, at the piled-up mail and dirty clothes and half-filled glasses of water and said, "I'm sure you can find something."

The boy was prompt. Frank gave him that. At nine a.m. sharp, Frank heard the rap of knuckles against the oaken door. He opened it to find the towheaded young man standing on his stoop in an old pullover sweater and a pair of faded jeans.

"My mom said I have to come over here," he said, casting a wary glance at Frank.

"Well, come on in, then," Frank said. "I'm not sure what to do with you."

Andy stepped inside. "I'd say let me go home, but she'd just send me back over here. So you better find something."

"You're a mouthy kid, aren't you?"

"So what? You're an old man who hits kids."

"OK, that's enough. Sit down."

Andy stared at him.

"I said sit down!"

Andy obeyed.

Frank sank into the chair across from the boy and rubbed his mouth and chin, considering his next move. Having no children of his own, he'd never had to learn how to deal with insolence.

"Is it OK if I call you by your name?"

Andy looked surprised. "Yeah, I guess."

"OK, look, Andy. I'm sorry for what I did yesterday. There is no excuse for it, and you have every right to be angry with me for it. So I'm putting that out there for you. If we're going to spend the day together, I'd like to put this behind us. Can we do that?"

Andy looked at the carpet. "Yeah, I guess."

"That's not good enough. Let's try again. Andy, I'm sorry for hitting you yesterday. Can you please forgive me?"

The boy looked up and bit off the words. "I accept your apology, Mr. Abrams."

With Andy's help, Frank toted two dozen bags of garbage to the alley for pickup. They folded clothes, vacuumed the house, dusted, cleaned windows, sorted mail and brought the place to a level of cleanliness that Frank hadn't seen since before Lucy got sick, when together they ran a tight ship, everything in its place.

In the kitchen, Frank poured the boy a second cup of hot chocolate. They had moved around each other stealthily for the first hour or so, but soon enough, the defenses had fallen away and the boy had begun chattering. Frank marveled at what constituted a young man's world these days—computers and text messages and a whole system of language that Frank couldn't begin to comprehend—but he also noted that the two primary concerns were the same as they had been when he was a twelve-year-old boy: girls, and the competitive challenges posed by other boys. From what Frank could gather, Andy was on high alert for the former and continually addled by the latter.

"You're a good worker," Frank said. "That's something to be proud of."

"Thanks, Mr. Abrams."

Andy pointed at a picture on the dining-room wall, a group photo of the Mission Command engineers in front of the space shuttle Columbia. "Are you in that picture?"

Frank turned and looked at the photo. "Yep, that's me and some of my co-workers after the first space shuttle went up and came home. It was taken in 1982."

"Which one are you?"

"I'm at the far left there, in the white shirt."

"They all have on white shirts."

"That's a joke, kid. Go on. Get up and take a closer look."

Andy walked around to the other side of the table and got close to the frame. Frank peered over his shoulder. It had been a long time since he'd looked closely at the photograph, and he was a little surprised by what he saw. He was so young then, yet ancient by NASA standards. He was well into middle age, fifty-five years old—a decade or more older than most of the men in the picture with him—and yet he was struck by how quickly the years had gone by and how much they had taken.

"What was your job?" Andy asked.

"I was a flight engineer."

"What does that mean?"

"Different things on different missions. I was one of the guys on the ground helping get the shuttle into space, communicating with the crew and helping them get home safely. When this picture was taken, I was getting close to the end of my career. I actually started with NASA in the beginning, more than fifty years ago. I saw all of it—Mercury, Gemini, Apollo and the first moon landing, the space shuttle."

"Cool."

Frank considered the boy's one-word summation of a long career. He hadn't thought about those days in a while. But Andy was right. If there had to be a single word for that part of his life, that extraordinary privilege, "cool" would do the job.

The next morning, as Frank headed up the sidewalk with his morning paper, he waved to Andy and one of the neighbor kids. They were rolling up snow boulders.

"Mr. Abrams," Andy called to him. "Do you want to help us build a snowman?"

"No, thanks, Andy. You guys have fun." He saluted the boys with the bundled newspaper and walked on.

"Come on. We'll let you choose his face."

Frank stopped. *What possible reason is there to say no*, he thought.

"I'll be right back, guys."

Up in the attic, Frank blew dust off a banker's box that had gone yellow with age, the corrugated walls caving in from neglect.

He began removing artifacts from another era of his life. Aviator glasses, cloth ribbons from his stint in the Air Force during the Korean War, among them a Distinguished Flying Cross and an Air Medal with three oak leaves, a visor hat.

He put everything in the hat and hustled back downstairs.

"That looks awesome!" Andy said.

Before them, a plump snowman—small head upon slightly larger torso upon much larger base—sported the brim hat, the medals on his chest, the glasses atop his carrot nose and a scarf around his neck and shoulders.

"He looks like a real jock," Frank said.

"What, like a football player?" asked the other boy, Aaron.

"No, that's what we pilots called each other in the Air Force."

"My dad was a pilot," Andy said, and Frank winced at not thinking before he spoke.

"He was," Frank said. "A damned good one."

The three of them stared a while longer, saying nothing. Finally, Frank said, "Well, we'd better not leave that stuff in the weather. You guys can divvy it up and keep it. I don't need it anymore."

The boys slapped high-fives and began stripping their snowman bare. As Frank opened the door to his house, he smiled at hearing the horse-trading taking place as Andy and Aaron weighed the worth of a pair of old sunglasses against an aviator's hat.

Andy's mother visited Frank that evening.

"I've figured out how you can make it up to Andy," she said when he opened the door.

"Come in," he said. "It's freezing out there."

For the second time, they settled into Frank's living-room furniture. "It looks like a different place," she said. "Did Andy do all of this?"

"Pretty much. I helped a little. He's faster than I am, though."

"Tell me about it," she said, laughing. "I'm just glad he still obeys voice commands. I don't know how I'll cope when he stops doing that."

"He's a polite young man. Maybe you have nothing to worry about."

"Maybe."

"So you say you have a task for me?"

"Right," she said. "Next month, December 7th, Andy's school is having a career day, and some of the kids are supposed to bring in a guest speaker to talk about different jobs and the schooling needed to get them. This is the kind of thing that Kevin would have done, and he would have been great at it. I'm nominating you to be Andy's guest speaker. What do you think?"

"Mrs. Elam, I'm flattered, but it's been a long time since I've had a career. I left NASA in 1987. I couldn't even begin to speak to how things are done there now."

151

"Oh, please, Mr. Abrams," she said. "Andy told me—"

"Frank."

"Beg pardon?"

"Please, call me Frank."

"OK, Frank," she said. "Andy told me what you said about helping with the moon landing and the space shuttle and all that. You'll be the biggest hit there. Those kids won't care when you last worked."

"I don't know."

"Well, I do. You owe Andy, and this is the payback I've decided on."

"December seventh, you say?"

"Yes."

Frank considered it, as if trying to remember whether he had a competing engagement, knowing full well that his social schedule was identical for the interminable future: wide open. "As it turns out, I'm free," he said.

Andy's mother stood up, walked over and hugged Frank.

Frank poured a cup of tea. "Forgive me, but I've forgotten your first name. Old men and their memories."

"Laura," she said.

"A lovely name."

"Thank you."

"Lucy, my wife, she liked to think about what our children's names might have been, if we'd had any. She liked that name very much."

"Why didn't you have kids?" Quickly, she slapped a hand over her mouth. "I'm sorry. It's rude to just ask like that."

"No, it's quite all right," Frank said. "We just never felt compelled. We had very full lives, even without kids. Then years go by, faster all the time, and you realize that you're old people and the chances of doing certain things are gone forever. So it was with children."

"You must miss her terribly."

Frank nodded. "I do. I suspect you have some appreciation for what it's like."

"It's so hard," she said. "I can still smell him in our room, and sometimes when I'm asleep, I dream that he's there with me. It's hard in the mornings to wake up to the fact that he's gone."

She looked at Frank. A quivering smile crossed her face. He picked up a paper napkin and handed it across the table to her.

"Are you getting along OK otherwise?" he asked.

She dabbed at her eyes with the napkin. "We're making it. You know, I really hated to reduce Kevin's death to numbers, but for a while there, I wondered how we would make it work. The insurance helped. People have been very nice, but I haven't wanted to impose. I'm getting back into the swing of things at work. I tell Andy, listen, you need to make good grades and get a scholarship. You know, to hedge our bets."

Frank picked up her cup and went to the kettle to refill it.

"I have to tell you, Laura, I was a pilot once, and what your husband did was one of the most heroic things I've ever heard of. A disabled plane, flying faster than it should—there's just no way to describe what a hopeless situation that is. Pilots train for moments like that, and they hope they'll manage to pull off the perfectly imperfect landing if that day ever comes, but the fact is, the human element—fear, indecision, clouded judgment—is powerfully difficult to overcome. He did it. I hope you're proud."

"More than I can say," she said. She looked down at her hands and tugged at a loose thread on her sleeve. "But you know what? I still feel cheated. I didn't have nearly long enough with Kevin, just eleven years. He was a miracle in our lives. I was a single mom. I'd been left by my first husband while I was still pregnant with Andy. We were barely scraping by after Ross left. I had to sell our house and move into a little apartment. And then we met Kevin, and he fell in love with us."

"Sounds like he was a miracle for a lot of people," Frank said.

Laura looked to the ceiling, as if she could see through it to the sky.

"I hate to say this," she said, "but I still wish sometimes that he'd been off that day, that it had been someone else's destiny. Even if it meant that fewer people came home."

On the appointed day, Frank drove to Lewis & Clark Middle School.

"You must be our astronaut," said the woman who checked him in at the office.

"Oh, no, ma'am. Flight engineer."

"Oh."

After a few minutes, Andy came in to collect Frank and walk him to the assembly room for the program.

"You clean up well," Frank said, pointing at the tie and blazer the young man wore.

"Mom made me."

"She's a smart lady."

Inside the assembly hall, rows of chairs faced a lectern and microphone. Along the walls, students, teachers, administrators and guests talked and ate Christmas-themed cookies. Strains of holiday music played above the chatter.

Andy rocked his head side to side in rhythm with the music.

"Jingle balls, jingle balls, jingling all the way," he sang-whispered.

"What's that?" Frank said.

"'Jingle bells.'"

"It sounded like 'jingle balls.'"

"It was. My friends and I changed the words."

Frank laughed.

Frank stared back at two-hundred-some-odd sets of expectant eyes. He wished that the principal hadn't built this thing up quite so much. ("This will be an experience we're sure you'll remember for a long, long time.") Frank rather enjoyed the speeches by the executive chef, the investment banker and the YMCA director. As he cleared his throat and began to speak, he had little confidence that his words would measure up.

He thanked the school leaders and acknowledged Andy—"my friend, Andy Elam"—and then he launched into remarks that he had been sweating over for weeks.

"I was teaching physics at Eastern Montana College here in Billings in 1958 when one of my Air Force buddies asked me to apply for an engineer's job with the National Aeronautics and Space Administration, which had just been created by President Dwight Eisenhower. I was thirty-one years old. So if I was thirty-one in 1958, you can figure out that I'm older than dirt today." At this, the assembly room filled with the laughter of seventh-graders.

"Actually, that's not true. I was a sophomore when dirt was a senior." More laughs tumbled in, and Frank felt more at ease. He looked over at Andy beaming back at him, and he gave the boy a wink.

One thing surprised Frank: The kids, while mildly interested in things they'd often heard about, like the moon landing, were absolutely entranced by the disasters and near-misses. Frank had seen most of them.

He lamented the loss of Gus Grissom, Ed White and Roger Chaffee on the launch pad with Apollo 1. "We got so many things wrong," he said. "But that drove us harder to get them right, to keep the program alive when a lot of people on the outside wanted to scrap it."

He talked about the lifeboat situation in Apollo 13 and how work on the ground—figuring out how to preserve enough power for re-entry, creating impromptu carbon-dioxide scrubbers and relaying those instructions to the crew—was essential to bringing those men back home safely.

He explained how one person, one very smart person, can make all the difference. "When lightning struck Apollo 12 in the first minute after liftoff, it scattered everything. Instruments weren't working. We couldn't talk with the crew very well. Telemetry—the way we measured things from Earth—was a mess. This guy I worked with, John Aaron, an EECOM like me, he'd seen those kinds of telemetry readings a year earlier during a test, and he remembered exactly how to reset them so they'd read normally. Nobody else in the room knew what he was talking about, but Alan Bean, an astronaut up in the capsule, did what John said to do, and everything worked out. If John hadn't been there, if he hadn't known what to do, we would have had to abort that mission. After that, we all called John 'a steely-eyed missile man,' which is just about the best compliment there is.

"And let me tell you something else: John didn't have any opportunity that you don't have right here. He grew up in a little town in Oklahoma, in an area called Booger Hollow." The students tittered. "I'm serious: Booger Hollow. He's just a smart man who has focus and drive and who was constantly looking to learn. Any of you can do the same thing."

By the time Frank reached the end of his remarks, a recollection of the Challenger disaster and how that wore out his emotions and sent him into retirement, he didn't want the day to end. When he said "thank you," the seventh-graders gave him a standing ovation.

Andy and Frank sat at a table in the assembly room, eating finger sandwiches and other snacks and drinking punch during the closing reception for the day's guests.

"You were great, Mr. Abrams," Andy said.

"Thank you, Andy. Thanks for inviting me."

"Can I ask you a question?"

"Yes."

"Those stories about saving Apollo 12 and Apollo 13, they made me kind of mad."

"Mad how?"

"Well, it doesn't seem fair that you can rescue rockets but nobody could rescue my dad's plane. Why is that?"

Frank took a carrot and put it on Andy's plate, which was otherwise filled with french fries. "Do you remember what I said today about logic and reason and how we kept our heads when things were going badly, that it was the only way to overcome the odds?"

"Yeah."

"That was your dad that day. I can't tell you why the plane he was flying lost control. But I know this: Your father was the rescuer for a lot of people on that plane, a lot of people who probably would have died if not for him. Those people, every day of the rest of their lives they will be thankful that they were on a plane flown by your dad. And even though you miss him, I bet one day you'll realize that you're thankful for that, too."

Andy bowed his head, and Frank reached out and tousled his hair.

On the drive home, Frank felt a surge of energy deep inside. He recognized it, remembered it: adrenaline, something he hadn't experienced in years. In combat, in Korea, such shots of power kept him focused on a target even as hell rained down around him. On the job, he could use it to block out everything except the problem on his screen.

Now, all these years later, adrenaline came back to him, and it carried an idea, one he knew he would work on as soon as he got back to the house. He would start with all of the old friends and colleagues whose offers of help he had turned away after Lucy passed on.

"You would have been proud of me today, old girl," he said as he made the last turn for home.

On Christmas Eve, Frank answered the knock at his door and found Laura and Andy standing in the falling snow in matching candy-cane sweaters.

"Trick or treat," Andy said, and his mother jabbed him in the ribs.

"You goof!"

"Come on in," Frank said, ushering them into the living room.

Laura handed him a plate of sugar cookies. "A small gift from a neighbor," she said.

Andy gave him a card.

"From both of us," the boy said.

"Do you want me to open this now?" Frank asked.

"Sure," Andy said.

Frank set the plate of cookies down and carefully tore open the envelope. He smiled at seeing the simple, Rockwell-esque pastoral scene on the front, and inside he found a handful of coupons printed on colorful paper: *Good for five home-cooked meals. Good for 10 games of cards. Good for a chat on the porch, infinitely redeemable.*

"These are great," he said.

Laura gave him a hug. "You're such a blessing in our lives."

"Read the card," Andy said.

Frank looked at the inscriptions.

Dear Frank, you gave us something that neither of us thought we would find under the tree this year. You've given us comfort and joy. More than that, you've given Andy a role model when I was so afraid that the best one he would ever have was gone. We'll never be able to repay you for that. Love, Laura.

Frank: You are a steely eyed missile man! Your friend, Andy.

They said their goodnights on the front stoop, and then Frank remembered that he, too, had a gift. He dashed inside and then came out with a sealed envelope.

"Read it when you get home," he said, handing it to Laura.

"OK," she said. "Will you be over in the morning to watch the unwrapping of the gifts?"

"I wouldn't miss it."

An hour later, after finally persuading Andy to give sleep a try, Laura slit open the envelope and read the letter inside.

To whom it may concern:

We who are proud to call Frank Abrams our friend—a more ragged collection of flyboys, number-punchers and pencil-necked geeks you'll never find—are pleased to announce the establishment of the Kevin Elam and Lucy Abrams Memorial Scholarship Fund at Lewis & Clark Middle School in Billings, Montana. Our initial pledge will ensure that the 2010-11 seventh-grade class—every last member of it—will receive a full scholarship to college upon graduating from high school. It is our hope that the community will take up the challenge of matching this effort so that this might be a perpetual gift that bears the names of a true hero and a woman we all dearly loved.

Laura came barreling out of the house, simultaneously crying and giggling uncontrollably. Arms extended, she fell backward into her yard. There, illuminated by a street lamp, she waved her arms and legs and carved a joyous snow angel.

"Thank you, Frank!" she shouted.

A few yards away, watching through the cracked window he never fixed, Frank Abrams toasted her with his coffee cup.

slumpbuster

It's the damnedest thing.

I'm crossing Montana Avenue, same as I do every other Tuesday for sure and a lot of the days in between. I've got my collar up against the cold because November's come on fierce, and I look back over my shoulder and see it. The Conoco refinery blazes up against the night sky, this blue-black color that I've never seen before, and I just stop. I stand there and look at it, and damned if it's not just about the most beautiful thing I've seen. I know that sounds stupid, a refinery belching who knows what into the sky, but that's what I see. True beauty, right there on the edge of the hardscrabble.

It startles me. All I want to do is stand there and take it in, think about it some, marvel at this perfect little moment I've been permitted to see, for whatever reason.

That's when the meathead in the Neon pulls up to me and leans on his horn. I jump back, staggering into a fighting stance, and he blows past me. "Get outta the road, dumbass." A middle finger presses against the frosted window. I scramble up the curb and give him the double six-shooter fingers, but he's out of there, and soon I'm looking across the street again. My perfect little moment, it's gone. It's all weeds in the sidewalk cracks and windblown newspapers and the bleary light that hangs over downtown, threatening, like an unpaid hospital bill.

I head for the front door at Feeney's and try to get my head back on my business.

"I told you if it happened again, that's it," Frank says, poking at me with a finger that looks like a chunk of polish sausage, and that reminds me that I'm about half starving, only I don't think about that too much because I don't know where Frank's finger has been.

"Yeah, but Frank—"

"But nothing, Hugo. That's it. I told you three years ago that you're too damn old for this, but you know, you did all right there for a while. But this—Hugo, this ain't all right. I'm telling you, for your health, you gotta stop."

He's looking at my right eye, which is no doubt mangled pretty good, but the eye isn't the half of it. I got laid out again, dropped by a left hook from a kid who, by rights, should have to ask permission to wash my jockstrap. Frank thinks I can't see the shots coming anymore, that the ones I used to duck or block are finding their way to my melon, and he seems to be right. Two fights in a row, I've been sent down. I don't think I lost consciousness this time; Trevor says I did, but that's the sort of thing Trevor would lie about. Whatever. I was down long enough that there wasn't any point in getting up. Frank's no dummy. He sees what's what.

"Frank, you don't know what you're talking about. A couple of bad rounds, man. It happens."

Frank's eyes narrow in on me, gaps in the slats. "Trevor says you was out."

"No, I wasn't."

"He says you was."

I have to be careful here. Trevor's a liar, a cheat. Trevor has a beef with me clear back to when we were kids, when we were both coming up, young, same age, same weight class, same path. It worked for me, and it didn't for him, and he's never forgotten or forgiven. Trevor's also the guy, now, who puts three hundred bucks in my hand every couple of weeks, fills the Babcock for his smokers on the basis of my name, and would never acknowledge the truth of the situation. Trevor's got a lot of reasons to see me done. Trevor is also Frank's only boy.

"Frank, I was there. I wasn't out. I didn't get up—no use in denying that. But my eyes, they were open."

Frank reaches across the bar with those sausage fingers and paws at the flesh around my eye, the one Trevor patched not thirty minutes ago, talking too much the way he always does. "Gettin' old, Hugo. How's that feel? That kid tonight, he's, what, nineteen, twenty? Shame to see you busted up that way. Real shame." I had to sit there and take it.

Soon after, apparently, Trevor called his old man, because Frank knew before I hit the door. "Stitchin' ain't that kid's strong suit," Frank now says. He brushes his thumb across the knitting, and I bite the inside of my lip. It may be days before I have the guts to look at Trevor's handiwork.

"Hugo, here's the deal: No more fights for you unless a doctor says it's OK—"

"Aw, Frank—"

Feeney brings his left hand down, a hammer on the bar. "Shut up. Just shut up. This is how it's going to be. You're gonna go down to the clinic, you're gonna see one of those nice doctors, and you're gonna ask for some of them head tests. I been reading about this. They do 'em for guys who play football, this whole round of tests where they ask you stuff like your name—"

"Hugo Hunter." I snap my heels together and salute.

"—and other stuff, too, smartass, and they brain-scan you or some crap. It's all scientific. Cutting-edge stuff. After the doctor does that and if he writes a note saying you can fight, you can fight."

I roll my shoulders inside my coat and look for some crack in Frank's delivery, some little opening I can move through and make him give up this idea of his, but Frank isn't showing any give here. I know this look. This is the deal.

"How am I gonna pay for that, Frank?"

I've seen this look, too. Disappointment. Annoyance. The look that tells me I have my hand out too much. I know this, and he knows it. The sigh leaves Frank like air squeezed from a tiny hole in a balloon. He sweeps the rag over the bar.

"Bring me the bill."

"Thanks. You'll see. It's nothing."

Frank runs the hose from the tap to the glass bottle without me having to ask. "You know, it wouldn't kill you to bring these back so I didn't have to give you a new one every time."

"I forget, Frank."

He sets the growler in front of me.

"Kitchen still open?" I ask. "Man, I'm hungry."

"I got some cold sandwiches. Turkey."

"Great."

He dips into the cooler and pulls up a cellophane-wrapped sammy. Wheat bread, moving hard from stale to ancient. I hate wheat bread.

"That'll do," I say.

"With the beer, seven-fifty," Frank says.

I look at him. No opening. It's Frank the Rock, a man with a face for poker but a leaning toward bloodsport. That face would drop in on me in the late rounds, there on the stool, when victory and defeat were an equal stretch. "Bear down now," he'd say. "It's yours for the taking."

"Put it on my tab?"

The face breaks. "Damn kids," he says, and he turns away from me. That's my signal to go.

I'm halfway through the door when the words hit the back of my head.

"You ever plan to pay this tab?"

I toss a backward wave. I want to come back with something quick, but nothing really occurs to me. My smart-assing has about kept pace with my fighting. I know what I want to do, but my body and my mouth don't seem to be cooperating anymore. Anyway, I'll be hard-pressed to pay for anything if I'm not getting in the ring, and even if I do, well, there isn't much to suggest that I'll be squaring that account any time soon.

I take the long way around to the South Side, along Montana Avenue parallel to the railroad tracks, to the underpass and on to the other side. It's a good half-mile out of my way, and I'm far past the turn-back point when the wind kicks up and the hooked glass handle of the growler starts grinding into my finger.

It's just as well. Cutting through downtown, even the little corner of it that stands between me and the house, means perhaps running into someone who just saw me get dumped on my ass, and I don't really want to face that. Or maybe it's just someone hanging outside the Rainbow or the Rex who wants to talk about the old days. I mean, don't get me wrong: It's nice to be remembered, especially after all these years, but some nights—and tonight is one of them—a guy just wants to take off his shoes, settle into the recliner and float away in a glass of beer.

The other benefit of going this way, and this one's a harder sell with the beer and the sandwich in my coat pocket, is that I'll get a little exercise in. When I retired, the running stopped cold. My knees couldn't take it anymore, and once you've reached the point where the good money's gone and never coming back, the motivation to get up and pound out the miles pretty much leaves, too. Life is no *Rocky* movie. I'll tell you that right now. Sure, I was like any other kid, screaming for ol' Rock to knock those bums out, but that scene where the kids run through the streets with him and up the steps? Straight-up lies. I know. There isn't an intersection here in Billings that I haven't crossed on the run, and not a single time did even one kid, let alone a whole neighborhood of them, fall in with me. I would've let them if they'd wanted to. Running is a damn lonely business.

Grammy's house sits dark on the corner, a view to the browned-over emptiness of South Park. It is, all at once, a welcome sight and a reminder of the things I haven't done. Time stands still around here. If I forget where I've been and what I'm carrying, forget about the piled-up years and the ache in my head, and if I pretend the porch light is on instead of busted out because I can't afford to replace it, then I can also pretend that I'm coming up on the house after an afternoon of chasing my friends around the park. I can pretend that Grammy waits on the other side of the door with a hot bowl of soup and a grilled cheese, that she'll make me bear down and do my homework, even the long division that's giving me fits. I can pretend that loneliness isn't welcome here.

But I draw closer and reality can't be dodged. The seasonals that used to bloom along the footpath are long gone, the dead husks of them whittled away by the four winters since Grammy last drew breath. Paint flecks away from the eaves, reminding me of the last promise to her that I didn't fulfill. I was laid up in the bedroom upstairs, blankets on the windows to keep out the sun. For three weeks solid I was in there after McGinley knocked me out—Jesus, McGinley. That lumbering ape. I could see everything coming, and it wasn't any use to me at all. He was so big, so much stronger than I was. I just couldn't keep him off. I'd hit him, move away, and he'd be on top of me again, crowding, leaning, that left hand crashing down on me, again and again.

Anyway, this isn't about that. I'm lying up there for three weeks, Grammy's bringing me my meals, because any kind of light hits my eyes and my head just feels like it's going to go off like a bomb. And she asks me, all gentle like, which was her way, if I'd mind painting the siding on the house. And I tell her, "Grammy, of course I will. As soon as this passes, I'll take care of it. I promise."

A week later, she's slumped over in the front yard, and a month after that I'm in Reno, fighting Olson just to pay off her funeral bill. And four years after that, I still haven't climbed up to those eaves with a bucket of paint.

I'll get to it one of these days. I told her I would. I will.

I shouldn't have drank the whole growler.

Maybe it's the indigestion, or maybe it's the dream. Whatever it is, I'm standing at the toilet at 1:17 a.m. and I'm making a mess of it, aiming with one bleary eye under a single dusty light from the fixture overhead.

A lot of people might debate me on this, but I think there are four things in this world that deliver a cocaine high (four things besides cocaine itself, I mean): sex, sneezing, knocking a man out, and peeing. Still, I'm starting to think there could be too much of that fourth thing, as I stand here draining out what I put in just a few hours ago.

I give it a shake and head back into the pitch darkness of the attic bedroom. The blankets hung by Grammy over the windows remain in place, useful far beyond her intention. I can't take sunlight on its terms. The headaches come on too fast. Frank's been asking me about them for a while now, and it's been deny, deny, deny. I don't want to go to the clinic—a doctor's interests rarely match up with my own. But this is the path available to me, so I'll do what I have to do.

I fasten my hands together and reach for the ceiling beams. My shoulders groan happily in the tingle. I feel better. I consider a return to bed, but there's nothing there for me now. I head for the stairs.

Everything in this house has a place. Mine is upstairs, out of the light of day. Grammy's is down here, in the bedroom she occupied from 1952, a bride who never saw her man come home from Korea, until she left us—left me—four years ago. I don't like to talk about her being dead. I mean, yeah, she is, but she lives here still. I can feel her moving through me in the silent moments, so much that I got rid of the TV so I'd never be distracted and never miss her. She finds me in my dreams sometimes, as she did tonight, and I'm frustrated that I lost her when I woke up. I can't bring her back. I can only wait until she returns.

I run my finger along the pictures and plaques on the west wall, her monument to me. It's a mashup of school portraits and boxing ribbons and stories from the *Billings Herald-Gleaner* clipped out and preserved in shadowboxes. And there, big as all life in the middle, is a picture of the two of us from March 13, 1997, when I rented out a ballroom for her seventieth birthday. She's silver-haired and beautiful, and she's kissing me on the cheek as I hold up a fist. Everything was looking up then. Everybody was happy.

I sit on the edge of her bed, and I breathe in deep through my nose, and she's there. She lingers still.

An early morning like this, I might be up for a drive to the West End and a corner booth at IHOP. But I sold the car, and I'm not sure where the next check is coming from, so I'd best hold tight to the money. I scrounge around in the kitchen and scare up some saltines and peanut butter, and I sit at the blue kitchen table and build me a few cracker sandwiches.

I eat them one at a time, peanut butter sticking to the roof of my mouth and ground-up crackers sinking into the fissures of my teeth. I sweep a finger through my mouth and loosen the residue. The back porch light casts a faint glow on the grown-over yard. Add that to my list.

I guess I'm going to have to start where I left off and talk it over with Frank. Yeah, he's done for me. But I've done for him, too, many times over. I need to remind him of what he owes. He won't open the place till the drink-at-lunch crowd starts milling around Montana Avenue, and that's a good number of hours away. No matter. It's sit static in here or be moving out there. No choice at all.

I grab my sunglasses and charge the door. The light's coming up. The roasting of sugar beets, the smell of a sick child, fills my nose. The refinery belches into the morning sky.

Nothing changes on its own. You gotta change it, right?

remember me in istanbul

He lay on his back and shimmied his head and shoulders under the nose of the car, his boots finding little purchase. Sand layered the asphalt, an offering of winter traction to wayward motorists. The snow was mostly gone now, turned into puddles by day only to freeze again overnight. His heel crunched the icy leavings as he gave one last kick.

Above him, she opened the passenger door a crack. "Well?"

"Still looking. Hold on a sec."

Damn her anyway, he thought. *This is her fault, all that yammering all the time.*

He sucked in air and tried to pull his right hand free to get a tactile sense of things. The streetlight he'd parked under offered slanted shadows, but there was no clarity, not at this time of night, not at this time of year. The crosswinds barreled down off the mountains and ripped through Livingston, same as ever, finding him there under the car. The trailings of hot oil and grease and gasoline filled his nostrils as he reached for the bottom of the radiator. Warm water slipped between his fingers and forged tiny rivers toward his elbow.

Well, shit. That's that.

He wormed out from under the car as if he were playing limbo. His head clear of the front end, he flopped over onto his front side and did a pushup to get off the street. She sat inside in the half-light, looking at him, and she shrugged. He gave a thumbs-down, and she lurched violently in her seat.

He dipped his head, again checking the exterior damage, and he smiled. The front fender and the grille—all that fine plastic American craftsmanship—split and buckled when the car collided with the hindquarters of the buck out on Interstate 90. She could be as mad as she wished, but this was good news on the balance. By pure serendipity, it had happened just a mile from the Livingston turnoff, and he'd been able to coax the car into town for a look. A few miles more, and they'd have been in the mountain pass, as good as stranded at this hour.

She was out of the car now. Another blast of wind billowed her T-shirt. "Can you call someone?" she said.

"No point until morning. It'll keep."

"Motel?"

"No," he said, and she looked away.

Surely he didn't have to remind her of their cash position, of the $287 in his wallet that was everything liquid, of the reason they were out here at all. He hadn't wanted to make the trip, right up to the moment when no more alternatives were available. Drive to Missoula, tell her folks that the yarn store—her yarn store, seeded by her father's money—had gone belly-up. Beg for a bailout. Try to resume some semblance of life before the failure, without continually divvying up the blame for it.

"So what, then?" she asked. She pinched the hem of her shirt against her flannel-clad hips. Still the wind found its way in.

He pressed a button on his keychain, and the lid to the trunk opened before being slammed back down by a gust. He walked past her, engaged the button again, and caught it this time. "Get what you'll need for tonight," he said. "I know somebody here who'll put us up."

"Who?"

"An old friend." He dug into the trunk and extracted a small duffel bag, which he opened and showed to her. She joined him and opened a larger suitcase, took out a shirt and jeans for the next day, and shoved them into the bag.

"Do I know this friend?"

"No. I knew her in college."

"Oh, her."

"Enough." He slung the bag over his shoulder and headed up the street. She fell in behind him, sneakers crunching sand.

"What you mean," she said, "is you fucked her."

A rather artless way of putting it, but yes, I fucked her, he thought. *And it was fucking great.*

"I'm not sleeping in a house with one of your old girlfriends," she said. She stopped under the streetlight, giving punctuation to her resolve. He could see the place from where they stood, two houses down from the intersection and across the street. He considered just pushing on, letting her stew over...over what? Over nothing, and none of her business. It was a senseless stand she was making, and there'd been enough of that already on any number of counts.

He turned to face her. "Fine. Go sleep in the car. I'll wake you up in the morning. Meantime, I'm going to be warm."

He made a diagonal crossing and moved along the sidewalk, closing in on the house. He was nearly to the empty driveway now, the front gate next, and through that the trellis Veronica had put there during the April they spent together, so tiny that even then, as now, he had to turn sideways and duck to get through it. After he knocked on the door, he heard the footfalls coming up behind him, signaling a rare victory for pragmatism.

"What if she's not here?" she said.

"She isn't." No light came on inside. No barking dogs. The house was empty.

"So what now?"

He gripped the door handle and turned it.

That the door would be unlocked was a certainty. She'd made that clear all those years ago, after his first overnight stay and his subsequent and obvious interest in a second. "Come over whenever," she'd said. "If I'm not there, the house will be unlocked. It always is."

The funny thing is that it hadn't seemed strange. Not if you knew Veronica. She collected people, friends, strays, itinerants, lovers, and her little house served as the gathering place for the motley lot of them. Her heart, she kept locked. But not her door.

He flicked on a light in the entryway. "Come on," he said.

"I'm not going in there."

"It's OK."

"What if she comes home?"

"It won't be a problem."

He held out a hand to her, inviting.

She motioned him toward the interior door. "You go first."

He found the place as he'd left it eleven years earlier, a little cracker box of a house, a small main room with two bedrooms shooting off west and southwest. Beyond the hanging glass beads in a doorway, a design flourish straight out of 1973, sat a kitchen draped in blue, her favorite color. Gas burners. Side-by-side refrigerator/freezer, Veronica's one nod to modernity and one rooted in her role as the nurturer of friends casual and closely held. He opened the fridge ("Don't," she said, still not getting it) and stared in. Jarred stuff—olives, capers, homemade jam—was all he found. Stuff that would keep.

"She won't be here," he said.

"Where is she?"

"How should I know?"

"Well, you fucked her, so I thought you'd have some insight."

"Stop it."

She moved away from him, into the dining room, her finger skirting the top of the table. He fell back to the kitchen counter, hands on the Formica, watching.

She pointed at the wall, painted a sort of aqua to leaven the baby blues proliferate in the room. "She sure takes a lot of pictures."

Black-and-whites, some familiar to him and some not, festooned the century-old plaster. Women, mostly. Some men. None of him, and for that he was thankful.

"Which one is she?"

"She's not there," he said.

"No?"

"No. She stays on the other side of the camera." It struck him now that all these years later, with no tangible record of her face, he couldn't remember exactly how she looked. The fuzziness of memory could be attributed, in part, to the fact that she was remarkable only in totality, not in her individual qualities. She wore her hair short when he knew her, a dirty blonde that he now pondered, wondering if it had yet been dusted in gray like his own. A round face, plump but not chubby. Mirthful. He never saw her wear makeup, not even an accent to bring up her eyes or sharpen her nose. She didn't need to. He remembered a soft neck, endlessly welcoming to a troubled head.

"Are you listening?"

He looked up. "What?"

"I said, I'm tired."

He moved toward the living room. "Spare bedroom's in here. I'll rustle up some blankets."

In the night, she nudged him with her foot.

"Wake up."

"I am," he said.

"Have you slept?"

"A little," and that was a little lie. He pushed himself off the floor by his elbows, bringing his head even with hers on the bed. He leaned in. "You OK?"

"Yes. I guess I am. I'm sorry I was a bitch."

"It's OK."

"I'm sorry you're on the floor."

"Don't be." It was a practical consideration. Veronica's day bed wouldn't have held the two of them.

"Can I tell you something?" she said.

"Yes." He watched her, the shape of her. The blackness of the room allowed him no glimpse of nuance.

She breathed in, expelled it, then drew breath again. "I'm mad."

"At me?"

"Yes," she said.

"For tonight?"

"Yes. That tonight was even necessary."

He slumped back down to his makeshift bed on the hardwood. "We've been over this and over this. You still blame me."

"No."

"It sounds like you do."

"No, it was my failure. I'll tell daddy that."

"Ours. I'll own half of it," he said. He reached up, tried to find her hand. She moved it away.

"I don't know how to fix this," she said.

He retracted his own hand. "We're not the first people to lose a business, hon."

"And I can't believe we're in this house," she said. "How did we come to this?"

When she finally found sleep, he left her there and wandered back into the main part of the house. He pulled a blanket from the couch and wrapped himself in it, and he remembered how close to the edge Veronica played everything. The thermostat kept low, even here in the last howls of winter. The food dollar she could stretch beyond any reasonable breaking point. The freecycled small appliances and the freezer full of game meat given to her by hunters clearing out space for the new season's haul and the late-'70s Honda that she nursed through several hundred thousand miles, that for all he knew she still had, wherever she was now. Waste not, want not, and she never did. She took what she needed, used what she took, and squeezed her nickels until they carried her to the places she wished to see.

He stood on the kitchen linoleum in his bare feet and he looked at the photos on the wall that had drawn interest earlier. He remembered some of them, the prints she had shown him on her many returns. Young women laughing in a West Bank coffee shop. A forlorn young man, head down, alone at a London Tube stop. *Tegucigalpa. La Nueva Guatemala de la Asunción.*

And there, bottom right, obscured by the kitchen table where he almost missed it, the Walls of Constantinople, the ancient precision of brickwork evident among the ruins. He hadn't wanted her to go. He worried about her, a single woman in a Muslim city, but no man yet had managed to put a fence around her. It wasn't just that. He'd wanted more than a concession on travel plans. He'd wanted her in a way that he hadn't before, permanently and exclusively. And her answer had been a flight to Istanbul and a postcard to tell him that she could never want what he wanted. If he really needed monogamy, she said, he should find a girl who would give it to him.

He moved closer. He knelt before the photo, and he reached for it, brushing fingers against the pane, and then he stood and returned to the bedroom. She was breathing in deep now, lost to sleep. He gathered the blanket about himself and took his place on the floor, and he smiled as he nestled his nose into the fabric and the whiffs of lavender, of Veronica, pulled him in again.

Come morning, he counted the bills as they left his wallet. The tow came to fifty dollars for a two-block ride. At the service station, the proprietor laid out the news, and it could have been a lot worse. "The front end is bashed all to hell but it's mostly cosmetic," he said. He could drain the remainder from the radiator, spray in some sealant and fill it up again. "That'll get you where you're going, and probably back again. Not a permanent fix, but it'll do for now." That came to eighty-seven fifty and an aw-shucks apology from the service-station guy, who said he knew how things could be tough these days. Two candy bars from the vending machine left them $147.50 to get where they were headed. Without some help, there would be no getting back.

He settled matters, and then they buckled in. The car started on the first turn, and he watched the temperature gauge slowly climb to midrange. The car warmed, and the reading held steady. He pulled onto the main drag and headed for the interstate.

"I'm going to sleep," she said.

"Good. I can't be distracted again."

"Don't be mean."

"I'm not. I'm just saying."

She sat up. "What did you say in the note to her?"

"I said, 'Thank you.'"

"That's all?"

"That's all."

"Did you love her?"

He fastened his grip on the wheel. "I thought so once. But that was a long time ago."

On the outskirts, he bore right onto the ramp and fought the crosswinds for speed. She reached for his hand as it found the gearshift. She laced her fingers in his.

"Can we be friends again?" she asked.

"Yes. Of course. I'd like that."

Cruising speed now, and with it came a change in elevation as they threaded the mountain pass. She leaned in and nuzzled him under the chin, and then she fell back into her seat.

"What?" he said. He reached for her. She withered against the passenger door.

"What's wrong?"

He cast a glance at her, and she stared back at him, through him, as if she wished him gone.

"You," she said. "You smell like her."

shorter fiction

the field

When Quince came rolling up into my front yard that morning, we were up to our neck in August, staring down a seventh-grade year that had crept perilously close when we weren't looking. I'm thirty-five years clear of it now, and I can still sense Texas on my skin the way it felt that summer, the heat bearing down, relentless. Quince would come up the street to my house sometimes to sit under the swamp cooler after his mama chased him out so she could sleep off another drunk.

"Derek...you gotta...come down...to...The Field." Quince squeezed the words out between gulps of air.

The Field, an undeveloped patch of ground on the northern edge of our neighborhood, came by its capital letters honestly. It was the perfect so-close-and-yet-so-far territory in our town. At the farthest edge of it, I was no more than a quarter-mile from my own house, but I couldn't see my street, couldn't cover the distance with any sort of speed, wouldn't have been able to call for help if I'd ever been set upon by older kids. It never did happen to me, but Quince and another kid we ran with, Danny Dutton, hadn't been so lucky. The previous spring, some high school guys from Meadowlakes, the subdivision on the far west side of The Field, had caught Quince and Danny walking their bikes through and had beat on them pretty good.

177

"I'm not going down there," I said.

"Derek, you gotta. Danny's down there. Burton, too. You won't believe what's happening."

"What?"

"You won't even believe it. Just come."

I slipped onto the saddle of my bike. "I'll follow you," I said.

We crested my hill and rode it down to the bottom on the other side, where it terminated at a barrier fence sporting the most disregarded KEEP OUT sign in our town. We walked our bikes around the fence, found the well-grooved trail on the other side, and set to pedaling again. Quince veered right, toward a line of trees.

"It's by the pond," he called to me over his shoulder.

Ahead, I saw Danny Dutton and Burton Mayhew standing by their bikes, waiting for us. Danny stood a head taller than the rest of us, on account of his being held back in second grade for poor marks. I never saw him without Burton, a smaller kid who was continually getting into scraps with anybody who cared to entertain him. One time, after I'd come home with a split lip courtesy of Burton, my father had said he had "short man's disease," said Burton's own daddy suffered from the same affliction back when they were kids. He said Burton probably felt threatened by me, so from that day on, I tried to be understanding of the little shit.

Quince and I skidded to a stop. "What's going on?" I asked.

Danny held a finger to his lips. Then, in a whisper, he said, "Do you know that older kid Darrell who lives over on Dutch Elm?"

I pictured the kid. Sixteen, seventeen years old. Tightly curled hair. Lots of acne. Smelled bad.

"Yeah, I know him."

"Well," Danny said, and he looked around suspiciously before he said this next part, "he's down by the pond, bopping his bologna."

"Huh?"

"You know," Burton cut in. "He's slappin' little Johnny behind the ears."

"He's jacking off," Quince said.

"I get it," I said. "How do you know?"

Danny grinned like he'd swallowed a delicious secret. "I've been following him. I saw him a few days ago down there. I was hopping a fence, cutting through some backyards, and I walked up the ridge there, and there he was, whacking it. He didn't see me. I started biking by his house, staking him out. I've seen him come out here three times in the last two days. He thinks he's alone."

"He ain't," Burton said. "We're gonna get him."

Danny lifted a canvas bag off his handlebars, dug around inside and retrieved walkie-talkies. One for each of us. He started handing them out.

"Let's surround him and scare the hell out of him," Danny said. I looked at the sweaty, dusty faces of my friends, and I saw three boys who wouldn't be talked out of mischief, not that day. I held out my hand and Danny filled it.

The volume turned low, the walkie-talkie spat out words and static in equal measures.

"Quince, you in position?"

"Check."

"Burton?"

"Check."

"Derek?"

The pond sat at the bottom of an earthen bowl. I'd climbed across the outside of it, kicking up dust from that caliche baked hard in the sun, to a clump of oaks along the rim. From my perch, I could see Darrell's supine bare legs, his blue jeans and white underwear down to his ankles. "Check."

"OK, boys," Danny's voice crackled. "count to five and then run at him like hell."

I must have counted slowly. I was at three when I heard that first banshee scream, and it chased me to my feet. As I rambled down the embankment, I tried to yell—I swear I did—but no sound escaped my mouth. It didn't much matter; my shrieking friends were upon Darrell, beating on him with fists, wailing, as he tried to stand. He finally did get to his feet, but the tangle of denim and cotton around his ankles tripped him as he tried to scramble away.

I just stood there, watching, as Danny grabbed at the kid's feet. Darrell kicked and kicked, and finally, the pants and underwear came off in Danny's hands, and Darrell got away for good, scrambling up and over the rim, lighting out for home in a KISS T-shirt, orange-striped tube socks and Keds, and nothing else.

I went home alone. Quince asked if he could come, and I lied and told him my folks and I were going to be heading for Lake Texoma for the weekend. He'd see me the next day and ask what happened, I knew, but I felt confident that I could conjure another fib if I had to.

The cold air in the house hit me as soon as I walked in, and immediately, my breakfast decided to retreat. I stumbled into the hallway bathroom and expelled it, my body recoiling in waves of wet and dry heaves. When it was over, I stretched out on the tile and set my cheek against its cool surface, and I went to sleep.

high above lake travis

We crept to the edge of the cliff and stared down at the lake. In this alcove, out of the churn of the speedboats and pleasure craft, the water shimmered, impossibly blue.

"Didn't you used to jump off here back when you were getting high?" Ryan said.

Edd rolled his head against his right shoulder in an ellipsis. "Yeah, man, but that's a big part of my past, big part of my past. I don't do that anymore. No more."

I felt vertigo kicking in and shuffled backward a couple of feet.

"Scared?" Ryan asked.

"Nah, man."

He turned back to Edd. "Jump, dude. Might be different sober."

Edd fell back parallel to me. "No way, man. I'm done with it. Done with it."

"I'll buy you a carton of Camels."

Edd tore off his shirt. "I'm there, dude, I'm all over it." Whooping, he slapped me in the chest as he launched himself off the cliff.

Feet first, his body sliced the water like a knife—calves, knees, thighs, torso, head, all of him pulled underwater, the surface returning to calm in his wake.

"That crazy fucker," Ryan said.

Edd bobbed back to the top, whipping his head in parabolas to shake the water from his white-boy dreads. He shouted up to us. "Don't forget my smokes, dude. My smokes. Come on. Let's go to 7-Eleven."

That we'd hooked up with Edd at all had been unlikely. Nearly half a million people in Austin, and we happened across one who'd shared a couple of AA meetings with my roommate a few years earlier, when he was an undergrad at UT. (I suppose we increased our odds considerably by posting up in a 6th Street pool hall.)

"Where you been, man? Where you been?" Edd said to Ryan after he ambled over to us. "Been a long time."

"Edd, I live in Dallas now."

"No shit?"

"Five years now."

"No shit?"

"No shit."

"Well, man," Edd said, his eyes bouncing wildly between me and Ryan, "that's a bummer. A bummer, man."

After dark, we headed out the Bastrop Highway to the airport. Edd said he knew how we could get up to the roof of the Hilton and watch the jets come in. I carried a six-pack of Cokes and Edd's Camels in my backpack.

The hotel lay squat on the horizon, four floors stacked in the shape of a doughnut. Once outside and atop the hotel, we clung to the edge, lest we be seen through the sunroof by lounging guests below. Edd found us a spot facing the flight path, the perfect vantage point. The wind picked up, brushing our sun-braised skin.

"I come up here sometimes and sit for hours. Hours, man," Edd said.

"It's awesome," Ryan said. He stood at the edge, hands fused to his hips.

The scream of an approaching jet shattered the peace, and light flooded the field to guide it in. I stood up to get a better view. Once the wheels were on the ground, the field went dark again.

"Awesome," I said.

"You stayed sober this whole time?" Ryan asked.

"Yep. Yep," came the answer from Edd. "What about you, man?"

Ryan looked past us. "One stumble, but otherwise, yeah."

"When was that, man? When?"

"Last year around this time."

I sat up. I hadn't known this about Ryan. Truth was, I didn't know much about him at all. Five months earlier, I'd answered his ad looking for a roommate and moved into the two-bedroom place he had on Lower Greenville. We worked opposite schedules, and on days off, I spent most of my time down in Huntsville, where my girlfriend, Elise, was wrapping up her last semester at Sam Houston State. When she went on a two-week mission trip to Mexico, it freed me up to say yes when Ryan asked if I wanted to mess around in Austin for a weekend.

"Jesus, man. Jesus," Edd was saying. "What'd you do?"

"Called my sponsor when I got on the other side of it, got my ass back into treatment right quick."

I tugged at a corner of the roofing material. A rubber piece, cooked rigid by the sun, came off in my hand. I whipped it side-armed off the edge of the hotel.

"It fucking sucked, man," Ryan said. "Came out, started at zero. You know the drill, right? 'My name is Ryan and I've been sober twenty-eight days.' Shit, man. I'd been three years clean and I blew it. Back to square one."

Edd took a drag off his cigarette. "One day at a time. All you can do. Desire, man. Desire. You want sobriety for a day, and you go get you a day. Then you gotta want it for another day. Desire. Another day, man."

"Yeah," Ryan said. "I know. But listen. Let me ask you a question: What did it feel like, jumping off that cliff again? Anything like before?"

Edd considered the question a while. A faint smile gathered at the corners of his mouth. "Didn't feel like nothing, man. Nothing."

"What do you mean?"

Edd mashed out his cigarette and flicked its carcass over the edge. "Man, it's like this. Used to be, I'd get loaded and climb up there and jump, and it was like I was flying, man. Flying. I went in there all kinds of crazy ways, man. On my head, on my back, on my face. I'm lucky I survived some of them, man. There's rocks down there, you know. Rocks. I never hit 'em, and I always found my way out. I was crazy, man. Crazy.

"But today, man, all I could think was, dude, this is a pretty stupid way to get a carton of smokes, man. Pretty stupid."

The field lit up again as another jet pointed its nose toward home.

Edd lit a fresh cigarette, his contorting face illuminated by the match. Ryan sat in a heap, boring a thousand-yard stare through the roof.

"Yeah," he said. "Flying, that's it exactly. That's what it feels like. That's what I miss." Edd opened his mouth as if to speak, and then I heard him swallow his words.

I pulled my collar up against the night and shoved my hands in my pockets.

Without warning, Austin had turned cold. So, so cold.

always, always other girls

Cooper and I didn't leave his house until dusk. It was an easy decision to stay buttoned up that long. Inside: Atari and IntelliVision, as much ice cream as we wanted and no chores, on account of Cooper's parents were loaded and had a maid. Outside: Texas in full-throated July, ready to pour humidity over us like so much syrup. We'd have stayed in all day and night had Cooper's mom not finally tired of us ping-ponging from room to room, agitating, our fast-twitch teenage muscles wanting to move even if our brains didn't. She came to us, gin and tonic in hand, and told us to get out.

I flung the basketball at the hoop and Cooper shagged the ball. He was the luckiest bastard I knew. A rubberized half court was rigged up in his backyard, with a fiberglass backboard and breakaway rim and netting all the way around to keep errant balls from escaping. I coveted that whole setup. The previous summer, before Cooper and I became friends, my old man had mixed cement in a rusty wheelbarrow and posted a particle-board hoop he'd found at a flea market. It stood twelve feet tall astride our driveway, which was at a slight downhill angle, and while I appreciated the old man's effort, once I met Cooper, I never used it again. A few years later, the old man took it down and jackhammered out the concrete. We never talked about that, and now, seventeen years after I saw him into the ground, I startle myself sometimes when I think that if I could speak to him just one more time, I'd tell him I wished I'd played ball with that hoop more than I did. I don't know. It just didn't seem like a big deal at the time.

I was working around the world— hitting shots on the periphery of the court—when Cooper made an audacious observation.

"We need to get us girlfriends this year."

I let fly with another shot that rattled through the hoop. "Good idea. How we gonna do that?"

Cooper gathered in the ball and whipped a chest pass to me at the top of the key. "I don't know."

I stopped shooting and slipped the ball under my arm. "Got your eye on anybody?"

"I was thinking about it."

"Who?"

"You know that girl Marci who lives up on Donerail?"

A hazy picture of a short, milky-skinned blonde popped up in my head. "She younger than us?"

"Yeah, she'll be a seventh-grader."

"I think I know her. Marci Barnes, right? You like her?"

Cooper held up a hand, calling for the ball. I gave it to him and we switched places.

His first shot caromed off the side of the rim. I chased down the ball.

"There are a few nice girls in that neighborhood," I said. "Anne Irving, she lives around the corner on Montrose. And then there's Brianna. She lives on Manuel."

"Brianna," Cooper said reverently. Never in a million years could either of us hope to get Brianna Odell as a girlfriend.

Cooper was finding the range now, and I promptly retrieved three shots in a row that passed through the net unmolested by the steel hoop.

"Nice shooting."

Cooper caught the ball in stride and dispatched another perfect shot. "Thanks. What about the aforementioned Anne? Do you like her?"

I corralled the ball and held it. "Aforementioned?"

"Yeah."

"How does a word like that even come up?"

"What's the big deal? You mentioned her before. Aforementioned."

"Yeah, but…"

"But what?"

I threw a baseball pass at him, hard. "I'm just saying, it's a pretty weird word to just say. You do that all the time. Have you ever noticed that?"

Cooper put up another shot that found the bottom of the net.

"Noticed what?"

"Come on, man," I said, throwing the ball back to him. "You're always using big words in class and stuff."

Another made shot. I threw back the ball.

"Like what?"

I didn't much care for this who-me act. "OK, here's one," I said. "Defrenes...defenstrated."

Cooper laughed. "Defenestrated."

"Whatever. I looked it up. Why can't you just say 'thrown out a window'?"

He shot again, another make.

"Why does it bug you?"

I tossed the ball back to him. "It doesn't bug me. It just seems..."

He pitched the ball at the hoop again. It swished through. "Ostentatious?" he said.

"Yeah. Goddamn it." I grabbed the ball.

"Well, Ben, I'm sorry to be so polysyllabic."

"Whatever, man. I don't care that you made that last shot. It's my turn. Get out of there."

I hadn't thought of that night in years. Today, I was headed to my mom's house—my house, long ago—after Cooper's funeral, and I had to turn right on Donerail and then left on Montrose before crossing Manuel into our subdivision. It all came flooding back.

Cooper never did tell Marci that he liked her, I don't think. By the time a new school year rolled around, there were other girls—always, always other girls. A few years after that, Anne Irving and I went to senior prom together, but she ditched me for John Courtney and I ended up drinking hooch in the parking lot with the guys from auto shop. The next morning, I woke up in an alley off Rosedale, my shoes, wallet and cummerbund gone, and I had to call the old man collect to come fetch me. We never talked about that, either.

We stayed friends, Cooper and I. We were as close as we could manage, what with my living in Fresno and his staying in Texas. Our kids are close, like cousins, and we'd occasionally take vacations together

—usually somewhere he and I could play golf while Deborah and Natalie did whatever the hell it was that they did. After I lost Deborah to cervical cancer six years ago, Cooper came and stayed with me for a couple of weeks when my grief was still inchoate (his word). He pulled me through that awful shit. I never imagined that I would lose him, too.

A lot of people came to say goodbye to Cooper, a lot of people I didn't remember and hadn't seen in nearly twenty-five years. Think about that. A quarter-century goes by so fast. It wipes away your youth, your looks (if you had any to begin with) and a good deal of your memories, but maybe not the most important ones.

Brianna Odell was there. She told me she'd moved back to that house on Manuel after her parents passed on. Her kids are in college now, her husband down in Itasca with some hot piece of ass he met at a chili cook-off. The whole thing sounds like the worst cliché ever, which is why I'm going over to Brianna's place tonight with a bottle of wine. Maybe that's a dumb thing to do, but I'm doing it just the same. I've about had my fill of these aforementioned regrets.

lingua franca

When Rusty says to me, "Look, Ronny, I want you to know that my interest in you isn't strictly prurient," I'm certain of two things.

First, I like him. I really, really like him in a way that I don't like guys, not anymore, not after all the dirty lies to get into my pants, the dirtier lies to get out of them later, the indignities and the humiliations and the disappointments. Which isn't to say that I've lost interest in guys. Guys are wonderful things in moderation, or so I hear. I haven't yet mastered moderation in much of anything, and certainly not guys, but there's still time, I think, which is why I try not to like them, Rusty aside.

Second, he's lying, just like so many guys before him, which surprises me exactly not at all. The thing is, I can't tell if this is the sort of lie that will lead where so many other lies have led, to my feeling broken and used and tossed aside, or if there is something more to this lie, some glimmer of belief on Rusty's part that there is something in me worthwhile, something he wants to get closer to before he has to tell the truth and admit to me that, yes, his interest in me is strictly prurient but that I'm also an awesome chick and he knew it all the time. I would be OK with that, and somehow, I have to let him know.

He looks a little bit like Jeff. That was what I noticed when Rusty first talked to me last week here at the Libertine. It's the way his jaws come together in a perfect point at his chin, as if the pieces of his face are locked together like Legos. I didn't want to talk to Rusty at first because of this, because Jeff was horrible to me, and Rusty reminded me of him. Jeff threw an alabaster vase full of potting soil at me, directly at my head, and only because he can't even get something like that right did it miss and shatter instead against the refrigerator. It fell to the linoleum in my kitchen, a debris trail of broken glass and dirt and plant life heading for death. I left it there for a week, long after Jeff left for good, because it was the only vestige I had of him. It took me a long time to get over that, and Rusty looking like Jeff was a mark against him from the start. But then he smiled, something Jeff rarely did, and I saw that he didn't look so much like Jeff at all. That was good, and so I smiled, too.

Rusty told me that he was an obesity researcher at the Southwestern Medical Center, and I believed him, and I never believe guys. But come on, obesity researcher? Nobody would make up something like that. I pointed at a fat bitch at the end of the bar and suggested that he talk to her instead, and he laughed and said it wasn't like that, and anyway, something called Occam's Razor told him that if she drank light beer and avoided the Hog Wings, her problem would probably be less acute. I asked him what the fuck Occam's Razor was, and he laughed again and told me that was a tool of deduction, whatever that is.

Anyway, tonight, he came back to the Libertine, and he remembered me and I remembered him, and we've been chatting—chatting, what a silly word—for a few hours and now he's telling me that his interest in me isn't "strictly prurient." I still think he's adorable and I still think he's lying, but I don't need to sort any of that out tonight, do I?

"What is your interest, strictly speaking?" I ask.

"To walk you home," he says.

"It's a long walk."

"No, it isn't."

"How do you know?"

"You told me, last week. You said it's two blocks away, right here on Greenville. Were you lying?"

"I wasn't lying," I say.

"So are you ready to go?" he asks.

"I am," I say.

November slaps us dead in the face as we leave the Libertine, and he asks if he can put his arm around me seeing as how it wasn't this cold when he came in and he didn't bring a jacket to offer me.

190

"Yes," I say.

And we're walking, and his arm has pulled me in closer, and I can smell him now, can smell the Irish Spring he scrubbed onto his body this morning. I like it. I like him. He's beautiful and he likes me back. Still I'm cold, and Rusty says he heard there's supposed to be an ice storm coming.

And I think, ice storm or not, I'm not bringing the plants in tonight.

this frozen place

The woman shook her boy. Half awake, he reached out, grasping at her hazy specter in the early morning dark. He couldn't reach her.

"Tyler, get up and get dressed."

The boy agitated in the cocoon of blankets, dropping his heavy legs off the side of the bed. "What time is it?" She didn't answer. She was gone. The hall light lapped at the edge of the bedroom through the open door she had passed through.

The boy walked on the edges of his feet to the dresser and opened a drawer, rifling through it like a blind man. His searching hands found a pair of woolen socks, and he sat on the end of the empty bed, pulling them on.

"Go get him." The man's voice, biting off instruction to the woman, traveled down the hallway to the boy's ears.

"I just have to put on my shoes." The boy fumbled with the laces as his mother came back into the room.

"Come on now," she said.

"What's going on?"

"There's been an accident."

The boy shivered in the backseat, worn flannel pajamas the only sentry between him and the cold, hard leather of the station wagon. He peered over the front seat at the clock in the dashboard. Four-twenty-three.

He could smell the vestiges of alcohol on his folks. They'd let him stay up till midnight to mark the new year, and his mother had sneaked him a taste of her whisky. He remembered now what she'd last said before sending him off to bed, how strange it sounded. He couldn't recall her ever saying such a thing.

"Let's hope this one's more bucolic than the last."

The gray slate of night still hung heavy in the car as the boy tried to clear his head of his cut-short sleep.

"Is it Trevin?" he asked, and instantly he felt stupid for having done so. *Who else could it be?* They were all accounted for. All of them except Trevin.

"What happened?"

The woman made a half-turn of her head and reached for her boy over the seat. He put his hand in hers.

"It was a crash, honey. We don't know anything else."

She gripped his hand. The boy looked in the rearview mirror. The lower half of his father's face twitched as he ground his teeth. He looked up and met eyes with the boy. The child smiled hesitantly, trying to send a signal—something, anything, that might give his father comfort. The man looked away.

Outside the car, a frozen morning chipped away at the fading night.

The white lights and antiseptic hallways of the hospital could neutralize everything except the roiling fear of a fractured family, who until an early morning phone call had been four. Now they were divided—three anxious on one side of a wall and one in distress on the other.

A deputy sheriff met them in the waiting room and dutifully delivered an account that told much and revealed little. Trevin, traveling too fast on the ice-slicked county road. Trevin, trapped in his car, which had been contracted by the collision with the oncoming pickup. Trevin, still with a pulse but otherwise unresponsive, airlifted to the hospital.

But what of the rest of it, his father asked, meek-voiced. *Where had he been? Who had he been with? Was he drinking? Had he fallen asleep? Did he know what was happening to him?*

The deputy held his Stetson and repeatedly creased the brim: "I don't know, sir. You'll have to talk to the doctor about that. I'm terribly sorry."

They heard that repeatedly in the week that followed. The boy had never before contemplated the congruence of the words, the horrible yet perfect way they fit together.

"That's terrible."

"I'm sorry."

"I'm terribly sorry."

The boy came to his mother and held his chin up. Wordlessly, she worked the tie in her fingers, fashioning the knot. The duty done, she clapped him on the shoulders and squeezed.

"You're a good boy."

He stepped through her grip and hugged her around the waist. She patted him on the back and then peeled him away. "We have to go. We'll be late."

They walked out the door, into the sun, joining his father. He mashed out a cigarette with his black shoe and led them to the car.

ponzi

In September of that year, our neighbor Wayne had this idea that he could get rich by selling groceries Amway-style, and he booted his twelve-year-old boy out of his own bedroom and put up shelves loaded with packages of spaghetti, cans of roast beef, soda pop by the case and other non-perishable goods.

Soon after, Wayne came over to our house and gave my folks the pitch, showed them how, if they just signed up a few friends and those friends signed up a few friends, and so on, they could make as much as $10 million a month, all by making a little bit on every transaction.

"Everybody needs groceries," Wayne said, mopping sweat off the folds of blubber on his neck. "It's the perfect plan."

My pop liked Wayne, liked going out with him occasionally and tossing back some suds, and he paid the ten-dollar membership fee and accepted the tabbed folder that contained the list of goods and prices, as well as several pages of helpful hints for enrolling friends in the program.

"We'll see what we can do with it, Wayne," Pop said, showing him to the door. "It's an interesting idea you have here."

The old man had said something similar a few times before. We still had a shed full of cleaning chemicals that Wayne had foisted on Pop in an earlier scheme. The stuff was supposed to get rid of deep grime on contact, and sure enough, it performed as advertised. It also ate a hole in our carpet. Pop put the stuff in the storage shed because, I think, he didn't quite know how to dispose of it, and he didn't want to hurt Wayne's feelings. A similar sensibility had driven him to sneak out of the house one night and open the door to the pigeon coop Wayne had insisted he build. The next morning, the flock had flown away, and Pop went across the street and told Wayne that they wouldn't be making that killing on squab.

"You're a soft touch, Leonard," Mom scolded him, and Pop mumbled something about how it didn't hurt anything. Mom often said that the old man "enabled" Wayne's irresponsible behavior; most of Mom's vocabulary came from the self-help books she consumed with the fervor of the newly touched religious. That idea never seemed to resonate with Pop.

Mom thumbed through the folder. "This isn't going to work."

"Why not?" Pop asked. "Seems like a decent idea. Like Wayne said, everybody needs groceries."

"Yeah, but look at this." Mom thrust the folder at him. "Now just look at that: Cheer laundry detergent for $2.49. I can get it for a dollar less down at Skaggs. And $1.50 for a two-liter bottle of Coke? I got it for 99 cents yesterday!"

It went on like that for another half-hour or so. After the first few broadsides by Mom against Wayne's plan, Pop looked for an escape. He tuned in to the Texas Rangers game on the radio, while Mom sat at the kitchen table and lingered over the list of products and prices. Their interplay was a series of exclamations in one room and knob adjustments in the other.

"Two-ninety-nine for Sanka!"

Pop turned up the volume on the radio.

"A buck eighty-nine for Doritos!"

Pop flipped over to Bill Mack on WBAP.

"A dollar-ten for a can of tuna!"

The old man turned off the radio and went outside.

"Rangers lost," I said. I held open a lawn bag so Pop could scoop a load of early fallen leaves into it.

"Figures," he said.

I shook the bag to settle the leaves and then tied off the top. Pop fished his smokes from his front pocket and lit up.

"I guess Wayne's idea has a few flaws," I said.

"Guess so." The old man exhaled a string of smoke from the side of his mouth, upwind of me.

"You know, he kicked Ethan out of his own bedroom so he could put food in there."

Pop didn't say anything, but I could see his jaws clench. He was chewing on something that was giving him trouble. Whatever it was, I knew I'd never hear about it.

"Men sometimes lose their way, Jon."

He crushed the cigarette into the brick of the house, behind the hedge where no one would see the mark.

"Come on," he said. "It's getting late."

meritorious

An hour after the campfire had been shoveled under, after the scoutmasters had retired to their adjacent tent and begun blasting peripatetic snores, the boys began plotting.

"I hate him," Quinton whispered, the first to break the silence.

Assent came from Rex, nestled in the sleeping bag across the hulking canvas tent. "I hate him, too."

Three of the other boys—Kevin, Bobby, Lance—mumbled in the affirmative.

"Who?" asked Alan, the tenderfoot.

"You know who," Quinton spat into the darkness.

"Don't be stupid, Alan," Rex whispered to the boy next to him. "That dick Carlson."

"I'm gonna get him," Quinton said. "And you guys better help me."

Thirty years later—and all the years in between—Alan Walton would remember how insidious it was, the anger that started that night with Quinton Harris, fifteen years old and the undisputed leader of the troop, and spread like a virus to the other boys in the tent, boys who spoke openly of high crimes beneath a shroud of darkness. As night tumbled into early morning, Ernie Carlson's punishment was agreed upon, with no leniency to be granted or even considered.

At the mess hall for breakfast, Rex approached Carlson.

"Hey, Ernie," he said, sitting down next to the instructor, who scooped scraps of fried egg onto his toast. "I found a really odd-looking plant yesterday in the woods. I think I remember where it is. I figured since you approved me for the plant science merit badge, you might recognize it. Can you take a look?"

"Sure, bud, no problem. Let me finish eating."

"Sure." As the Eagle scout, now a twenty-year-old college student, wolfed down the last of his eggs, Rex looked him over and let doubt edge into the picture. Carlson had a couple of inches and twenty pounds on the biggest of them, Quinton. They'd have to take him down quick, without hesitation. Quinton was game. So was Rex. He wasn't sure about the others.

"All right, bud," Carlson said, standing. "Let's see this thing."

Rex led the young instructor out of the Jamboree camp, into the hill country.

"How far are you from Star?" Carlson asked.

Rex picked up the pace. "A few more hours of community service."

"That's great, bud. You're doing great."

They crested a bald knob and headed into a thicket of live oak.

"You were really back in here, huh?" Carlson said. "We must be a half-mile from camp."

Rex aimed for the heart of the dense growth of trees. "Yeah, I kind of lost track of time. Anyway, here it is."

Carlson, lagging, jogged a few steps to catch up. "Where?"

"Here," came the voice from behind him. When Carlson turned, Quinton smashed a rock between his eyes. Carlson fell in a heap at his feet. The others—Alan, Kevin, Bobby and Lance—emerged from behind the oak that had hidden them all, looking at Carlson's twisted body and at the wreckage of his face.

"He's dead," Alan said.

"Don't be stupid. He's not dead," Quinton said. "Look at him. He's breathing."

Rex sat in the dirt, unable to catch his own breath. Lance began whimpering. The others just stared.

"I want to go back to camp," Lance wailed.

Quinton stepped over to the boy and plowed a fist into his nose, dropping him. "Nobody's leaving. Now help me get his clothes off."

These are the things Alan Walton thinks about decades after the fact, the things that wake him up in the early morning darkness, tormenting him with doubts about the way he's raising his own boys. He tries to do the right things, tries to set a moral foundation and hopes that his sons make the right choices.

And yet...

The boys who set upon Ernie Carlson that morning were fine young men. Boy Scouts. All from nuclear families and from good Baptist churches, God-loving and pure. Even Quinton. And still they beat a man, undressed him, lashed him to an oak tree using knots Carlson had taught them, and slathered his chest and neck and face and testicles with bacon grease, leaving him there for an August baking.

Alan wrestles with the guilt and gives himself no mercy even for his later act of leading the head scoutmaster to the spot a few hours later, to a naked, bitten, bloody, parched Ernie Carlson, who had screamed himself into collapse. Alan's shrink and his pastor tell him that he did the right thing—no matter how late it was, he did the right thing—and that he should give himself some grace. He can't.

He remembers it all. Above all else, he remembers Carlson begging, pleading, as the boys left him.

"I'm going to die," he said, sobbing.

Quinton turned around and smiled—*God, he smiled*, Alan thinks now—and said "Be prepared."

anything for a friend

Eddie Dorsett was a dumb kid. Nobody could dispute it. More than that, Eddie Dorsett was a fat, slothful, whining, shilly-shallying, booger-eating zero of a kid, the lowest of the third-graders for certain and a prime contender for the lowest of the entire Rutherford Hodges Elementary student population, no small dishonor. In the fall of '78, you could argue, Hodges Elementary was overrun by layabouts, hoods in training, crumb factories, carpet rats and crackers, and Eddie Dorsett, the sniveling little shit, was one of them. Maybe the worst of them.

So it was not without reservation that I stepped between Eddie and Mike Brill that October before Brill could blacken Eddie's other eye.

"Leave him alone."

Brill, the tallest kid in our class but one whose constitution wouldn't allow him to take on anyone but the weakest kids, stopped his advance on Eddie. "What's it to you?" he said. His cohorts—wingmen, I guess you'd call them today—looked at Brill and each other, uncertain what to do. I'd counted on that. If the three of them had been capable of rubbing together two cogent thoughts, they easily could have given me the ass-kicking they intended for Eddie.

"Just leave him alone," I said. "He hasn't done anything to you."

Brill stepped backward, something else I'd counted on, as he tried

205

to save face. "It must be save-a-dork week. Or join-a-dork week. You joining up with the dorks, Rodney?" His slope-headed sycophants laughed and slapped Brill on the back, even as they walked backward with him.

I didn't say anything to that. I just kept my fists clenched, all the message the likes of Mike Brill needed. He threw a couple more sneers at me for good measure, and soon enough, he was on the other side of the recess yard, tormenting Roger Prager, who probably deserved it.

I turned to Eddie, still on the ground where he'd fallen into a defensive posture like the pill bugs I'd spent much of the summer crushing between my fingers.

"Get up," I said. "He's gone."

Eddie flopped onto his back, sat up and then scrambled to his feet, looking for all the world like a miniature version of Boss Hogg in Tuffskins.

"Thanks for that," he said. "Nobody ever stuck up for me before."

I didn't even look at him as I walked away. "Don't mention it."

The fat little fucker mentioned it. Somebody did, anyway. Mrs. Dorsett came by the house that night with Eddie in tow. (Mr. Dorsett—whose existence could be divined by the malformed mound of genetic material standing in our living room but who'd never been seen by me or anyone I knew—was out of town, his wife said.) She had these enormous pillows of fat hanging from her upper arms, and they became cellulitic metronomes, moving in time as she swung those fleshy stubs of hers around, excitedly telling my folks what I'd done for her boy.

Mom stood next to me and patted me on the head as Mrs. Dorsett unspooled the account of the thing. She got key details wrong, notably when she said Eddie was backed into a corner rather than cowering in the dirt.

"Did you hit that boy, Rodney? Did you give him what for?" Dad asked. "No."

"Too bad. Sometimes with a boy like that, a punch in the nose is the only thing that will get through."

I looked at Mrs. Dorsett and she was nodding, and it was only by the grace of my upbringing that I didn't ask her why she was nodding at me when she should have been stuffing that good advice into the ears of her idiot son.

"Well, I'm just so sorry about what those awful boys are doing to

Eddie," Mom said, reaching out and patting Mrs. Dorsett's doughy arm. I looked at Eddie and he had half a finger jammed into his nostril.

The next morning, Mom laid it out for me.

"The Dorsett boy is going to start spending the night over here a few nights a week."

I spat out my toast. "What? Why?"

"That family is in a bad way, and we can help. His mom got an offer to work the night shift at the hospital, and Eddie's dad is gone a lot, so he's going to stay here."

I looked at Dad. He tugged the sports page higher, covering his face.

"Why us? Doesn't she have family?"

"I'll tell you why, young man. First, no, she doesn't have family here in town. Second, we do not turn our back on neighbors in need. And third, you're friends with the boy. You can help him."

"I'm friends with him?" I looked again at Dad. He shook the paper but made no signal that he'd be joining the conversation. "I'm not friends with that freak."

"Rodney!"

"Well, I'm not. I can't believe you're doing this." I shoved back from the table and slipped behind Dad, breaking into a full-on sprint for my bedroom.

That night, I lay in bed, staring into the gray darkness at the bunk above me, now occupied by the smelliest kid I knew. Holy hell, it was bad, like the stench of my father's loafers and a full diaper battling it out for airspace.

"Rodney?"

"What?"

"Will you be my best friend?"

I closed my eyes and bit my upper lip.

"Well, will you?"

I opened them. "How many friends you got?"

"Well...I guess just you, pretty much."

"Well, Eddie," I said, with the resignation of a condemned eight-year-old, "I guess that makes me your best friend." The mattress above me, protuberant from Eddie's ample ass, jiggled happily.

"Thanks, Rodney."

"Don't mention it."

"Rodney?"

"Look, Eddie, let's just go to sleep, OK?"

"OK." He shifted in bed and the mattress morphed above me.

"Rodney?"

"What?"

"You're not mad at me, are you?"

"No. Go to sleep."

"OK."

I waited, eyes open. Ten minutes. Fifteen. Twenty.

Finally, blessedly, came the sound of slumber. Naturally, Eddie snored, but under the circumstances, I was more than willing to accept that.

"No, I'm not mad at you," I whispered into the darkness. "I just think you're a P-U-S-S-Y."

closing time

He took a sip off the longneck and handed the bottle to her. She lifted the cold glass to her forehead and held it there a few seconds before taking a gulp of her own.

"Crazy hot," she said.

"Yeah."

They leaned against the hood of his pickup, which sat heavy on its wheels, the back of it filled with the things that he'd held out of the yard sale.

"When're you leaving?" she asked.

"Early. Get on down the road. Shut 'er down early."

She handed the bottle back. "No chance you'll stay on a bit?"

"No." He took a swig.

"Don't backwash that thing, mister."

He tilted his head to her, his cheeks bubbled up, holding the beer. She was grinning at him. He swallowed and handed the last of it to her.

"You've had my spit in your mouth before."

She drained the last of it. "Boy, you are romantic." She leaned toward him, putting her shoulder into his bare right arm. He lifted his arm and she wriggled in, close enough to smell the day's work on him. He wrapped her up, pulled her in tight.

"You want me to stay tonight?" she asked. She pressed her chin against the chambray.

"You want to?"

"I do."

"It's just a sleeping bag on the floor. House is empty."

"I know. It's OK."

"I'm leaving early. Won't get much sleep."

"You already said. I'm not thinking of sleep."

That night, she lay her head on his chest and listened as his heartbeat wound down.

"I'm gonna miss this," she said.

"We said we weren't talking about that." His words rumbled in his chest, leaving her with an odd sense of stereo—the unadulterated sound entering the ear exposed to the open air, the more guttural, interior version coming through the other.

"We're not. Not really."

"Then what're we talking about?" He sat up a bit, propping himself on his elbows. Rousted from her resting spot, she sat and faced him, the sheet she'd wrapped herself in falling to her waist.

"Nothing. I just ..."

"What?"

"I don't know. I guess I didn't believe you were really gonna go back. I mean, I know you said you were, but..."

He sat up fully, pulling in his knees. He dropped his head and kept it there awhile. She pulled the sheet back up and draped it over her shoulders, covering her breasts.

"Look," he said, "I never led you on about anything."

"I know."

"I appreciate everything you've done for Mom. I couldn't have managed all of this without you, and this thing, I never expected it..."

"Neither did I."

"But it's done. She's gone. I've closed down the house. It's time for me to go."

"I know."

"So what are we talking about?"

She looked down at the carpet. "I just thought I...You know, when I came back here, I knew I'd never leave. I was hoping you might feel the same way. I thought I could be honest with you, that's all."

"To make me feel guilty?"

"No."

"What, then?"

She looked up at him. "Because you made me feel safe enough to say it. Because I think…"

"What?"

"I think I love you."

"Love? This isn't love."

"It might be for me. You don't know."

"So, what, I'm supposed to say I love you back?"

"No."

"What am I supposed to say, then?" For the first time, there was bark in his words, aggressiveness, anger. It frightened her.

"Whatever you want to say."

"You're an emotional extortionist, you know that? We talked about this. We said it wouldn't be weird."

"It doesn't have to be weird."

"It's already weird!"

She stood and wrapped herself tight in the sheet that smelled like him, like her, like them. "I'm going to go. I'm sorry. I shouldn't have said anything." He reached for her leg, but she backed up out of his reach. "I'm sorry. I'm sorry about your mom. She was a great lady. I'm sorry. I'm really sorry."

She turned and ran for the door in short steps. He watched her go.

He groped in the dark, found the watch and pressed the light button on the side. Two twenty-one a.m. He pushed himself off the spread-out sleeping bag, his back scolding him. He rolled up the makeshift bed and tied it off. He slipped silently into a T-shirt and his jeans, patting the front pockets and finding the outline of his wallet and keys.

In the cab of the pickup, he fired up a Marlboro. He blew a cloud of smoke and watched through the rearview mirror as it diffused.

The engine turned over, and he set the truck in gear. At the bottom of the driveway, he turned right, under a street lamp spraying the asphalt in sullen yellow, and he remembered a night, thirty-odd years earlier, right around this time of year, when he and the girl next door ran circles under that light, catching moths in a Mason jar. He remembered, and he wondered what home would look like tomorrow, when he got back to it.

nice cans

Puddles Palmer and I scooted along the high cinder-block fence, our bellies scraping as we inched our way toward the far corner, where we'd be covered by the night and an overhanging oak tree.

Puddles—not his real name, as you've probably gathered, but the kind of nickname a fat kid got tagged with in our neighborhood—kept stopping short, picking underwear out of his ass or taking a breather. This had the unfortunate byproduct of my crashing into his Keds with my nose.

"Dammit, fatass, keep moving," I spat at him.

"Sorry." After a few feet more, Puddles stopped again. I slapped his Vienna sausage leg.

"I don't think we should do this, Richard. Let's go somewhere else."

"The hell you say. Keep going. We're almost there."

Finally, we reached the spot where the fence merged into a corner. There, the oak tree's leaves in full bloom, we were out of sight of the adults just ten yards away. We were able to sit on the broad top of the fence and take in the scene.

Puddles' mom, Paulina, was throwing another of her summer pool parties, and we'd invited ourselves in. On the stereo rigged up to two big speakers—Paulina, on account of her divorce settlement, had some great toys—Mick Jagger had just started telling us about these Puerto Rican girls, and I sat there and did an informal census of the neighborhood.

Paulina, of course, was there, along with Teddy Carson, the guy she was currently balling. I counted Bill and Megan Romersma, whose place backed up to ours and whose son, Jared, Puddles and I had ditched earlier, because there was no way we were going to get away with this if that little tattletale had come along. Randy and Sue Jepperson were there, too, a younger couple on our block who didn't have kids yet. And over in the deck chairs were my mom and pop, both of them a full decade older than anybody else. Mom was thirty-five when I was born; I was her miracle baby. Dad? I wasn't even out of junior high yet, and he was almost sixty. Their presence might have surprised me if not for the fact that Dad would go anywhere somebody else was supplying the Jack Daniels.

"You're sure they're gonna skinny dip?" I said.

"They did last time." Puddles said this glumly. He wouldn't even look at me.

"Come on, Pete," I said, chucking him with my elbow. "This is going to be fun." I hoped the invocation of his given name might cheer him up; there's only so much "Puddles" and "fatass" anyone can take.

"I wish we'd just stayed at your house."

"Come on, man. Don't be chicken."

Puddles plucked a leaf from one of the overhanging branches and tossed it to the ground.

Paulina was the first to doff her top, and I realized at once that my brilliant plan might have a fatal flaw: the considerable boner that had staked a claim in my shorts. Teddy soon followed, tossing his trunks on top of her bikini. The Romersmas and Jeppersons, perhaps more discreet than Paulina and her beau, slipped out of their swimwear while in the water. Mom, as I expected, stayed above the naked fray. Dad, halfway pickled, took off his pants, tossed them into the increasing heap and sat back down.

"Now," I told Puddles.

"But—"

"Now!" I said.

Fatass turned on his considerable rear end and dangled his legs off the side of the fence. I gave him a shove, and he hit the ground on the other side.

For the first time, I grew tense. Puddles' trip around the perimeter of the fence took longer than I expected, and just as I was about to jump down and go after him, I heard the sound I'd been waiting for.

The first firecracker of the package of fifty went off with a meek "pop." But then the fuse hit its stride, taking them out two at time. Puddles was safely on the other side of the fence; he'd simply lit them and tossed them over.

Paulina screamed, her boobs jiggling. By the time everybody else scrambled out of the water and moved in to take a look, I was off the fence and at the pile of swimwear, shoveling it into a plastic bag. I got the bag, and myself, over the fence without being seen.

I hooked up with Puddles at the bottom of his driveway, where he was holding the jar we'd stashed in his front yard.

"This is so great," he said.

"No shit, Sherlock. Give me the stuff."

I set the bag on the ground and opened it wide. Then I turned the lid on the old peanut butter jar, slowly so I didn't spill the contents, and wrenched it open.

"Ready?" I asked.

"Ready," Puddles said.

I poured the contents onto the clothes. Puddles and I had been pissing into that jar for a week, sneaking into my wooded backyard and letting fly with the whizz, then capping it and leaving it in the sun to cook. The stench nearly sent me to my knees.

I closed and tied off the top of the plastic bag.

"Shake that up real good," I said to Puddles. He picked it up and did something on the order of a spastic flamenco.

We walked the bag up the driveway to Puddles' backyard fence and threw it over.

In the hindsight of maturity and experience, I'd like to tell you that there was some huge punishment that came of that night, but the truth is, there wasn't.

Fatass blamed it all on me, naturally, and so his mother blamed me, too. Teddy Carson barked at me a few times when I walked by his auto-body shop, told me he'd kick my ass when I came of age, but that winter he got shot between the eyes by a near-sighted hunter in the Piney Woods, and that pretty well ended any threat he held over me.

Mom told Dad to deal with me, and so we stood on our back porch, Dad's index finger sunk into his Jack and Coke, and we talked about it.

"Why'd you do it, boy?"

"I don't know. It was there to be done."

"That's no kind of answer."

"Are you going to ground me or something?"

Dad pulled his finger from his drink and flopped his arm around my shoulders. "Naw. Hell, no. You're a good boy, generally."

"Thanks, Dad."

"I just want to know where the hell you came up with a stunt like that."

I shrugged. "I don't know. I just wanted to see Puddles' mom naked. The rest sort of fell into place."

Dad took a sip and wiped his mouth with his sleeve."Yeah, Paulina, she's got some nice cans." He looked at me, using his drink hand as a point of emphasis. "Don't go telling your mom I said so."

night patrol

I didn't want her to go and she didn't want to stay. It was her irresistible force against my immovable object, but maybe I'm going to say now that physics is a liar. It wasn't a stalemate, not at the end. She left, and all my wishing for a different outcome—a comfortable one that didn't change anything—went for naught. She was out of there.

Had I gotten clingy? Yes. You want to make me cop to something I don't want to admit, there it is. I knew she was slipping away from me in small movements. I could feel the distance between us even in half slumber, when my hand would find only a cool sheet where her body used to be. I would open an eye, waiting for it to absorb the scant light in the room, and I would see her on the far edge of the bed, the topography of her hips now a battlement to keep me at bay. I would sidle up and slip my arms around her, and she would pat my hand. Come morning, I would be alone.

Where did we go wrong? I have no idea. OK, that's a lie. I have some idea, and I'm willing to take on a considerable burden of blame for it. I lost my fuse, OK? I did. I took the test for lieutenant, finally listened to her about getting off patrol and trying to build my career in the department. She could point at a half-dozen guys who'd shared a car with me who had moved up and out. Casey, in particular. She was always bringing up Casey. Chief in North Richland Hills now. Didn't I want that, she asked me.

No, I didn't, but I took the test, and I passed it—I'm not an idiot, OK?—and my captain swung by and said, "Hey, congratulations, Dave. You're finally getting off patrol." Yeah, well, fuck you very much, you know? I didn't want this. Still, I took a desk in homicide, and I hated it. Homicide is a big clusterfuck, and nobody wins but the lawyers. Patrol was where the juice was. I knew the folks on my beat, knew their businesses, knew their kids and knew what was going down. That moment when you flip the siren on and light out some back street, your synapses firing and your temples throbbing and your dinner in near revolt? That moment is pure adrenaline. It's a drug. And I wanted it, always.

For two years solid, I sat at that desk, my brain atrophying, and then I come home eight months ago and packed boxes are sitting in front of the door and all the stuff is off the walls—even the big picture from Hawaii, the one where we're looking like a couple of sex gods. I love that picture, and she took it.

"The moving van will be here in the morning," she said. "I'm spending the night at Amber's."

"Why are you doing this?"

"Because I can't let myself love a man who doesn't care."

"I care."

She didn't say anything else. Irresistible force.

The department owed me seventy-two personal days, and I took maybe eight of them before I went back and asked for a transfer back to patrol. The skipper didn't understand it, but I must have looked like a guy you don't say no to, because he didn't waste more than a minute trying to talk me out of it.

I know where she lives. She didn't try to hide it. She doesn't think I'm a threat to her, and maybe I'm not. Sometimes when I'm running backup on a call and I end up in her neighborhood, I take a swing by. Just to check things out. Just to make sure she's OK. And then I drive back to my zone.

I didn't want her to go. Even now, I want her to come home. I told her that when we signed the last of the papers, when she finally got the divorce she wanted. You'll miss me, I said. You'll be home soon.

You know what she said?

"Isn't it lovely to think so?"

left turn

When I told Amber I was leaving her for Caroline, she was pretty broke up about it. Part of that, I'm sure, was because she really expected that we had some sort of future beyond furtive screwing at night after her old man fell all the way into his bottle. I mean, I'm not going to sit here and lie and tell you I didn't cut the edges off the truth to get into her pants. I did. I was nineteen and dumb and horny as all hell, and I leaned on any advantage I had when it came to screwing. If I could somehow go back and visit the kid I was then, I'd kick his ass for a lot of things, but what I did or didn't tell Amber would be pretty low on that list, I have to say. Was I using her? Yeah, in a manner of speaking, but no more than she was using me.

Also, I imagine she was pissed off that I told her as we lay on the bed in my motel room, out of breath, the swelter of night moving across our bodies like a mop. Had I said something before, she might could have saved a little face by telling me to go to hell before we tumbled into the covers. All right. Again, I was no gentleman. Send me to hell. Whatever. I lay there on my back, my arm around her, and listened to the bug zapper do its work while Amber cried. I felt bad about that. Not bad enough to stay, but bad.

More than anything, though, I think she was just upset that Caroline was a car.

"So that's it, then? You're leaving?"

I'd driven back to the Wagon Wheel from the gas station across the street, after pumping Caroline full of high test. My pop's green canvas flight bag, the only thing of his I got after he was blown all to shit in Nam, sat on the concrete stoop outside my motel room door. Once it was in the backseat, Caroline and I would be pointing our noses north.

"Job's done. No reason to stay."

I did the once-around on Caroline, rubbing out a couple of splashes of fresh tar on her fender. A robust yawn while driving through Kit Carson would cause you to miss the little shitbird town, but damned if the whole Colorado Department of Highways hadn't converged on her that summer to rebuild Highway 40.

"You could stay for me. Better, I could go with you."

I slipped past her and hooked my arm through the bag's handles.

"I ain't ready for that."

She stepped into my wake, her voice rising, talking to the back of my head. "You were sure ready for everything else. I guess if it was beneficial to you, nothing else matters, huh?"

I dropped the bag into Caroline's back seat and slammed the door. "You were, too, goddammit! You're the one who came sniffing around my door that first night."

"Fuck you, Ray."

"Exactly."

"What?"

"I said, you fucked me, Ray. Me. Ray. You fucked me."

I shouldn't have said it. Amber, she flew into a godawful rage. She reached for the keys to Caroline, which I dangled out of reach. Then she reached for my shirt and tore the breast pocket off that.

"You love a car," she screamed at me. "It'll never love you back, and nobody else will, either."

She stomped off into the motel office, where her mother, a little rodent of a woman who hadn't said two words to me all summer, was no doubt watching and wishing me dead.

I unbuttoned the shirt and threw it into the backseat, then opened my daddy's bag and found a T-shirt I could slip into. I slid into the seat and coaxed Caroline to life.

Where the motel parking lot T-boned the highway, I took a quick look left and right and then laid down a scratch as I aimed Caroline toward Denver.

I've replayed that moment so many times in my head, and always, it's the sound of rubber first and the quick, screaming pain next, a split-second behind, as Caroline's back window shattered and the diffused glass shot into my skin. I whipped my head around and saw Amber there, straddling the yellow highway line, the pistol held in both hands. I stomped on the gas and Caroline was equal to the task, and we got the hell out of there, and that's the God's honest truth.

So, anyway, that's what happened. I was digging pieces of glass out of my shoulders and neck and hair for days, and a new back window set me back some dough once I got to Denver. But I'm not pissed anymore. I did what I had to do in leaving, and I guess Amber did what she felt like she had to when she shot at me. She was five or six years older than me, which means she'd be getting close to fifty now. She's probably on grandchildren now, probably already told her girls, if she had any, to stay away from the likes of me. I like to wonder about what happened to her, since I really have no way of finding out now. The way her old man drank, he couldn't have been long for the world. Maybe she got the Wagon Wheel. Or maybe the guy she hoped would take her away from Kit Carson showed up and did just that. I don't know.

Me, I've been here for twenty-three years, waiting out my days. Caroline's long gone. I get a new bunkmate from time to time. They always end up going, and I always end up staying. It'll be that way until it's not, until the day I don't wake up when they do bed check.

I have all the time I could ever want to think about anything I want. More often than not, I think about Amber.

fatboy

Lester always figured I caught all the breaks, being the little brother, and I guess that's why even when we both were in our thirties—sitting around the backyard table in August, our parents and our wives and our kids all cringing as we fought like children—he felt compelled to lay his bet against me.

It started when Dad looked disapprovingly at my second plate of brisket. "You're carrying an extra tire, aren't you?" he said, loud enough to catch the attention of Kim, who'd been on my ass about it for years.

"Yeah, I guess," I said. "I'm gonna do something about it."

Here came Kim. "When?"

And here's Lester: "Yeah, fatass. When?" The big hypocrite. Nobody was giving him shit about his fourth beer.

"All right," I said. "When's the Cowtown? February?" The adults' eyes grew wide at this mention of the town's annual marathon, and I scurried for cover. "By February, I'll do the 10K. How about that?"

Lester popped the top off his Shiner, and it clinked to the concrete. "Ha!" He tipped the bottle onto his lips and sucked prodigiously from it, and I wondered how he managed to stay alive without hydration.

"Care to put some money on it, smart guy?"

We settled on a wager of a grand, and I could see the worry blasted across Kim's face. One, her birthday was in February. Two, we didn't have a grand.

Anyway, that's Lester. It's hard to believe he and I crawled out of the same womb. I was a reader. He wasn't. I pulled mostly A's in school. He dropped out midway through his junior year. I never had much of a head for business or finance, so I've spent my life being the smartest guy working for the man. Lester, he was a business genius. The guy was continually launching companies—the bus service for bachelor parties and proms was a particular success—and then selling them at a huge profit down the line. An entrepreneur, that's what he was.

I think now that his biggest gripe with me lay in our relationships with the folks. Now, look, I'm sure Mom and Dad fawned over me some; Mom had been told after Lester that another pregnancy would kill her and the baby, so when I showed up, healthy and happy and all, I was the miracle. I'm sure that was tough on Lester. I'm sure that awful name they saddled him with—a gift from Dad's dad—didn't help. But that wasn't much my fault, was it?

I remember one time, Lester was still slogging through high school, and he came home late one night from work. He throws the lights on, and I come barreling out of sleep, cursing him up and down, and he walks over and punches me square in the nose. What is it the kids say now? At that point, it was on like Donkey Kong. Dad came in, wearing a T-shirt and his underwear, squinting through his one blind eye, and separated us. He told us that he'd be cracking heads if he heard another peep.

Lights out, Lester's in his bed and I'm in mine, and I can hear him whispering. "One day. One day they won't be here to protect you. And on that day, I'll be right in front of you. And I will beat the living shit out of you. Count on it."

So, yeah. Do I hate Lester? Hate's a tough word. I sure as hell don't love him.

February came around. I was down about twenty-six pounds, and I'd managed to cover ten kilometers a few times on my daily runs, but I hadn't yet done it under any sort of pressure. Lined up with the pack, looking at Kim and the kids and Mom and Dad watching from the throng, it was a different deal. My heart was kicking like a dog getting his neck scratched.

Then the gunfire echoed, and off I went Finished in sixty-two minutes. Holy hell.

Oh, boy, Lester was hot. Kim wanted to have a celebratory lunch, but I insisted that we drive out to Arlington and collect the money while Mom and Dad were there to corroborate things. The sour bastard had it on him, and he pulled the bills from his wallet like they were nothing, but I could tell from the way his face steamed up that I'd gotten over on him.

"You got lucky," he said. "Doesn't matter. Now that it's over, you'll be back on the doughnut patrol."

I used the money to take Kim to Puerto Vallarta. Every day, I sent Lester a postcard and told him how much I was enjoying his cash. A dick move? Yeah, maybe. So what?

And every evening at dusk, I walked down to the beach alone and set out, striding across the sand. Lester always saw the worst in me. His prerogative. This, too, I would outrun.

better be home

I wouldn't say that things with Marla were written in the stars. For one thing, that's a really dumb phrase. But beyond that, it's completely inaccurate. Our friendship was written on a first-grade blackboard in 1976, where Mrs. Appelbaum etched our weekly vocabulary words. Marla, who had the desk next to mine, leaned across the aisle and said her first words to me in the five weeks we'd been in school.

"Mud spelled backward is dumb."

I laughed out loud, and Mrs. Appelbaum and her pointy-framed glasses turned around and asked me what was so funny. I guess Marla must have admired my courage in quietly accepting the punishment of writing a hundred times "I will not laugh in the middle of my lesson" because, after that, we were pretty much inseparable.

(Besides, I got Marla back a few years later in Mr. Byrd's class, when we were watching a filmstrip and I leaned over to her and said "Focus spelled backward is suck-off." Marla couldn't stop laughing. She used her feet to propel her desk across the room and buried her face in the wall, and Byrdie about lost it.)

People ask me sometimes what it's like to meet your wife when you're six years old, and I have to admit now that I don't really understand the question. Marla and I, we were just friends for most of that time. She made me laugh. I let her crib off my math homework. Marla couldn't do numbers; it's why the checkbook belonged to me.

What I'm saying is, it's not something we planned. It's something that happened.

To a lot of the people we went to school with, Senior Prom '88 has become this big thing, the Night During Which Gordie Knocked Up Marla, and while it most assuredly was that, the truth of the matter is that we hadn't even intended to go together. That prick Jeff Caslon broke her heart because he decided to go with Carla Edwards instead, and I hadn't made plans any more ambitious than getting stoned out of my head with Parker White, so I found a tux at the last minute—blue with a ruffled shirt, because I was just that sexy—and I took my friend. You can chalk up what happened next to any number of things, but being as I was there, I put more credence in the bottle of vodka than I do in the fucking Richard Marx songs that our class of corporate-rock sheep insisted on playing that night.

The point is, we did what we did, and the result was what the result was, and I married her. That was twenty-three years ago, a number that astounds me. I'd like to say I thought I would do more with the years, but truth be told, I've hung in as best I could. Marla eventually became a radiology tech and made some pretty good bread. You know those houses that dot the north end of town, that sprang up there like a rash? I swung the hammer on most of those, and I also spent more than a few winters wondering if I'd ever find another job. On the balance, though, we did fine. Better than many. Not as well as some.

When Keri, our daughter, brought that boy home from college and told us he was the one, it didn't hit me the way I thought it would. She's beautiful, Keri is, and she looks just like her mother. I remember sitting there thinking, "You know, she's found someone she can connect with, and that's all I care about." Keri will be going off to grad school, and I'm just so proud. I can't quite believe I have a twenty-two-year-old daughter—I'm only forty-one, for Christ's sake—but it is what it is, to use another totally useless phrase.

I guess Marla saw things a little differently, though. Maybe I should have picked up on it, the distance that seemed to move into the house after Keri brought her young man by. Marla seemed antsy about things, impatient, unhappy. I figured it was just a phase—hell, I've done the same thing—but I came home a few weeks ago and found the note, and if this is a phase, it's sure as hell going to be unpleasant.

The specifics of what Marla had to say ought to stay between her and me, I suppose. It'll be easier that way if she does come back. But in general, she said we got together too young and have become different people. I don't feel that way, but I guess I should take her at her word. She said she needed time and space to figure some things out, and I guess whether to stay with me is one of them.

She left Stumpy, our collie mix, and I've been appreciative of that. Dog spelled backward is God. Sometimes I talk to him—God, I mean— but so far, nothing's changed. Maybe he sees things Marla's way. I've always said she's a lot smarter than me.

by the roots

I heard that song yesterday, the one where the guy talks about wanting to open his mouth wide enough for a marching band to come out of it, and it got me to thinking about some things. If I could spread my mouth open that wide, I'd like to think that all the words I've never found at the moment I needed them would be right there, queued up perfectly, waiting for the chance to come around again. Maybe Kate would tell me again that I'm incapable of real love, and instead of standing there, struck dumb as she walked away, I would open wide and hear myself say, "No, just incapable of loving you." I thought of that on my own, a half-hour later. Not that it did me any good.

People talk about "real love" the way politicians talk about the "real economy." It doesn't mean anything, except in their own heads. Even then, the idea of "real" is specious at best. It's not a measure of authenticity, just a reflection of their desire that it be something other than what they have. That's what it was with Kate. After three years, she didn't want me, didn't want my troubles, didn't want what I could give, despite everything that happened. She wanted something else— what, she had no idea. That mythical thing became "real love," and I became another guy on a park bench, looking for something that was gone, gone, gone.

I loved Kate once, and though she's probably been telling her friends otherwise, she loved me. For a while there, we had dreams—and while anyone can have dreams, we also had plans. It all seems moot now. The life we built together exists in parts, like in a scrap yard. Our house, hers. Our car, mine. The crib we bought, given away. I sealed off the room we'd painted blue with clouds on the wall, and I moved the crib into the garage. I couldn't stand to look at it, couldn't stand to accept money for it. Just take it, I told the man and his wife, who looked for all the world like Kate and I did a year earlier. Effervescent. Apple-cheeked. In love. I hope it lasts.

I think I could love again. Not now, but someday, maybe. I have to learn to live with regret, and that's not easy when you pile up new ones every day. Today included. I'm sorry that I wished to say I was incapable of loving Kate. That's not what I want, and I take it back.

I wish I could pluck a dandelion from the grass below my feet and blow on the flowering part, and the spores I set free would float around on the wind until they found someone who needed love or comfort or a friend. They would ride in her hair or on her clothes, all the way home, and would become what she needed, the way I could not.

the way it breaks

My mother, she had a particular saying that nettled me when I was a kid. If I was acting up, giving her trouble and whatnot, she'd say, "Leon, you're being uncouth." Lord, that used to torque me off something fierce. It wasn't just that I didn't really know what she meant. It was the way other people, adults, would look at me, their eyes all narrowed and accusing. I'd hang my head and sulk, and Mother wouldn't look at me for a while, and I'd think how much I hated her for making me feel that way. Now she's twenty-five years gone and I'm older than she ever was, and I think maybe I should have enjoyed her overly corrective ways while I had the chance.

It was her favorite word, uncouth, and she wasn't one to use it sparingly to preserve its power. By the time I bothered myself to look it up—or, rather, its brother couth—I could only chuckle at the airs she was putting on. Sophisticated and refined? Hell, we didn't live in a house without wheels until '74 and then only because my daddy crawled out of the bottle long enough to hook a union job at the refinery. For the first time in my life, I didn't have to go to school in the same threadbare clothes my brother Lawrence wore a year earlier. My point being, nobody in our house was couth, Mother included. We all were what she continually accused only me and Lawrence of being, and I don't care who you are, that's pretty funny.

It tore us all to the marrow when she passed on. It was one of those things that you don't even get to see coming. I'm standing there at the kitchen counter, making a bologna sandwich. Friday afternoon. I'm minutes from leaving the house, thinking about heading up to the hill and drinking some beer and maybe seeing if Linea Arroyo's gonna let me into her pants. Mother says, "I don't feel well," and behind me I hear her hit the floor, and before I turn I know. She's gone. I go down there and I hold her, and she's at peace. I never saw that before.

I probably don't have to tell you that daddy found his way back down to perdition. Lawrence, he took the refinery job that daddy vacated, because somebody had to make some effort at keeping our heads above water while we were bereft, and I was still in high school, a fact that didn't seem to matter much to anyone, least of all me. Come May, I went straight from the graduation to the county community college, because I figured I had three options: start pouring my own drinks out of daddy's bottle, go join Lawrence on the line, or keep my ass in school. What's that thing that makes a dilemma different from an ordinary old problem? The fact that every choice is unappealing? That's where I was. Burying myself in a book seemed the least bad way to go.

In the end, it made sense, I guess. It kept me here but gave me a little bit of direction. I've never been much beyond this patch of earth, except for the occasional ride over to Rock Springs for a nice dinner, but I latched on with the sheriff after I got my associates degree in '89, and I figure I've got a good shot at his chair here in a few years when he finally gives himself over in full to that damn garden he's always puttering around in.

I'm not going to say it's been without its good points. Every day after shift, I can stop by and see Daddy. I'd be lying if I said I thought he'd be around this long, but if I learned anything from Mother, it's that every moment is a gift. He can't much see anymore, and he talks more and more these days about when he'll get to be with her again. I figure that one's in the hands of the man upstairs. When the time comes, I won't begrudge it. I've watched Lawrence's kids grow up, and looked the other way a couple of times when I found them in a bit of malfeasance. We've spun off another generation of Harroldses, and that's something, I guess.

Every now and again, I'll meet eyes with Linea. She's got grandkids now, and they're always hanging off her cart at the IGA. I look at them, and I see traces of her and of Warren, her husband, and I think, hell, she and I could have done better than that, if things had broken another way.

our disquieting

Even now, all these years later, it's easy to remember when it all went down. July 1979. Jimmy Carter had just told us all that we were in a funk, only he didn't use that particular term, because "funk" isn't a Jimmy Carter kind of word. No, he said it was a "malaise," and he caught all kinds of hell for it, too. So now, I hear the word "malaise" and I think of Jimmy Carter and I think of that night in July 1979 and how my father and Roger Englund almost whipped the hell out of Rex Langley.

Dad and Roger, our next-door neighbor, worked their way through the better part of a case of beer while they talked about how Jimmy Carter was running us into a ditch. Dad said he'd be voting the next year for Anybody But Carter, and that was a hell of a thing to hear, as the old man, a union guy through and through, had voted Democratic clear back to Adlai Stevenson in '56. I remember Roger egging him on, talking up this California cowboy who was going to turn everything around, and it gives me no joy to say that, in retrospect, Dad couldn't have been more wrong. Two years later, Reagan fired the air traffic controllers, and Dad was out of a job, and Mom was just indelicate enough to point out that Carter might have been a sniveling pantywaist but at least he never fired Dad.

At some point, Bobby Englund and I found our way out of the house, neither of us giving a good goddamn about Jimmy Carter or Ronald Reagan. I wanted to head up the street to Cyndi Ham's house, because I heard Lauri Popelka was spending the night there. But Bobby wanted to go down the street to the Tangled Briar subdivision. There was an empty lot between Rex Langley's house and Megan Witten's, with a huge, gnarled oak tree—biggest one in the county, I do believe—that we could climb onto and see everything in the neighborhood. So that's what we did.

Now, I've asked myself plenty of times in the intervening years whether Bobby knew what he was going to do when he suggested climbing that tree, and the truth of the matter is, I just don't know. When I knew him—and I'll grant you, that was a long time ago—he wasn't the sort of kid who plotted out his cruelty. Sure, he could be mean and stupid, just like all of us, but I didn't get the sense that it was a compulsion deep inside him. On the other hand, I heard a lot of stories after the Englunds moved away about Bobby's mom and how she liked younger guys, and some of those stories suggested that this was why, in the middle of winter in '80, the Englunds pulled Bobby and his sister out of school and up and moved to Missouri. But it was all just talk, for all I knew, except that Rex Langley's name often came up when discussion started moving in that direction, if you get what I'm saying. So let's just say that if Rex was laying Mrs. Englund, maybe Bobby knew about it, and maybe that's why he did what he did. And maybe Roger knew it, too, which would explain why he did what he did.

All I know for sure is that Bobby had a slingshot in his back pocket and a handful of marbles in his front pocket, and when Rex Langley came outside that night, Bobby loaded up and sent one of those glass beauties into the small of Rex's back, dropping him to his knees.

"What are you doing?" I spat at Bobby. "He's gonna kill us."

Under his breath and loading up his next shot, Bobby said, "If you shut up, he'll never know where they're coming from."

He might have been right about that, if he could have held his aim. But the next shot missed Rex altogether and took out the front passenger-side window of Mr. Langley's Gran Torino, and from that Rex managed to judge the trajectory and, even in the fast-coming dark, find us in our perch.

Rex lit out, adrenaline compensating for whatever damage Bobby had done to his back, and in the next moment, Bobby and I were rappelling down the tree. We were in big trouble, I knew. The question was whether we could cut off the corner of the vacant lot before Rex closed the distance; if we could, we might have a shot at making it to the house.

I fell to the ground first and beat it out of there, making it to the street a good twenty yards ahead of Rex. Bobby, much slower than me, got to the street, too, but Rex was nearly on top of him. Bobby screamed, and I ran faster, and I heard him go down, and still I ran.

On my porch, I yelled "he's beating up Bobby!" through the screen door at Dad and Roger, and they were off the couch and past me before I could even register it, the faint traces of Miller Lite trailing them. I chased them back down the street.

What I saw next was just...well, surreal's probably the best word. Bobby sat on his rump in the street, his lip split, crying. Roger had Rex pinned up against the Curleys' spite fence, his right arm big as a maple ham against the kid's chest, holding him in place. Dad had one hand against Rex's throat and the other unfurling a spindly finger that he jabbed into the boy's nose.

"I don't want to ever catch you around these boys again," Dad said, his index finger punctuating every word. "Do you understand?" Rex, his face tear-tracked and crimson, trembling, tried to nod and couldn't even manage that.

And then, instantaneously, the fury drained out of Dad, and he released Rex—"Roger, let him go"—and he said, swear to God, "I'm sorry. Go on home."

Late that night, from my bedroom, I listened to the voices of Mr. and Mrs. Langley in our living room, heard the rise and fall of their anger as they came in looking for a fight and left with grudging acceptance that Dad had messed up but had done no lasting harm to their boy.

I don't know how things went over at the Englunds' place, and Bobby made it clear he wasn't going to do much talking on the subject of Rex Langley, so here, thirty-two years clear of it, I don't have much more clarity than I had then.

Dad, I know, held the shame deep. The only thing he told me was that I'd pay for Mr. Langley's car window, and though I had nothing to do with it, I didn't fight him, because he had that look of finality, and I knew that look all too well.

Sometimes, at night, I'll stand over my boy when he's sleeping, in the shadows so I don't cause him to stir, and in those moments, I think I can see every side of it. Dad was protecting his son. So was Roger, and maybe he was protecting something more, too. And so were the Langleys when they came to our house and asked Dad why they shouldn't just go ahead and call the cops.

I think about that night a lot, and for a lot of reasons. The biggest one, I think, is that there was a lot of anger in the air that night, a lot of anger about a lot of things, and in retrospect, we're all pretty lucky it didn't end up a lot worse for everybody.

That's when I get up and go to Eric's room. I look at my boy, and I know that, right or wrong, no matter what, I stand with him. He's my heart.

from the author

The first ten stories at the front of this book—starting with *Somebody Has to Lose* and ending with *Comfort and Joy*—came into the world several years back as a collection titled *Quantum Physics and the Art of Departure*. For a long time, it was my "other" book. I loved it just as much as the others, certainly, but it wasn't one likely to shine brightest or get talked about most. That's been OK by me.

They're joined here by two relatively new, standard-length short stories, if there is such a thing, and a scattering of very-short fiction that I wrote mostly back in 2011 and 2012. I lopped off half of the original title for the collection, shortening it to *The Art of Departure*, and now you hold this fresh version in your hands. Thanks for picking it up.

So why take a modestly successful story collection, one that's been a consistent if plodding seller and has won some critical acclaim, and recast it?

Two reasons, I suppose.

First, I can. The rights to most of my longer works are encumbered in various ways (I'm not complaining), and these stories have remained my babies for lo these several years. If you're as interested in the mechanics of publishing as you are the craft of writing—and I am—the opportunity to dabble is hard to resist.

Second, that old title long grated on me, even if I have only myself to blame for it. *Quantum Physics and the Art of Departure*. It's a reliable laugh line for me to say, at readings, "If you want to ensure that your book is widely ignored, put 'Quantum Physics' in the title," but damned if that isn't the truth in some uncomfortable ways. I've often said that there's no actual quantum physics in the book, and now that's true in fact and in name. *The Art of Departure*. Better title. And now, I think, a better book, too.

Beefing up the short stories and offering some shorter fiction brings all of my smaller-scale work, so far, together under one roof. In preparing this new edition for publication, I got to walk back through these stories, in some cases years after I last read them. What I'm struck by now, nearly five years on from their original release, is the evolution of a world of fiction. Every book I've released has touched every other book. You can see that here: Jim Quillen, the violent father at the center of the novel *The Summer Son*, makes a crucial appearance in the story *She's Gone*. Ray Bingham, the self-righteous inmate in *Star of the North*, tells a little more of his story in the short piece *Left Turn*. Hugo Hunter, the titular character from the novel *The Fallow Season of Hugo Hunter*, first showed up in the short story *Slumpbuster*, published in the Spring 2013 edition of the *Montana Quarterly*. That one's here, too. I hope you like it.

Short fiction is an irregular pursuit for me; the stories don't often come, but when I'm so compelled, it's some of my favorite work. The ideas often arrive with fully formed arcs, but there are enough surprises to keep the endeavor interesting, with some of the nausea and uncertainty and slog of writing a novel neatly shaved away.

I keep hoping someday I'll hit another rich vein of short fiction. The only way, I suppose, is to keep digging. Hand me that pick and shovel, won't you?

Craig Lancaster
Billings, Montana
August 2016

Photo by Casey Page

Connect with Craig Lancaster

On the Web: www.craig-lancaster.com
Twitter: @AuthorLancaster
Facebook: www.facebook.com/authorcraiglancaster